SERIES

California Dreaming

California Dreaming

An A-List Novel

by
Zoey Dean

poppy

LITTLE, BROWN AND COMPANY
New York   Boston

For Hair Guru to the Stars, Mr. Raymond.

Poppy

Little, Brown and Company
Hachette Book Group USA
237 Park Avenue, New York, NY 10017
For more of your favorite series, go to www.pickapoppy.com

First Edition: April 2008

The Poppy name and logo are trademarks of Hachette Book Group USA.

alloyentertainment

Produced by Alloy Entertainment
151 West 26th Street, New York, NY 10001

Cover design by Andrea C. Uva
Cover background photography © Marianna Day Massey/ZUMA/Corbis
Cover model photography © Bill Ling/Getty Images

ISBN-978-0-316-11353-3

10 9 8 7 6 5 4 3 2 1
CWO
Printed in the United States of America

There must be thousands of girls like me, dreaming of becoming a movie star. But I'm dreaming the hardest.

—Marilyn Monroe

Fear of Flying

Saturday morning, 2:47 a.m.

Anna Percy was trapped. Also, barefoot.

Behind her was the slammed-shut door of the long, white-walled jetway. Ahead of her gaped the open door of her Bali-bound flight. A petite flight attendant with dark, thick waist-length hair, clad in a double-0 navy blue uniform, was calling to her in lightly accented, chirpy English.

"Hurry! We're pulling back from the gate! Hurry!"

Rather than hustle the remaining ten paces toward the beckoning flight attendant, Anna froze. Her last words with Logan Cresswell, the boy who had brought her here, the boy who was presumably waiting for her in the first-class cabin of this Air East Indonesia flight, flashed through her mind.

"There's a flight back to Bali that leaves LAX at three this morning. That's three hours from now . . . Come with me."

Anna was not the kind of girl to break up with one guy—the exquisitely complicated but equally compelling Ben Birnbaum—only to run away to Bali with another one. Everything in her future was planned out, thank you very much. She was exactly seven days from returning to New York City after living for eight surreal months in Los Angeles. Then, she'd start her freshman year at Yale, which had been her dream ever since she could remember dreaming at all.

Yet here she was, on the jetway. The international-departures building behind her, the plane ahead of her. Her Chanel pumps? They'd been tossed aside a few moments before, as she'd made a mad three-hundred-yard dash down the airport concourse from the TSA metal detectors to gate 87.

After these months of attempting to reinvent herself in Los Angeles, including some admitted experimentation with things both remote and dangerous—as benign as ordering a double-double animal style from In-N-Out Burger, as scary as learning to surf on the waves of Malibu, as death defying as ascending the steps of the Getty in a pair of Prada stilettos—now she was about to do the most remote and dangerous thing of her life. A mere ninety minutes before, she'd made the snap decision to join an old Upper-East-Side-childhood-neighbor-turned-recent-romantic-interest, Logan, for a trans-Pacific flight to Bali.

She wasn't sure Logan was even on the plane. The airline's gate attendant had told her it was against security regulations for her to confirm that he was on the flight. Anna had tried to reach him by cell, but evidently, the captain had already given the order for cell phones to be turned off, tray tables to be locked in their upright positions, et cetera, et cetera.

"Miss! Please hurry!" The petite flight attendant's voice went up an octave and a half, and she gestured with both hands.

Anna's heart was pounding as she covered the last five paces of the jetway. She took a deep, fortifying breath and stepped across the threshold. There, the beautiful Balinese flight attendant broke into a relieved smile, welcomed Anna aboard with a gentle bow, and thrust a ribbon-tied bird of paradise blossom into her hand while she scanned Anna's ticket stub.

"You'll want to take your seat quickly in the first-class cabin, Miss Percy. You're the last one to board, and we'll be taking off shortly."

Anna thanked her and pivoted left in the direction of first class. She sighed, grateful that the twenty-two-hour flight across the Pacific and the international dateline would at least be comfortable. Since she hadn't had time to pack— this trip had been the very definition of a last-minute decision—she still wore the white eyelet lace Betsey Johnson baby doll dress she'd had on earlier in the evening.

She glanced around the cabin. There were nine rows of first-class seats, two across. Directly in front of her, another immaculately coiffed attendant in the same navy blue uniform served tall, chilled mimosas to a well-dressed elderly couple, regaling them with details about Bali's fabulous gem shopping and wondrous natural beauty.

Where was he?

Bald man in a tweed business suit. Not him.

Swarthy guy with a heavily tattooed neck, wearing skinny vintage jeans and studded bracelet. Definitely not him.

Huge man in backward Lakers baseball cap atop a Lakers uniform. Nope. Tiny woman in a maroon warm-up suit sitting beside him. Double nope.

Short, dirty blond hair. Broad shoulders. Piercing blue eyes. Slight cleft in the chin. Faded jeans and plain black T-shirt.

Logan.

Anna smiled. There he was, stretched out in the second row of the luxurious white leather seats, next to the window. The seat on the aisle—*her* seat—held two hardcover books and a Yankees baseball cap. In that moment, she realized he wasn't expecting her to show up.

"Please, to your seat, Miss Percy," the petite, raven-haired flight attendant whispered discreetly. "We'd like to depart."

The flight attendant moved off. Logan didn't look up from his copy of the *Los Angeles Times*, open to the sports section.

Anna was just about to move to her seat and announce her arrival when another memory struck home. It had been in a first-class cabin that she'd met Ben Birnbaum. That flight had been the one on New Year's Eve that had brought her from LaGuardia Airport to LAX. Ben had been a savior on that flight—he'd helped get rid of her deeply obnoxious seatmate, a thirtysomething record producer, by pretending to already know her. By the time the flight ended, she felt as though she *did* know Ben. And she also knew that she wanted to be with him.

But Ben was in the past. Just a few hours before, he had broken her heart again, this time by kissing his old flame, Cammie Sheppard. Anna had met Cammie her first night in Los Angeles, and it had been hate at first sight. On Cammie's part, anyway. Mostly because Ben was clearly into Anna, and Cammie had been Ben's last girlfriend. But also partially because Cammie was the type of girl who needed someone to hate. At times during the last few months, their relationship had thawed to almost peaceful coexistence. At other times . . . not so much.

"Come with me."

That's what Logan had suggested to her and it seemed like the perfect escape. Yet she'd said no. Expectations awaited her. Home to New York. Then Yale. But then she'd seen Ben and Cammie in a corridor at the new club they'd opened together in Culver City—Bye, Bye Love—having a close encounter of the third kind.

That was enough to send her to the airport. Why not? She could always fly back to the East Coast in time to start at Yale.

The white leather seats were so lush and roomy that Logan didn't at first notice her moving in next to him. "Sorry I'm late. The traffic on the 405 was just *insane*," she announced nonchalantly, flipping a lock of her long silky blond hair.

He looked up and, in one fluid movement, rose and pulled her toward him. "Anna." He breathed her name and the next thing she knew his lips were on hers as they melted into a tight embrace.

"Umm, sir? Miss?"

The flight attendant tapped Logan on the shoulder, and they broke apart sheepishly. "Please have a seat. You don't want the other passengers to show you what they think of your public display of affection," she chided, winking at them as she moved away.

They sat, belted in, and a different flight attendant began the pro forma announcement that always came as a plane was taxiing to the runway. Then the captain came on—Anna was surprised to hear a slight Southern accent—to explain that they were number three for takeoff and it was a gorgeous night for flying. She mused whether they'd be able to see Tahiti or Fiji en route. Probably not, she decided. They were flying west. It would be dark a lot of the way.

"Hey." Logan put his hand atop hers as they waited at the end of the runway for the tower to clear the one to take off. It felt good. Safe. If Logan wanted to hold her hand for the next twenty-two hours, she decided that would be okay. He laced his fingers with hers. "Why'd you change your mind?"

"I have an impetuous side," she replied lightly. Then she frowned. "Actually, that's not true. I am trying to *develop* an impetuous side."

This was closer to the mark. Impetuousness did not have its own chapter in the *This Is How We Do Things* Big Book (East Coast WASP edition.) Everything about Anna—from her natural butter blond hair, which she wore very straight and shoulder length, to her refined ivory features and slender body—seemed to denote her prim and proper upbringing. She had the carriage of a ballet dancer, wore little makeup, and favored her grandmother's diamond stud earrings over anything flashy and new. She'd rather go to the Strand bookstore than to Bergdorf Goodman (back in New York), or to the B. Dalton bookstore than to Fred Segal (here in Los Angeles). She loved literature—give her Faulkner or Wharton or Twain over a Bruce Willis movie any day.

Her time in Los Angeles hadn't changed that. But it had changed her, freed her, to the point that she was able to make impulsive decisions like the one that had brought her here, to this very moment.

"Me too." Logan grinned, his intense blue eyes twinkling. "Impetuosity—is that even a word?—is highly undervalued."

"You're suitably impetuous. You got accepted to Harvard and decided not to go," she challenged.

Anna had practically been with him when he'd made the decision. She had been at a Yale freshman gathering in Manhattan, and he'd been at the same kind of gathering for incoming Harvard students. They'd met up afterward and Logan had confided in her that he felt uninspired by what he'd heard and who he'd seen.

"Gotta see the world first. You know, starting with my dad's new eco-resort." He shrugged playfully.

She laughed. Logan's dad, Vaughn Cresswell, was a hotelier whose name people mentioned in the same breath as those of Marriott and Hilton. "Not exactly roughing it with a sleeping bag and two matches."

"Touché," he agreed. "Anyway, it's a hell of a lot better trip with you along. I'm glad you're here."

He gave her hand a little squeeze as she stared at him. Logan was tall and blond, on the preppy side. They'd known each other when they they'd been little. When Anna had been in New York a couple of weeks ago, she'd run into him in front of her family's brownstone on the

Upper East Side, which just happened to be next door to *his* family's brownstone. She hadn't seen him in years, and was shocked to discover he'd grown from a skinny, rather quiet boy into a junior version of Daniel Craig—blond, with intense blue eyes, ears that stuck out slightly, a sexy smile, and the kind of sinewy muscles you didn't expect on an intellectual.

Spending time with him was a bit of a shock. She'd forgotten that there were guys who shared her love of books and meandering philosophical conversation. Most of her Los Angeles peers knew everything there was to know about television and the movies, could spout off the latest box-office results and Nielsen overnights, but couldn't identify Henry James on a bet.

"So have you told your parents about this little walk-about?"

Anna felt a bit queasy. Her parents were going to go insane when they found out—in their own idiosyncratic ways, that is.

Her mother, Jane, was currently in Florence, Italy, with the latest in a long line of very handsome and much younger artists whom she "promoted." In this case "promoted" meant "supported in every way possible," and "every way" probably indeed meant "every way." But Anna had to admit she chose well. Just about every artist she "promoted" got invited to the Whitney Biennial, the Whitney Museum's exhibition of the latest and best in modern art from around the world, which took place every other year.

What would her mother think? Her mother would be apoplectic that she'd even *considered* ditching Yale. That is, after she recovered from shock. Then she'd scold her for traveling without luggage or toiletries.

As for her father? She'd spent the last eight months living with him at his Beverly Hills estate. Well, that was a bit of an exaggeration. Jonathan Percy worked such long hours as an investment advisor that she barely saw him; it wasn't like they sat down together each evening for a family dinner. In some ways, her father might be more forgiving than her mother. Jonathan was considerably more open-minded than his ex-wife, and even had a lovely marijuana habit that he often indulged in the gazebo in his backyard. Still, Anna was pretty sure that his open-mindedness would probably not extend to what she was doing this very minute. The Airfone call that she'd make to him in the morning, once she'd put three thousand six hundred miles between them, was going to be interesting indeed.

"They'll be okay with it," she finally surmised.

"Bullshit."

"Well, that too."

Anna and Logan continued to hold hands as the captain announced they were number one for departure. The engines roared as the Airbus barreled down the jet-black runway, blue and white guide lights flashing by faster and faster, until the plane lifted off effortlessly into a slight breeze coming from the west, out over the inky Pacific, leaving the city behind them. Anna could see the clear demarcation of the Pacific Ocean where it touched the coastline. The pilot made a sweeping turn to the north. To the east, Los Angeles stretched out in all its gleaming, pulsing glory. To the west was the blackness of night.

As the plane rose to its cruising altitude, Logan enthusiastically told her about his father's resort on Bali. Four-poster beds strung with dreamy-yet-practical mosquito nets; thatched-roof bungalows that opened onto white sand; lazy afternoons on the resort's private sailboat; moonlit dinners of fresh fish and tropical fruit served by a chef named Dolph, whom his father had imported from the finest four-star restaurant in Düsseldorf, Germany. As she leaned back into the pillowy leather seat and closed her eyes, Anna could visualize the lush island's aquamarine coves and a hammock tied between tree branches thick with mangoes. She felt her body relax. She had made the right decision. She was sure of it.

With an audible *ding,* the seat-belt sign switched off.

A male flight attendant lifted a small microphone and began chattily describing the flight's amenities. With the push of a button, the seats would recline into twin-size beds. Down pillows and comforters were available, as well as scented aromatherapy eye masks and shearling travel booties designed exclusively for the airline by Donna Karan.

"Let me bring you some slippers," the flight attendant said to Anna in a hushed voice as he finished his announcement. He wasn't much taller than the diminutive woman who had welcomed Anna aboard. Anna thanked him; she was so comfortable, she'd almost forgotten she had nothing covering her toes.

"Champagne?" The first female flight attendant was making her way down the aisle with a service cart. "We're pouring Taittinger or Moët tonight. As you prefer."

She poured them each a well-chilled crystal flute, with a fresh orchid blossom adorning the rim. Logan raised his glass.

"Here's to adventure."

"Impetuous adventure," Anna agreed.

They clinked flutes and drank. Anna knew she should be nervous, upset, anxious, and second-guessing this mad, last-minute decision. But she really didn't feel that way at all. She drained half of her champagne and leaned into Logan. He put an arm around her. "I'm happy."

Such a simple thing to say, but for Anna, who tended to overthink *everything*, being here in this moment and being happy was something miraculous. She smiled up at him.

"Me too."

They were already in Bali, out sailing at sunset. The sun was tomato red as it sank into the water, and the air was redolent with the aroma of coconuts and gardenias and salt.

"Anna!"

Anna felt Logan shaking her arm urgently and snapped awake. She'd been having the most delicious dream.

"What's going—"

"Shhh! Listen."

Anna realized that the captain was in the midst of a long announcement to the passengers.

". . . malfunction. Now, what's caused this malfunction, we can't tell in the cockpit. And they can't tell us from the ground, either." While his tone was light and confident, there was no mistaking the seriousness of his words. "But here's what it's going to mean," he continued. "We're going to do a big ol' U-turn and head back to Los Angeles, dumping as much fuel out at sea as we can. Don't worry about the fish, folks. It's a big ocean."

"Oh my God!" Anna heard someone behind her exclaim.

"There's always a chance that my hydraulics will return, and it's a fine night out there. But if I can't get the gear down, we're going to come in on our belly and that's never a picnic. Had to land a Tornado fighter this way once. I'm glad that it was only once, and that I'm here to tell you about it. They'll be ready for us at LAX, but you should all be prepared. So we'll keep you posted from up here. Our flight attendants will review the safety precautions, and I'll be back from time to time. Don't worry, folks—we'll do everything we can to get you home safely."

Anna suddenly felt the blood run cold in her chest. She didn't know all the specifics, but she'd heard enough to be afraid. There was a problem with the plane, a serious problem that would likely force a belly landing.

Logan gripped her hand tightly and she could tell he was trying his best not to betray his own fear. Her mind was already on overdrive. Was this the punishment she received for trying to be impetuous?

In the back of the plane, Anna could hear people clamoring in a dozen different languages, looking for more information, translating for one another—it was the sound of panic about to erupt.

"We could die," she said quietly, slumping back in the white leather seat and staring ahead, stone-faced.

Logan leaned in to kiss her cheek. She hoped he'd contradict her, tell her she was silly, tell her everything was going to be okay.

"Probably not," he replied, but his face gave a different reaction.

Anna blinked and sat up straighter. She reached for the Airfone. "I've got to call my dad. It could be goodbye."

Do It Again and You're Dead

Saturday morning, 2:58 a.m.

"**M**y Eduardo, *Eduardo mio. Mi querido Eduardo.*" Samantha Sharpe mumbled to herself in a mix of English and limited Spanish as she sped west on Wilshire Boulevard toward Eduardo Munoz's building—one of those Manhattan-esque apartment houses that lined both sides of the Wilshire corridor between Westwood and Santa Monica.

It was a heady feeling to be doing sixty miles an hour on a street where traffic generally crawled along at a teeth-gnashingly slow pace, her Sirius satellite radio tuned to the blues, the windows cranked down, and the balmy late-August night air hitting her in a rush.

"Her Eduardo" lived in one of these white high-rises, in an apartment owned by the government of Peru and reserved for members of its Los Angeles consulate staff. Eduardo was a member of the staff for the summer, compliments of his father, a high-ranking official of that mountainous South American nation. Sam had met him at a resort in Baja California during the spring, where he was vacationing from his studies at the Sorbonne in Paris.

"*Mi Eduardo. Querido Eduardo. Guapo querido Eduardo*," Sam repeated.

Your Eduardo.

That was how her boyfriend—no, her *fiancé*—Eduardo had signed the handwritten note that she'd found on the last page of the mystery delivery she'd received not three hours before, while standing in front of Cammie's club, Bye, Bye Love. A thin Latino man in a black pin-striped suit had presented her with an artist's portfolio, saying only, "I have a delivery for you."

She and Anna had opened it, Sam in a state of near-paralyzing shock, on a round stone table near the club. It was filled with artists' renditions of bridal gowns, each worn by a girl sketched in Sam's likeness. Her favorite was strapless, with a bodice encrusted with pearls and diamonds, and an Empire waistline. But the others were almost as dazzling.

Until the moment she opened that portfolio, she had been absolutely, totally, utterly convinced that Eduardo was cheating on her. In recent weeks, a gorgeous Peruvian designer named Gisella had made a habit of hanging around him, and when Sam had gone to New York City with Anna a couple of weeks before, she'd encountered Eduardo and Gisella in a cozy booth at a Midtown restaurant, looking rather intimate. In a scene worthy of a cheesy soap opera, she'd dumped him on the spot, without giving him any chance to explain.

His explanation was, of course, almost achingly simple. He had been working with Gisella in secret to create these bridal gowns. To top it all off, he'd been understanding of Sam's dramatic outburst. In his apologetic explanatory note he'd written, *Somewhere in your family tree, there is hot Latin blood—of this I am certain.*

At this point, she wouldn't have been surprised to find out his teasing supposition was correct.

Sam's stomach rumbled in nervous excitement as she reached Eduardo's new building, the Edgemont. It had a circular driveway, and a valet was on duty despite the late hour. He took her Hummer and parked it while Sam pushed through the glass revolving door and into a mirrored lobby.

A white grand piano rested in the center of the deserted lobby. Gigantic vases of freesias, lavender, and roses adorned every available table. Soft classical music wafted from speakers hidden in potted trees. Behind the white marble guard desk stood the doorman on duty, the size of a linebacker for the Oakland Raiders, with a shaved head and thick bushy eyebrows. "Good evening. Welcome to the Edgemont," he greeted Sam as she entered. His voice was melodious, and he wore a classic black Ralph Lauren suit. That it was nearing three in the morning didn't seem to faze him at all. "May I help you?"

"Eduardo Munoz, please."

"Just a moment." He picked up a white telephone, made a brief call upstairs, then smiled at Sam.

"Go on up. It's apartment 14-G."

She strode to the gleaming gold-doored elevator and took in her reflection. After bidding goodbye to Anna at Bye, Bye Love, she'd driven back to Bel Air for a hair, makeup, and clothing detour at her father's estate. She'd hunted around in her studio-apartment-size walk-in closet for the perfect outfit, finally choosing a vintage emerald strapless chiffon party dress she'd found at Decades on Melrose that somehow made her look something approaching petite, particularly if the lights were low. She paired it with Marni wedges that lengthened her legs by four inches, then showered, did her hair, smudged in some Tarte bronzer and spritzed her cleavage with Thierry Mugler Angel. She smiled at herself approvingly. There was no way she was going to let Eduardo see her looking anything less than fierce.

The elevator arrived with a ding, and as it took her fourteen flights upward, her heart flew into her chest. She tumbled out of the gilded box, barely registering the hallway's lush beige carpet, or the reproductions of paintings from the Los Angeles County Museum of Art that hung at twenty-foot intervals on both sides. Fourteen-G was to the left, at the end of the corridor. She stood outside Eduardo's door and knocked, her heart pounding.

She was about to fish in her Rebecca Minkoff clutch for a breath mint when the door opened. There he stood, impossibly handsome with his inviting dark brown eyes, olive complexion, and mussy dark hair, in a white Marc Jacobs linen shirt with the sleeves rolled up and tan Ermenegildo Zegna brushed cotton pants. She hadn't seen him since their horrible breakup in New York more than a week earlier, and wanted to find the most wonderful, romantic, perfect thing in the world to say to him.

"You asshole."

He laughed and pulled her into the entryway. She had forgotten how good he smelled, how warm his skin felt against hers. He wrapped his arms around her bare back and spun her in a half-circle, so that she stood facing him in the foyer.

"I love you, my Samantha," he whispered into her ear, then gently moved her long hair and kissed her neck. "Don't ever, ever, *ever* do that to me again," Sam warned.

He grinned and held a hand up as if taking an oath. "On my honor," he agreed, trying hard to look solemn.

Then he kissed her again.

That was easy. Why had she been so insanely jealous, so certain that he was playing her? Perhaps it came from being the daughter of America's Most Beloved Action Star, Jackson Sharpe. Or maybe it had something to do with growing up as a size twelve in a town where none of the other second-generation female royals wore anything larger than a size four. Perhaps it came from knowing deep in her heart that despite the perfect caramel streaks and hair extensions put in by Raymond himself at his new salon on Rodeo Drive—who would ever have thought that neighborhood would stage a comeback?— and the brows done by Valerie, and regular oxygen-and-fruit exfoliation facials at Thibiant day spa, she was still not beautiful.

"You look gorgeous." He tracked one large hand to the curve of her waist, then slid his fingertips to her ample hips. "Come. I've prepared a feast."

"With pleasure. But what if I hadn't shown up?"

He smiled at her. "I knew you'd come. And I'm glad you did."

She slipped an arm through his as he gave her the

tour of the apartment. It was one bedroom, with a wide-open combination dining room and living room with a tile floor and a picture window that looked out onto Wilshire Boulevard, and beyond that, the Santa Monica mountains. There was a glass table with four chairs, a low couch covered with authentic Peruvian pillows and a green quilt, and a flat-screen television on the wall. The kitchen was white-on-white and ultramodern. Nowhere did Sam see a feast. Which could only mean . . .

Eduardo opened the bedroom door. It looked like something out of a *GQ* spread. Sleek, modern furniture with a walnut finish, a king-size bed with a headboard covered in distressed chocolate leather. In the corner, a desk held his PowerBook laptop and a Bose iPod Sound Dock. There was also a candlelit table covered with a white tablecloth and laden with an astonishing spread. Two black upholstered teak chairs were placed side by side.

"Come. Let's eat. And drink. And talk." He took her by the elbow and steered her to the table.

After he gallantly pulled a chair out for her and helped her into it, he poured her two crystal glasses. One was fresh mango juice, the other was Stag's Leap chardonnay. There were platters of smoked oysters, Russian salads of various types, three kinds of cheese, and a French baguette fragrant with rosemary.

This was another thing she loved about him: he actually encouraged her to eat.

"I have a plan that I think you will like," Eduardo began, slipping an oyster into her mouth.

"Which is?" Sam prompted. She took the glass of juice and swallowed half of its sweet, fragrant contents in one gulp. "I'm game for anything. As long as I don't have to leave this apartment." She glanced at him through her L'Oréal Paris–mascaraed lashes seductively. "Make that this bedroom."

He smoothed some caramel-streaked hair off her face. "I'm thinking more long term. You want to go to film school at USC in the fall. I must return to the Sorbonne for my last year there."

"And you go back in like a week," Sam added miserably, feeling like a warm shower had suddenly run cold.

"We could have the long engagement you envisioned when I first asked you," Eduardo continued, running his finger around the rim of his wineglass. The flickering candles cast eerie shadows against the bedroom's white walls. "But I think this will make it so much harder for us to be apart. I never want to have the kind of misunderstanding we just had again."

The thought of what had happened in New York made her wince.

"I think we would not have had such a misunderstanding if we had moved past being engaged," Eduardo finished.

Sam had another oyster halfway to her mouth, but gingerly set it back on the plate. "I'm not sure what you mean."

"I mean marriage," Eduardo said simply. "I mean . . . let's not wait to be wed. Sam, my beautiful Sam . . . marry me *now*."

Sam gripped the countertop with her petal-pink fingernails. Now? Marry him now? Okay, not right this instant, but when he said *now*, he didn't mean in a year.

He wasn't talking about months—he was talking about weeks. Maybe even days.

She sat up straighter in the cushioned teak chair. What was he envisioning, a shotgun wedding in Las Vegas? She had no aspirations to get hitched at the Little Chapel on the Strip, with an Elvis impersonator preacher officiating, thank you very much. It was all . . . just . . . too *soon*. She inched closer to him and gently put a hand on his leg. "Eduardo, you know that I—"

She was cut off by the jarring ring of her cell phone.

"Who's calling at this hour?"

Caller ID was useless. It was a blocked number. Sam brought her Razr to her ear. "Yes?"

"It's Anna."

She sounded like hell. Had something happened with Ben? "Anna! It's three-thirty in the morning. What's up?"

"Are you watching the news?" Her voice was quavery.

"No, I'm not watching the news. I'm at Eduardo's, and it's really, really late."

"Turn on the news. I'm on the Air East Indonesia jet. Flight 1976."

"What the hell are you doing on an airplane?" Sam was flummoxed. She looked over at Eduardo, as if his concerned-looking dark eyes might hold the answer.

"I decided to fly to Bali. With Logan. It was a sudden thing. I thought it was a good decision, but now we have mechanical problems. We're an hour away from LAX and we're going to crash-land. I'm scared."

For a brief moment, Sam thought her friend was playing a joke on her. But Anna wasn't a prankster. She was in danger. "Anna, stay calm." Sam turned to Eduardo. "Honey?" She tried to keep her voice as steady as she could, knowing her friend could overhear. "Could you go put on one of the local news channels? Anna's on a flight that's having some mechanical difficulty."

Eduardo covered the thirty feet to his bedroom's forty-two-inch Sony plasma TV in less than a millisecond, and the screen glimmered to life. The local CBS affiliate was on with breathless coverage of the Air East Indonesia jet that was about four hundred miles off the coast and headed for LAX without functional landing gear. There would have to be a crash landing, the anchorwoman said, and then the coverage switched to a brief interview with a retired Continental airlines pilot who was pontificating on the chances of the plane coming through this landing unscathed.

"Tell me what they're saying," Anna demanded.

Sam's heart thudded in her chest, and she felt even more nervous than she had standing outside Eduardo's door half an hour ago. "I don't think that's a very good idea, Anna."

"Sam, I am on this jet, and I need to know what's going on. The pilot isn't telling us much. Please?"

Sam breathed deeply. How did you tell one of your closest friends she was about to die? "They're saying that—that—you're going to—"

There was a slight pop as the connection was lost.

The hand holding her now-silent phone trembled. "I lost her. They're crashing—" Tears began to flood Sam's eyes.

"No, they're not," Eduardo declared, his voice strong and reassuring. "Don't panic. They're showing radar of the plane on the television. It's in the air. It's heading for LAX. The pilots on board are very experienced. No one is crashing."

Sam stared at the TV as though it were some kind of oracle. In the lower left-hand side of the screen was a radar image, along with an arrow pointing to Air East Indonesia flight 1976. Eduardo was right. The announcer intoned again that the plane was maintaining its altitude and was still on course to LAX. It was due to arrive in an hour. The TV station put up a digital clock in the lower right-hand side of the screen, counting down the minutes and seconds to the plane's scheduled arrival time. It reminded Sam of the constant clock on the show *24*. But this wasn't prime-time TV, and there was no Jack Bauer waiting in the wings to save the world.

Sam stood, tottering a little on her sky-high Marni wedges. "We're going to the airport." She started toward the door.

"I don't know if they'll let us in," Eduardo commented, but he had already turned off the television. "They might close the terminals."

"Let them try to stop us."

"I'll drive." He picked up his keys from the nightstand and held the bedroom door open for Sam, placing a gentle hand on the small of her back as she drew near him. "Let's go."

Sam paused as they stood in the open doorway. "Eduardo? Wait."

He stopped and gazed at her with his chocolate brown eyes.

It was as if this terrible thing that was unfolding with

Anna suddenly made the world seem clear in a way that had been impossible only a few minutes before. The plane could crash. This wasn't bullshit. And here was a guy whom she loved dearly, who wanted to marry her. That wasn't bullshit either.

Who knew what the next minutes and hours would bring?

"If Anna survives, we're getting married at the end of the week." Sam heard herself say. "If she doesn't—"

"She'll make it," Eduardo assured her. His voice was full of confidence and his eyes shone. "She has to. She's supposed to be at a wedding a week from tonight. Ours." He draped an arm around her shoulder. "Come. Let's go."

Ménage à Blah

Saturday morning, 3:45 a.m.

Cammie Sheppard let her bejeweled satin Cesare Paciotti platform sandals dangle from her forefinger as she watched the night auditor—a hip Vietnamese accountant named Tran, whose shaved head and steel-toed motorcycle boots belied her chosen profession—of Bye, Bye Love, close out the cash register in the main bar. Cammie was wearing an emerald green Randolph Duke beaded mesh spaghetti-strap mini-dress, and some-time during the late-night/early-morning hours she had twisted her nearly waist-length strawberry-blond curls up on her head and skewered them with a pencil. By now, tendrils had fallen from the makeshift barrette and tumbled artlessly—which Cammie knew to be the most perfect kind of artful, because it looked as if you hadn't tried at all—down her slender back.

A few hours ago, the dancing, gossiping bodies of the L.A. elite had filled the club's immaculately designed dance floors to capacity. Opening night had been a smash-ing success. The crowd of Hollywood insiders, models, actors, and designers had met even Cammie's impossibly high standards. When your father was Hollywood's top agent, as famous as the megatalent he represented, you tended to reach for the stars. And if you were Cammie Sheppard, you got them.

"Hey." Ben Birnbaum eased up next to her. All six-plus feet of him looked fantastic, in a black Giorgio Valentini suit over a bloodred Bye, Bye Love T-shirt, which featured a razor slicing through the center of a heart. His electric blue eyes were lively and only his tousled brown hair gave away the late hour and the long night they'd had. "We're a hit." He grinned lopsidedly, his lip swollen on the right side where her ex-boyfriend, Adam Flood, had slugged him just a few hours ago.

"Interesting choice of words," she noted, twirling the stool so that her bare knee playfully knocked into his thigh. "And, for the record, I always knew we would be," she purred.

"We make a great team." He gave her a smile that reached his eyes, running a hand through his disheveled hair. "You are one of a kind, Cam."

She stood and wrapped her arms around his neck. "Well, Ben," she began, as Tran made a discreet exit through the club's large metal door. "We really ought to celebrate."

Her suggestion was thinly veiled: Cammie Sheppard code for *Let's go make insane monkey love.*

Cammie and Ben had been a couple during her junior and his senior year at Beverly Hills High, and had spent the year doing pretty much that, everywhere and anywhere. They'd gotten a rep for it. When he'd broken up with her during that same year, she'd vowed to get him back someday, a feat that at the time had seemed simple enough. Until boring, blue-blooded Anna Percy came along. Ben had fallen for her almost immediately upon her arrival on New Year's Eve. But his fling with Anna was now clearly over, and tonight he had kissed Cammie like he had finally come to his senses, all five of which were clearly focused on *her*. Best of all, Anna had walked in at exactly the right moment, when Cammie and Ben his engaged in a full-frontal lip-lock.

"We could go back to my place," Cammie added, letting the loose tendrils of her curls brush his strong shoulders. Only twenty minutes separated her and Ben from picking up where they'd left off just a year ago. She traced a delicate finger over the soft cotton fabric that stretched across his chest.

"What about Adam?" Ben asked suddenly, pulling back to look at her.

Cammie withdrew her arms from his neck. Damn. The last person she wanted to think about right now was Adam Flood.

She had never expected to fall for the tall, lanky, smart, sweet basketball star. He was definitely *not* her type. He read books. He played chess. He did volunteer work. He even liked his parents. Under ordinary circumstances, she would never have given him the time of day.

But somehow, he had gotten to know her, come to care about her, seen beneath her facade to something hidden underneath. He made her feel vulnerable, like she was walking around without her usual armor of carefully applied makeup and designer clothes. Sometimes Cammie wondered if the girl Adam saw was the girl she might have been if her mom hadn't died when she was much younger. Other times, she thought the whole you-see-the-real-me thing was a clichéd crock of shit. Most of the time, in fact.

They'd been together for the last part of the school year. Then Adam had left for a camping trip to Michigan—Michigan!—with his parents. It was tolerable for a while. Then annoying for a while longer. Then, when he told her he'd not only decided to extend his stay, he was also thinking of passing up Pomona College, just outside L.A., to actually *go to school* in Michigan, it had become completely insufferable. Finally, Cammie had given him an ultimatum: Be home by a specific date or be gone.

He had chosen gone. And then had chosen this night to show up at the club and punch Ben out for kissing her.

"Adam who?" Cammie said coolly. She nibbled on Ben's earlobe and brushed her lips against his. Slipped just the tip of her tongue daintily into his mouth. If that didn't underscore her answer, words were pointless.

"Your dad home?" he asked huskily.

Cammie raised a perfectly plucked eyebrow seductively. "Different wing of the house, remember? I could have the Mormon Tabernacle Choir up to my room for a sing-along and my father wouldn't hear anything."

He laughed. "I need to lock up. I'll meet you in front."

She gave him a smoldering look. "Don't take too long."

She could feel his eyes on her as she sashayed out of the body-shop-themed bar. Cammie and Ben had enlisted the help of students from Cal State's design department to come up with a look for the club's interior, and they'd chosen to incorporate its history as an auto-body repair shop. There were license plates all over the walls, tables made of former car hoods, and even a two-car racing track that circled its interior. The most ambitious part of the concept was that once a week it would be completely revamped in a different décor and style, with only the general floor plan staying the same. The scheme was meant to ensure the club's lasting success, as its patrons got the comfort of a familiar atmosphere with the feeling they were discovering a new place.

Cammie looked proudly at their handiwork as she made her way toward the exit. She was barely eighteen years old, and she and Ben were the co-owners of the newest and hottest club in L.A. It might not last. But for now, they were the king and queen of Hollywood's nightclub scene, and Cammie was more than ready to claim her throne.

When she hit the cool night air, she leaned against the club's hard brick exterior to wait for Ben. She bent over to put her shoes back on. They'd of course be coming off again—along with her green party dress—as soon as they made it back to her place, but she knew that the act of removing clothing was half the fun.

"Cammie."

She looked up quickly to see a startlingly familiar face. Adam was walking toward her, his hands shoved deep into the pockets of his faded, baggy jeans, still wearing his favorite Ramones T-shirt. Unlike Ben, Adam looked tired—weary, even, like he hadn't slept in days. His lanky frame was slightly hunched, his size-twelve black Converse All-Stars dragging across the asphalt.

"Have you been out here all this time?" Cammie asked. She set the Cesare Paciotti platform sandal she held in one hand down on the sidewalk, momentarily caught off guard.

He nodded.

"The word *stalker* comes to mind," she said icily, regaining her composure.

He sighed and crossed his long, basketball-muscled arms over his chest. "What is *wrong* with you?"

"With *me*?" Cammie felt her cheeks redden in anger. "You're the one who showed up here and punched Ben, remember? So what the hell is wrong with *you*?"

"Look, I shouldn't have hit Ben." Adam rubbed his face wearily. "That was a stupid asshole thing to do. It's not even my style. I just . . . I lost it, seeing him kiss you."

He had a possessive look in his brown eyes, as if nothing had changed over the past few weeks and he had every right to punch anyone who showed interest in her.

She opened her Stila-glossed lips to protest but was cut off by her customized Razr's current ring tone: The Who's "Baba O'Riley." Cammie pulled her phone out of her emerald green clutch.

"Just a sec, Adam."

"The call can wait," he said impatiently, narrowing his eyes.

"No. You can wait." She lifted the Razr to her ear. "Yes?"

"It's me. There's a problem." Cammie was surprised

to hear Sam's voice sounding so stressed. "After she left the club tonight, Anna got on a flight to Bali. Don't ask how, it's complicated."

"So what's the problem with Anna?" Cammie asked, annoyed, leaning against the wall again.

"What problem with Anna?" Adam interjected quickly. He scratched at the star tattoo under his left ear, a gesture which she knew meant he was nervous.

Cammie frowned. Adam and Anna had been an item for a few weeks earlier this year, until Anna had lured Ben back into her clutches and promptly dumped Adam. That's how Cammie saw it, at least. Then she and Adam had hooked up. And now it looked like Cammie was with Ben again. It was the Beverly Hills version of six degrees of separation. Laughable in a way. Delicious in another, since she knew Anna cared most for Ben. And now it was Ben-and-Cammie and Anna-and-no-one—just as it should be.

"Her plane has a mechanical failure." She could hear her friend's voice catch in her throat. "It's coming back to LAX. It's going to crash-land, if it gets that far."

"*What?*"

"What is going on?" Adam demanded.

Cammie sank a little against the brick wall as adrenaline rushed through her veins at breakneck speed and everything around her flashed into ultrasharp relief. The late-night traffic on Venice Boulevard. The salty aroma of the ocean, as a few wisps of predawn fog rolled in from the Pacific. The brightly lit exterior of the club, which a couple of hours before had been a seething hub of famous partygoers. There were still a few stragglers hanging around, couples who'd had too much to drink. She and Ben had thoughtfully moved some folding chairs to the club exterior for just this eventuality.

Through her daze, Cammie noticed music that carried through the club's front door. Ben had put on some sort of blues mix for his clean-up-and-close-up work. Eric Clapton's "Key to the Highway" segued into the Climax Blues Band version of "So Many Roads."

"It's Anna," she turned back to Adam. "She's on a plane that's having some problems."

"Big problems?"

"Very."

"Is there a TV inside?"

"I think Ben can get reception on one of the video monitors. If you're going in—"

Adam didn't stick around for the rest of Cammie's sentence. He raced inside to turn on the news. Cammie momentarily wondered if Ben would kick his ass when he saw him. Probably not, once Adam told him what was going on.

"Cammie, are you still there?" Sam's voice sounded tinny and far away.

"Yeah. What are you doing now?"

"On my way to the airport with Eduardo. You want to come? We're just passing Culver City. We could stop and pick you up. The plane's supposed to make an emergency landing in forty-five minutes or so."

Cammie automatically slipped into her platform sandals, her body naturally springing into action. She was tempted to say yes. But Anna wasn't her friend. Anna had never been her friend. There'd been grudging respect, and there'd been that unwanted and unholy bond through the guys they'd dated, but that was it. It seemed somehow wrong for her to join Sam at the airport, like she'd be pretending to be someone who she wasn't.

"I'll stay here," Cammie decided. "I'll watch on TV." She kicked a toe idly against the brick wall of the club. "I'm praying for her," she added. The words were out of her mouth before she could stop herself. *Praying*? And yet . . . she found that she meant it.

"Okay," Sam said. "I'll call you."

Sam hung up and Cammie found herself outside alone. The night air felt suddenly chilly and she folded her arms across her chest. Anna Percy was up in the air, on a plane that might not make it safely down. It was ironic in a way, as the only thing Cammie had wanted from Anna since she set foot in Beverly Hills was for Anna to suddenly be gone. But not like this. She never would have wanted anything like this.

"Cammie?"

She turned around. Ben was standing in the doorway. He saw her shivering and came over to throw his blazer over her shoulders.

Cammie felt herself relax at the sudden warmth. For a fraction of a second, she considered not telling him what had happened. They could pick up right where they'd left off, get into his car, and speed the twenty minutes to her house. But now that didn't feel right either. "Sam just called. Anna's on a plane heading back to L.A. that has to make a crash landing."

"Damn," Ben breathed. He looked like he wanted to say more, but instead clenched his square jaw. She thought she could see a vein pulse at his temple. "Come back in—it must be on the news."

She hitched a thumb toward the entrance. "Adam's here. He just ran in—did you see him?"

Ben shook his head.

"You okay?"

"Fine, whatever." Ben was already heading back inside, pulling Cammie with him.

She drew Ben's blazer tight around her tiny size-two waist as they made their way inside. "Let's try to stay positive, all right?"

Ben merely grunted in response.

The ten-man crew they'd hired for cleanup at the club had done their work, and the place was spotless again, without a single remnant of the scandalous night that had passed. Adam sat alone at the main bar, his eyes glued to the TV, and he barely looked up as they approached. Cammie felt her breath catch as she saw an illuminated image of the Air East Indonesia jet against the sky. It was being tracked by a couple of Air Force fighters with enormous spotlights, and the announcer was somberly holding forth that this was not an ordinary landing-gear problem. If the plane reached the mainland—and this was still a big *if*—there would be a dangerous belly landing.

Cammie and Ben slowly dropped onto the empty bar stools next to Adam, the silence of the club still unbroken. Ben wordlessly poured out three shot glasses full of scotch, and Adam took his gratefully with a tip of the head to Ben.

On the wide screen that hung above them, a reporter

at LAX picked up the story with a live remote. She talked through all the crash-landing preparations, careful to call them "emergency landing" preparations, but everyone knew what she was talking about. Firefighting equipment lined both sides of the runway: the plane had burned off the maximum amount of fuel it could in order to reduce its flammability and weight, and foam had been sprayed at the far end of the landing strip.

"The pilot will have to exercise extraordinary skill if there is to be no injury or loss of life," the reporter explained. "When we come back after this break, we'll have some statistics for you on this type of forced landing. Historically, it's a sobering record."

The station cut to a commercial for Coca-Cola, a bunch of smiling teens looking carefree as they sipped from the trademark bottles in the backseat of a red convertible.

"This is so fucked up," Adam muttered as he extended his empty shot glass to Ben for a refill.

"Extremely," Cammie agreed as she drained her glass.

"Ben?" Adam finally looked Ben in the eye.

"Yeah?" Ben paused midpour.

"I'm sorry about before, man." He nodded his head at the TV screen, as if to imply that bigger things had put the night into perspective. "I shouldn't have done it."

"Forget about it." Ben shook his head, his eyes emotionless. He passed the full shot glass over to Adam, and Cammie couldn't help but think that the proffered olive branch took a very different form in L.A. than in Michigan.

"You know what, guys? I'm outta here." Ben got up

slowly from his seat. "I can't watch this shit. You can stay if you want. Cammie, don't forget to set the alarm before you leave. I'll call you in the morning."

"Where are you going?" Cammie asked, getting up as well. She took off Ben's blazer and extended it toward him.

"Home." Ben shrugged his broad shoulders, taking the jacket. "This is too depressing." He didn't even look toward the TV as he said it, as if afraid of what images he might see next.

Cammie nodded her strawberry-blond curls. "I understand."

She really did understand. You either had to have a sick voyeur gene in your body to watch a friend's plane during its final forty minutes in the air—or you didn't. She knew she had it, and it didn't surprise her that Ben didn't.

"Thanks," Ben replied dully. "Have a drink or three for me." He kissed her gently, then turned and slowly moved toward the door. She watched him for a moment before turning back to the most horrible reality television she'd ever watched. The most riveting too.

Sliding into Home

Saturday morning, 4:30 a.m.

"**A**pproximately one minute prior to landing, our captain will give the command 'Brace!' When he does, you must assume the brace position. Place your feet flat on the floor, put your head on your lap, and clasp your arms under your knees."

Yet another of the Airbus flight attendants was giving the instructions into an oversize handheld mic. She was petite, with honey blond hair in a glossy ponytail at the nape of her neck, and a smattering of freckles across her nose. She looked like a high school cheerleader, Anna thought, who should be explaining the way the human pyramid was going to work, not how to save your life in a plane's crash landing.

Crash. Plane crash.

Oh God.

Anna reached for the sleek white Airfone again. Since she couldn't get service on her cell, she'd tried to call her dad twice already on the Airfone, but had gotten a busy signal both times. She'd been able to reach Sam at least.

Just hearing her voice had made Anna want to cry. How could this be real? How could it be happening? How could it be happening to *her*?

As Anna pressed her father's number into the phone with sweaty hands, she nearly laughed at the absurdity of it: this was what it took for Jane Percy's daughter's palms to perspire. When she heard the dull clanging of the busy signal, she hung up again.

"I can't get through, either." Logan put his cell back in the pocket of his jeans. The flight attendants had confirmed that it was fine to use them in this emergency, but had said that the Airfones had a better chance of success. For Anna and Logan alike, nothing had worked, except the brief call to Sam.

Logan's normally tan skin looked pale, and there were a few droplets of perspiration near his blond hairline. He leaned back against the seat, breathing shallowly through his mouth, and Anna turned to face him, concerned. He tried to give her a reassuring smile, but it didn't reach his eyes. Instead he squeezed her hand.

She turned to gaze across the aisle at an elegant, slender woman with hair pulled back in a tight bun. Sitting impossibly straight in her charcoal Brunello Cucinelli shawl-collar cardigan, she looked like a former ballerina. As Anna watched, the woman extracted a set of ruby-colored rosary beads from a signature brown leather Louis Vuitton clutch. Next to her, a man whose stomach overflowed his seat belt—and his wrinkled lavender Armani shirt—was pounding his third Absolut on the rocks. The flight attendants had told him half-sternly that this one would be his last. His response: "Seriously?"

Funny. Anna was either going to laugh or cry or scream or—

"Hey." Logan nudged his shoulder into hers to get her attention. "We'll be fine. The plane lands, we skid like there's no tomorrow, we slide down the emergency chute, and we have a great story to tell at parties."

"Flashover's gonna get us," the heavy guy mumbled to no one in particular. "Gases get trapped in the cabin and auto-ignite. It's not the crash, it's the fire. We're toast. No way out of this sucker."

The older, elegant woman next to him closed her eyes and continued with her rosary. Her lips moved but she made no sound.

"I thought this kind of thing was only supposed to happen in the movies," Logan mumbled.

Anna searched for a pithy, dry response, but nothing came. All she felt was fear. It was like a pit of acid in her stomach, growing and growing and growing as the plane zoomed closer to Los Angeles. She leaned back in the seat and closed her eyes, trying to rein in her thoughts.

"I thought . . ." she began slowly, her throat suddenly dry. "I thought I had all the time in the world to do whatever I wanted. Go to school and get married and start a family." Anna could feel hot tears fill her eyes, and she blinked them away. She looked down toward her lap, the white of her sundress making the world seem like a snowy blur.

Logan tightened his grip on her hand. "What seems ridiculous to me is fighting with my dad, my sister. We argued coming back from East Hampton, because she made me wait for her for two hours while she made out with some pretentious asshole from Berkeley who did performance art. I railed at her all the way home. Told her what a jerk he was and made fun of him. Why did I do that?"

"I'd like to talk to Susan," Anna murmured. "To tell her I love her. And my parents. And Cyn—"

"Cynthia Baltres." Logan nodded "I remember her. Didn't she bring her mother's fancy bag to first grade?"

Anna managed a small smile. "She did. And in second grade she didn't wear panties under her skirt and kept mooning all the boys in the cloak room." Anna's smile quavered as she thought about the possibility of never seeing Cyn again. Why hadn't she kept in better touch with her childhood friend? Why hadn't she e-mailed her or texted her or called her every day? She regretted that now. Friends—true friends—were so important. She thought about Sam and gulped hard. Eduardo had sent that portfolio of wedding gown drawings to her. She'd looked beautiful in the sketches, her black-and-white alter ego wearing those gorgeous white flowing dresses. But if Anna didn't make it through this, she'd never get to see her wear one in real life. Instead of being there, watching her friend walk down the aisle with Eduardo someday, everyone would be saying, "Poor Anna."

Anna shook her blond head as if she could shake off the morbid vision. A man sitting in front of them had his eyes closed, listening to music, and Anna suddenly wished she'd brought her own headphones so she could tune everything out. She tried to think of a song to sing to herself, any song, and a random melody flew into her mind. What was it? Some country thing . . .

"One of our housekeepers loves country music," she told Logan, remembering. "She walks around singing this song all the time—something about how you should live like you're dying." Anna felt a sudden relief as she thought of the lyrics. She leaned her head heavily against his shoulder and felt him kiss her temple, his slight stubble grazing her skin.

The plane hit a patch of turbulent air and pitched forward. Anna gasped and somewhere behind her, people screamed. The heavy guy across the aisle grabbed a barf bag and used it. Anna had to look away. In the row ahead of him, two men were praying in Hebrew, rocking back and forth as they did.

"I'm here," Logan told Anna, his voice firm. "I've got your hand."

Then another face—not Logan's—filled her mind. Dark brown hair, laughing blue eyes, and a strong jaw. Her stomach started to ache. And then her heart. Would she never see Ben again?

Logan slid an arm around her shoulder, and the fabric of his black T-shirt felt soft against her skin. "We're going to be okay, Anna."

She looked up at him like a child hearing a bedtime story, wanting to believe him. "How do you know?"

"I just do," he answered her without a flicker of doubt in his steely blue eyes. He was no longer sweating, or breathing like a marathon runner. Anna had no idea where his sudden resolution had come from, but it comforted her.

"Okay, it's a deal then." She nodded slowly, as if she had the power to control such things. "We're going to be okay. And from this day forward, we'll live like we're dying."

"We will," he echoed. His eyes were drawn outside the plane's small circular window and he pointed with his free hand. "Fighter jets." Anna followed his gaze. On both sides of the plane, fighter jets had scrambled from Edwards Air Force Base to escort their plane to the airport. She had a sudden vision of Logan as a little boy, playing with his toy planes, and she felt her lips curl into a small smile.

"Ladies and gentlemen, this is your captain. I need your complete attention." The captain's formerly easy, conversational tone had turned steely and serious, and the whole cabin looked up in rapt attention. "So, here we are. We're ready, the airport is ready. We've been through this many times, but it can't hurt to repeat it. Our landing gear won't lower, so we'll make a belly landing on the runway. There's foam on it to soften the impact, and there's a steady fifteen-knot headwind, so that should help our cause. Fuel's been dumped to lessen the fire danger."

"Lessen. All he said was lessen," the heavy guy across the aisle muttered, attempting to loosen his navy blue power tie, which clashed with his lavender dress shirt. He swiped a meaty arm across his sweaty forehead.

"When we come to a stop, the safety slides will deploy. Get to the emergency chutes as fast as you can—and do not stop for your carry-on luggage!"

Nervous laughter rippled through the cabin. "Better than screams," Logan noted haphazardly. He gave Anna's hand a final squeeze.

"That's it, here we go," the pilot concluded. "See you there. Hang on. Stay alert. Move fast, and good luck."

"Put your head down, Anna," Logan urged, and she did, hands behind her bare knees, just as the blond flight attendant had instructed. She rested her head on the cottony fabric of her white dress and closed her eyes, trying to imagine she was floating on a cloud.

The plane made a sweeping left turn in the sky, and Anna felt her body twist, but she kept her head where it was and her eyes squeezed shut. She started to feel everything careen downward, and she knew instinctually that the plane had begun its descent. The descent felt like the descent of most any other flight, except that the cabin was deadly silent, with the occasional whimper, moan, or cry. With her eyes closed and other senses alert, Anna had never felt so in tune with her own body. She could hear her heart beating, and it seemed to sync itself with the platinum Chopard watch she wore on her left wrist, its ticking loud in her ear. The moment that the plane hung in the air felt like an eternity of peaceful stillness, and Anna couldn't help but wonder if this was what heaven was like.

The plane's belly slammed down the runway with a screeching roar, and Anna had to press her head hard against her knees to remain in the brace position. She could hear metal being torn away as they skidded eastward at a hundred and fifty miles an hour, the screeching noise reminding her of a fork being raked across the surface of a metal bowl. There were a few stifled sobs and screams around her, but mostly everyone had managed to stay quiet, as if they were all waiting for the worst.

Please, Anna found herself thinking. *Please.*

"Stay in seat! Stay in seat!" a flight attendant was admonishing, and Anna drew her head up slightly at the sound. Sparks filled the air outside the windows on both sides of the plane. Around her other heads began to lift, realizing they'd touched the ground. The plane continued at its manic pace, and out the window they skidded past the first bank of fire trucks. There was a flash of red light outside as the fire trucks roared into action, all sounds replaced by that of their sirens blaring as they gave chase.

The slide continued. *Just let it end,* Anna pleaded silently, *either way.* There were so many sparks now, it felt like being trapped in the middle of a Fourth of July firework.

And then, suddenly, they stopped. Anna looked to either side of her for confirmation, and all of the other passengers seemed equally shocked.

"Go, go, go!" The flight attendants were all yelling at once, flashes of navy blue uniforms as they sprung up from their seats and waved the passengers to the emergency exits. "Down the chutes! Down the chutes and away from the plane! Down the chutes!"

Anna and Logan jumped out of their seats immediately, and she could feel his steady hand on her back as they raced toward the emergency chute two rows in front of them. The emergency door of the plane gaped open, a black square of night outside, with the chute emerging from it like a tongue.

Standing in front of them was a little girl with her two front teeth missing, chestnut hair in messy pigtails and tears in her eyes. She paused at the chute, even as the flight attendants called to her to get on the slide.

Where were her parents? Anna had no idea. She put a hand on the little girl's shoulder and urged her forward.

"Jump! Jump!" The flight attendants pointed to the chute.

"Go, sweetie," Anna urged the child, and the little girl slid down before her. Anna was next, with Logan behind her.

She jumped, and felt herself hurtle through darkness toward the ground. It reminded her of her favorite slide in one of the Central Park playgrounds she loved to go to growing up, except now she had no idea where she would land.

"I'm right behind you—"

Anna heard Logan's voice, but lost the end of his sentence as she reached the bottom of the slide. Two firemen in yellow flame-retardant suits grabbed her by the elbows and hoisted her to her slippered feet. It felt like an eternity ago that she'd tossed her pumps in the airport trash can, and for a second she wondered if they might still be there. But that was the only clear thought she had. Everything was happening so fast, Anna could only keep moving. Huge spotlights illuminated the plane and the fire engines' sirens wailed on. "Run! Run to the buses!" a fireman on a bullhorn was shouting to her.

It was utter chaos, people running, some falling, many crying. Anna saw three or four yellow school buses parked in a row a good four hundred yards away. Logan was pulling her along, faster and faster. All around her, various passengers were doing the same, escorted by policemen holding orange flashlights.

A slender man in jeans and a button-up shirt had plucked up the little girl—he looked like her father. She clung to him as he ran with her wrapped in his arms, her brunette pigtails bobbing as they sprinted forward.

"We're going to make it," Logan exulted as he tugged at her arm, his blue eyes wide as if shocked by his own statement. And in that moment, Anna realized he was right. They *were* going to make it. From the size of the crowd of people gathering by the school buses, it seemed that every single passenger on the plane was there. She looked back toward the crippled plane, a hunk of gleaming metal resting lamely on the runway. The firemen were pouring white foam on its body as a precaution, and it looked like huge tufts of marshmallow gushing from the enormous canvas hoses. But, Anna realized, if the plane was going to explode, it would have already happened.

"Holy—"

"Shit." Logan finished the words for her. He laughed joyfully and hugged her hard, pulling her slender body into his strong frame. "Holy shit."

There had to be at least two hundred firefighters on the scene. The chief was announcing that if they boarded the buses, they'd be taken back to the international arrivals terminal.

Anna and Logan waited to board the buses, and she felt like they were on an elementary school field trip. Around her, she heard the sound of gathering applause, and turned to see the entire flight crew—twelve flight attendants, the pilot, and the copilot—walking wearily toward them together in their matching navy uniforms. The pilot looked like he was out of central casting. Chiseled chin, regal bearing, silver hair. His copilot was Indonesian, and had a huge smile on his face. The passengers greeted them with wild applause and cheers, and Anna joined in, yelling at the top of her lungs, even though her throat still felt scratchy and dry. The copilot took a bow; the captain merely doffed his cap.

Fifteen minutes later, the white lights of the airport felt blindingly bright as they emerged in the baggage-claim terminal to an enormous crowd. There were hundreds of friends and relatives, as well as representatives from what seemed like every newspaper, magazine, radio, and television station from Los Angeles to Bangkok. Anna craned her neck, looking for her dad. When she'd finally gotten ahold of him on the bus earlier, she'd found that Sam had already called him: he'd told her he would be in the baggage claim, just past the TSA doors.

Finally she spotted his brown hair and lean frame, his blue eyes searching the crowd wildly for Anna. He wore Calvin Klein jeans, a faded white golf shirt, and chocolate-brown Ugg slippers—Anna realized that he must have been too stunned by the news to put on actual shoes. Well, that made two of them.

Jonathan's face broke out into a huge smile as he spotted his daughter, and he held his arms out to her. She had only been safe in his embrace for about ten seconds when she heard her name shouted from another part of the crush. "Anna! Logan!"

They turned to see Sam and Eduardo approaching breathlessly, Sam looking radiant in an emerald chiffon party dress she hadn't been wearing earlier. Anna pulled away from her father just as Sam tackled her, wrapping her in a bear hug.

Anna nestled her head into Sam's brunette waves and inhaled the scent of her Juicy Couture perfume. The hug went on and on, until Anna finally pleaded for mercy.

Sam smiled, the expression on her face one of utter joy and amazement, as if she couldn't believe she was really looking at Anna. "I know this is going to sound selfish, because it should be all about you right now," Sam began, grinning from ear to ear, "but I'm so glad you're here, because later this week Eduardo and I are getting married, and I want you to be a part of it."

Anna looked at her friend, stunned for the second time that night. But this time it was a happy kind of shock. "Congratulations!" She grabbed Sam again and hugged her tightly.

It was too much. This night. Her father. Her friends. All the people around her, laughing and crying and hugging. Anna saw the man still carrying the little girl in the pigtails, who was crying to a woman who looked like her mother. For a moment, Anna almost dissolved in tears too. But she was too overwhelmed to cry. She didn't know what she felt, beyond being so, insanely glad to be alive and on the ground.

She looked from Sam to Eduardo to her father, and finally rested her eyes on Logan, who'd been so quietly patient during her whole reunion. She'd almost forgotten the thing she most wanted to say. "Thank you."

He cocked a blond eyebrow. "For what? Inviting you to Bali on a flight that nearly got you killed?"

"For being so wonderful when I was losing it. You got me through it."

"We got through it together."

Anna felt entirely comforted. Surrounded by her friends, her father beaming appreciatively at her, and with Logan by her side, it felt like the complete opposite of an hour earlier. Wearing airplane slippers and a sundress, in the midst of a sea of people in the international-arrivals terminal of LAX, she felt truly free. So she did what she never would have done at any other time in her life: she grabbed Logan and kissed him.

He kissed her back.

It was a kiss of hope. A promise for the future. It was, more than anything else, a kiss of life.

The Parent Trap

Saturday evening, 8:45 p.m.

As Sam pulled up to the valet stand at the Beverly Hills Hotel, the hallowed grounds where the Hollywood elite had partied, mated, dated, and overdosed for years, she decided that this had been one of the more insane days of her life.

First Anna had nearly died. Then Anna had survived. Then she and Eduardo had called his parents to deliver the news that they were getting married in a week. His parents, Pedro and Consuela, had cut short a vacation in Cabo and caught a flight to Los Angeles that afternoon, renting one of the hotel's most exclusive bungalows for a week. Sam next called her estranged mother, Dina, who agreed to fly in from North Carolina immediately. A cozy dinner for six was planned—Sam, her fiancé, and both of their parents—at the Polo Lounge in the back of the hotel, at 9:30 p.m.

As Sam had waited for Anna's plane to land, one part of her brain was so deeply steeped in Hollywood that she'd felt removed from the terror, as if she were watching one of her father's big-budget action movies, and whether or not the plane crashed, whether or not people survived, was nothing more than a plot point. But another part of her—a part she liked—had been terrified. She'd cried, she'd felt nauseated, she'd even prayed.

But now that it was over, with a very Hollywood-esque happy ending, Sam was back to worrying about her own life and her upcoming nuptials. Eduardo's parents were light-years different from her own. Would they hate each other? Would worlds collide?

Sam slid out of her Hummer and handed the keys to the red-uniformed Italian valet who wore, she noticed, those supposedly invisible braces on his teeth. *Wannabe actor*, she thought. Sporting the Invisalign was always a dead giveaway.

A uniformed doorman opened the glass doors to the hotel for her, and she strode through the lobby of the Pink Palace—the nickname for the pink-hued hotel that had seen so much Hollywood glitter and decadence over the decades of its tenure on Sunset Boulevard in the heart of Beverly Hills. It had certainly earned its nickname, with its pink-and-white carpeting, dusty rose-colored gold-framed chairs, and enormous arrangements of native California flowers (many of which were, of course, pink). The only thing that wasn't pink were its majestic yellow pillars. The lobby itself was something of a hangout, and tonight it was crowded. Martin Scorsese was at the fireplace having a drink with Matt Damon, and Jessica Alba sat in a low-slung chair in the corner, chatting with a couple of friends. Sam had known the indoor part of the Polo Lounge would be equally crowded, so she'd asked Eduardo to book a table on the quieter terrace, where the green-and-white striped tablecloths, huge white umbrellas, and wrought-iron seats promised a quintessential Los Angeles dining experience.

Sam caught a reflection of herself in a spotless columned mirror flanked by massive vases of freesias and orange blossoms. She wore a zebra-patterned Givenchy cotton T-shirt under a cantaloupe raw silk jacket with lantern sleeves, Chanel black trousers, and cantaloupe-and-black polka-dot Gucci heels. Casual enough to be hip, grown-up enough to suit a "fiancée," and flattering enough to minimize what needed to be minimized.

Sam tore her gaze from her own reflection. Where were her parents? They'd said they'd meet her in the lobby. She nibbled unconsciously on a recently manicured fingernail. Her stomach flip-flopped. If she was this nervous about dinner, how nervous would she be at the actual wedding? Her side of the aisle would likely be quite a bit more complicated and more crowded than Eduardo's. For starters, her father. Jackson, had a virtual harem of ex-wives, one of whom was Sam's biological mother, Dina, who had left America's Most Beloved Action Star when Sam was still in elementary school and moved to North Carolina. Though Sam had seen her at graduation, that meeting had been the first one since Sam had been in elementary school. To say that she was estranged from Dina was an understatement. Yet when she'd called her mom early that morning, Dina hadn't hesitated. There was a ten o'clock flight from Asheville to Charlotte, and a noon flight from Charlotte to LAX.

With the time change, she could be at the Beverly Hills Hotel by four.

Frankly, Sam was shocked that Dina was showing up at all, as she had really only called her out of obligation. It kind of begged the question, If it was so easy for her mother to hop on a plane when Sam asked her to, why the hell had she hopped out of Sam's life in the first place?

Sam asked herself now: How did she feel about Dina dropping back into her life? She felt . . . nothing. Didn't care one way or the other. She wasn't about to invest any emotional energy in the woman, since apparently it had slipped her mind for years that she actually had a daughter.

Well, at least her father hadn't offered Dina a room at their Bel Air estate. That would have been too weird. Instead, he was graciously picking her up here at the hotel. But they *were* having a drink together at the Ivy, before meeting everyone at Pedro and Consuela's bungalow and then adjourning to the Polo Lounge for dinner. Sam checked her Omega Constellation watch. They still had ten minutes.

At the lobby bar, CNN was on a strategically placed flat-screen TV. The crash-landing of Anna's jet in darkness at LAX was still the lead story—the reporter described it as a miracle and the captain as a hero. Sam paused for a moment to watch: dozens of television cameras had caught the landing from every conceivable angle, and it was being rehashed and analyzed like a key play at the Super Bowl. She'd seen this footage a hundred times since last night and couldn't imagine what Anna had gone through. She'd tried to call Anna at around noon, but her father had said she was asleep. Sam couldn't blame her. Though from a strictly budding director/storytelling point of view, she was dying to find out what it had been like.

"Sam!"

She started slightly at the sound of her father's deep, resonant voice and turned around to be greeted by a rare sight: her father and mother together, striding across the pink hotel lobby toward her. They'd seen each other at graduation, of course. But Sam couldn't remember the last time they'd actually spent any time together, let alone sat down for a drink and a civil meal. That they were doing so now, simply because Sam had asked and said it was important, filled her with a kind of light, bubbly feeling. She didn't trust this feeling.. Experience had taught her not to trust in such things a long time ago. But still, for the moment, *in* the moment, it felt good.

Dina was as Sam remembered from June. Her dark brown hair, streaked with gray, was still frizzy, her clothes—a simple, loose-fitting black pantsuit—three years out of date, and her simple black fabric shoes built for comfort. She was incongruous next to the buff, charismatic Jackson. His presence pretty much commanded the attention of everyone—even seasoned Beverly Hills matrons—in the lounge. He had the kind of chiseled jaw that seemed to exist only on movie stars, and boyishly cut sandy hair that hung fashionably shaggy over his eyes. Today, he wore black Armani jeans and a baby blue silk shirt; black-and-white rattlesnake cowboy boots added a good two inches to his natural height of six feet. He was a man whom age had treated well. The few lines on his face were all character and charm, especially the crinkling around his sparkling cerulean blue eyes.

As they moved toward her, and she toward them, Sam could see several guests stop their conversations to watch. A ponytailed girl, no doubt a tourist, lifted her Nokia to take Jackson's picture, then shrieked to her friend, "Oh my God!" Sam figured this photo, or a similar one, would probably end up in some gossip rag with a headline that read, JACKSON SHARPE AND EX-WIFE #1 MEET FOR SECRET TRYST, or some such bullshit. Well, hell. That was the price you paid for getting twenty mil a movie.

"Hi, Mom." Sam hugged her mother. It felt forced. It *was* forced. Sam considered changing her maternal greeting to "Dina." That would be better. And more honest.

"Hey, pass it around," her father teased, and held his arms out for her. She hugged him, too. Wow. They were just such a hap-hap-happy family. Except that she hardly ever saw her father. And her mother had abandoned her long ago. But, you know, other than that . . .

"I think Eduardo must already be with his parents. They're in the Paul Williams bungalow out back," Sam declared. "So let's go."

She took a tentative step in the direction of the glass doors that led to the bungalows. But Jackson and Dina weren't moving.

"Just a sec, sweetie," her father began. "Your mother and I have been talking about this whole marriage thing. . . ." He shifted his weight to one leg and thrust his hands deep into the pockets of his black jeans.

"And we wanted to talk about it with you," her mother chimed in, nervously patting her semi-frizzed blond hair.

Okay, this was surreal. Sam had anticipated the "you're

too young to get married" rap. But that her mismatched parents were standing there as a parental unit, out of concern for the daughter they had not exactly nurtured together? It was beyond bizarre.

The truth was, Sam had given the "you're too young" speech to herself many times since Eduardo had proposed a few weeks ago on the Santa Monica Promenade, and had given it to herself a few more times since Anna's plane had safely landed last night. She'd said yes to a marriage in a week under some duress—the impending death of one of her best friends. Honestly, Sam thought in retrospect that if Anna's plane hadn't made it, she would have been at a funeral in New York City in a week and not at her own wedding. But now she was seeing an exchange of vows with Eduardo as some kind of predestined thing. Anna had made it. That was a miracle. Maybe her own marriage was meant to be, too.

Or some such quasi–New Age, it's-all-destiny reasoning.

"We hope you're willing to listen," her mother added, shifting back and forth on the rose-and-white carpet.

Sam shrugged. "Fine, Dina," she replied, trying out the first-name thing. It definitely felt better than "Mom." Dina didn't flinch, and Sam leaned coolly against the yellow marble pillar behind her, waiting for the avalanche to descend.

And so it began. First, three minutes from her father, followed by three minutes from her mother, and not a single surprising statement. You could have torn it out of *Modern Maturity*: what to say when your eighteen-year-old daughter says she's getting married and you think the idea is insane. It was, Sam thought, awfully rich coming from them. What the hell did they know about marriage and family?

When they finished their monologues, Sam did her best to stay cool. "I respect your opinions," she began. "And I'll consider them."

Her dad looked surprised. "Well, that's great, Sam."

It was also a crock of shit, but Sam wasn't about to add that sentiment. "We still don't know what Eduardo's parents are saying to him. Let's go out to the bungalow, have a drink, and we can talk about it together," she suggested evenly.

"What about the wedding preparations?" Dina pressed.

Yeah, those. Sam had thought about that, too. She had no venue, no caterer, no guest list, no invitations, no wedding gown, no bridesmaids, no maid of honor—who would it be? Cammie? Anna? If it wasn't Cammie, she'd be so pissed. Most Hollywood weddings took at least a year to plan. How was she going to pull this off in time for next Friday night? The idea was preposterous.

But then, her whole Hollywood life was pretty preposterous. Sam had learned, early and often, that the answer to . . . well, pretty much *anything* was that the application of copious amounts of money solved most problems.

"I'll figure it out," Sam responded. "Can we just go to the bungalow now?"

"Fine," Jackson agreed. "But I doubt that your mother and I will change our minds."

They left the lobby and walked along the gaslit asphalt path through the hotel's fragrant gardens toward the bungalow. Giant bouquets of yellow and orange nasturtiums hung from tall stone planters and perfumed the air. Sam walked a few steps ahead of her parents, but she could feel them behind her, bearing down on her. She clicked along in her three-inch stilettos, and had never walked a hundred yards faster.

Eduardo's father answered Jackson's discreet knock on the door. "Welcome," he greeted them. "I'm Pedro Munoz." Eduardo's father was just as Sam remembered him. He had an elegant but friendly-looking face, silver hair and a mustache, and his English was accent-free. Tonight he wore an immaculate gray Canali suit.

"And I'm Consuela," added Mrs. Munoz, appearing behind her husband in the open doorway. Tall and slender, Consuela wore a simple fitted black Prada dress that fell to just below her knees, and black suede Ferragamo pumps. Her dark hair was twisted off her face into an elegant bun at the nape of her neck. Her inflection only occasionally betrayed that she was not a native English speaker.

"And me you already know," Eduardo chimed in. He stood, nervously shifting from side to side, a few feet behind his parents. He was attired more casually, in vintage Marc Jacobs jeans, a fitted white V-neck, and a black Dolce & Gabbana velvet blazer. Even so, the three of them were dressed far more formally than anyone else in the room.

Sam had met Eduardo's parents once before, when she and Eduardo had taken an impromptu trip to Peru right after graduation. They lived in a fantastic white villa on a mountainside overlooking the capital city that had all the creature comforts of a Bel Air mansion and then some. Pedro Munoz was a high-placed government official, and Consuela owned Lima's most prestigious art gallery.

Each had been educated abroad—Pedro at St. Paul's and then Dartmouth, Consuela at a boarding school in the south of France and then the Sorbonne, with a two-year stint at Carnegie-Mellon in the middle.

Sam's parents introduced themselves, and then they all stepped inside, where the air was at least fifteen degrees cooler and smelled of oranges and bergamot, thanks to a thick scented candle flickering on the coffee table. The room could have been designed in the 1920s; there was something timeless about its crystal chandeliers and polished brass sconces. The furniture, all buttery yellow and pale apricot, was plush but sophisticated, and tufted stools and velvet throw pillows gave the seating area an almost *Alice in Wonderland* feel. A baby grand piano stood in one corner, and through the bathroom door Sam glimpsed a mint green Jacuzzi tub and a tower of plush towels piled almost to the ceiling.

When she'd been in Peru back in June, Consuela had been the perfect hostess. Tonight, she outdid herself again, bringing a pitcher of iced limeade and a fruit platter from the kitchen as Sam joined Eduardo on the lemon silk brocade couch, and Dina and Jackson settled into cream-colored club chairs. Pedro perched on a peach chenille love seat. Eduardo kissed Sam's cheek and entwined his fingers with hers.

"You look beautiful," he murmured, low enough that none of the parentals could overhear.

Sam smiled. He knew exactly the right thing to say. Though she'd felt reasonably calm when she was in the lobby with her parents, the walk down the path to the bungalow had been a nerve-racking experience, and she was now so anxious that she could actually feel a drop of sweat traveling into her two-hundred-dollar black-and-beige lace La Perla push-up bra.

"So," Consuela began as she sat next to her husband on the peach love seat and crossed her slender, elegant legs. "We come together to discuss a happy occasion. We are very fond of your daughter."

"Then we already have something in common," Jackson said in his resonant movie-star voice, glancing over at Sam with paternal warmth. "Because we're fond of her too."

Sam tried very hard not to roll her eyes, but Consuela smiled and looked charmed.

"We understand our children would like to be married soon." Pedro took a sip of the fresh limeade that Consuela had poured for him. "It's a lovely idea."

"Why have a long engagement when you know exactly what you want?" Eduardo added rhetorically, smiling at Sam and squeezing her hand.

Dina cleared her throat and crossed her legs, revealing perhaps the ugliest red-and-black zigzag-patterned trouser socks Sam had ever seen. She was momentarily stunned by the notion that someone related to her *by blood* had actually gone into a store, picked out these socks, and said to herself, *Yeah, wow, these are cute— I definitely want these.*

"Sam is very young. We thought she'd wait until after college even to think about marriage," Dina said slowly, twirling her own glass of limeade in her small hands.

Sam looked at her mother, unable to handle the combination of the ugly socks and this latest statement.

"How would you know?" she blurted, instantly regretting it. She didn't want to look like a snotty little bitch in front of Eduardo's parents. Well, too late.

"It's true that Sam and I haven't seen a lot of each other." Dina looked from Pedro to Consuela, neither of whom betrayed a sign of surprise. "I hope to change that in the future."

Sam rolled her eyes and nuzzled her head into Eduardo's shoulder so that she wouldn't have to look her mother in the eye.

Consuela smiled easily, as if she hosted estranged mothers-of-the-bride for drinks all the time. "Well, what better way to help family come together than a wedding?" She graciously picked up the fruit tray and circled the group with it, offering the fresh strawberries and mango, along with a cocktail napkin. "And I cannot think of a better spot on earth for newlyweds to live than Paris. Paris is a city made for lovers," she said enthusiastically, nodding her glossy dark head.

"Paris?" Jackson was about to pluck a juicy orange slice of mango from the fruit platter that Consuela was offering, but withdrew his hand quickly, surprised. "Who said anything about Paris? Sam's not moving to Paris," he finished, more firmly.

"What my father means is that Eduardo and I talked about being long distance for a while," Sam hastened to explain, leaning forward on the brocade couch. She ran her fingers through her hair nervously. "I'm planning to go to USC while he finishes out the year at the Sorbonne."

Pedro frowned, stood stoically, and moved toward

the fireplace. He put his hands into the pockets of his well-cut gray suit. "You here in California and my son in Paris? What kind of marriage would that be?"

Consuela nodded as she put the fruit platter back on the glass coffee table. "I agree. A new marriage is too tender a thing to endure such strain. Eduardo's father and I are no strangers to airplanes—we own one, as you probably know—"

"I've got a Gulfstream myself," Jackson put in.

"This is not about planes," Sam interjected hotly. She felt Eduardo put a calming arm around her shoulder. That helped. A little. But she was feeling squeezed in both directions.

"What I was saying," Consuela continued patiently, "is that it is one thing to have a long-distance relationship when you have been married for many years and one of the spouses must travel. It is another thing in the first months. Don't you agree, Eduardo?"

"No, Mom, I don't," Eduardo replied. He had a firm look in his dark eyes that spoke volumes. Sam breathed a little easier.

Sam saw Consuela bristle, and decided that, like her own father, Eduardo's mother was probably used to getting her way most of the time.

"Here's what I want to know, Sam." Her father leaned forward and held her gaze, earnest and focused. "What's the point of rushing to get married—which I still am not in favor of, by the way—if you're going to live thousands of miles apart? If you're going to do that, why not just wait to get married until both of you are done with school? You only just finished high school.

You have plenty of time. Maybe you wanting to live apart like this is a sign that you don't really want to get married." Sam stared back at her dad. Looking particularly young in his baby blue shirt and patterned cowboy boots, he made her feel like she was being counseled by one of her Beverly Hills High classmates, not her father.

Dina stood up and moved a step toward her, so that she was hovering by the side of the couch. "I agree, Sam. I agree completely with Jackson."

"Thank you," Jackson said as he rose and stood by his ex-wife.

Jesus Christ. It was happening. Her mother and father—who'd barely communicated for ten years—were presenting her with a united front. It was maddening. Enough so that she decided she'd rather piss off her parents than piss off Eduardo's. She stood, too, and reached for the limeade pitcher.

"Would anyone like more to drink?" She turned to face Consuela and Pedro across the coffee table, her back facing her parents. "I'll think about France. Maybe that really would be the best thing."

Eduardo's response was a beaming smile. His parents nodded in tandem and Consuela indicated that she'd like a refill. Sam leaned over to pour Consuela a glass of the pale green drink, and as she did so sneaked a glance at Jackson and Dina. They each looked like someone had just peed in their limeade.

Sam smiled to herself. Their expressions alone were almost worth making the move to Paris and skipping USC altogether.

Almost. But not quite.

Girl of the Milennium

Saturday evening, 10:45 p.m.

"Step away from the police line! Step away from the police line!"

A special off-duty officer of the Los Angeles Police Department, chosen by Cammie and Ben as much for his rangy good looks as his man-in-black authority, barked into a loudspeaker. "The club will not open for fifteen minutes. Step away from the police line!"

Cammie stood alone, surveying the madhouse scene outside Bye, Bye Love's second night of operation, smiling with satisfaction at the hundreds of people trying desperately to get into her club. She wore a black Azzaro by Vanessa Seward swing halter top studded with crystals, with black Imitation of Christ skinny jeans and black Jimmy Choo ankle boots with lethal-looking scarlet stiletto heels. She'd piled her strawberry blond curls on her head haphazardly, allowing a few to fall across her forehead and down her back.

Behind her stood her and Ben's brainchild, a low, squat, building, with auto-bay doors facing an asphalt tarmac, and an old-fashioned, low-rent sign announcing BYE, BYE LOVE as if it were an oil-change special. There were gas pumps in front that had been rigged up to dispense pure spring water, and the windows had been painted over—bloodred on the outside, black on the inside—to heighten the club effect.

News of Bye, Bye Love had spread like some kind of virus through the cell/text/Internet/tele-friend grapevine that was club-hopping Los Angeles. Within twenty-four hours it was *the* club, and if you didn't know about it, or you did know about it but couldn't get in, you were relegated to the great unwashed underclass of the subhip.

"We wanna get in!" a Valley denizen in a tartan micromini and a matching bustier wailed.

"Guest list first," replied the rent-a-cop.

"I've been here since noon!" The Valley girl wasn't quitting.

"Yeah, we've been here since noon!" her friend joined in. She wore a cobalt blue Juicy Couture tube dress that did nothing for her dumpy figure and had VE—visible extensions, the cheap kind, glued in. Both girls screamed "before" photo in the makeover section of a fashion magazine.

"Then you can wait a little longer," the rent-a-cop growled from behind his too-cool shades.

As if they'll get in at all, Cammie thought with a satisfied smirk.

The Valley girls were not alone in their desire to infiltrate the club's exclusive clientele. Venice Boulevard was jammed bumper-to-bumper. The valet-parking operation that Cammie and Ben had hired already had a full lot, except for spaces being held for VIPs, so prospective parkers were being shunted off to neighborhood side streets. A five-abreast line snaked down the sidewalk to the west, which was fine, since Cammie and Ben had anticipated this chaos and arranged a special VIP entrance through the back alley. It was guarded by a phalanx of security guards to ensure that no riffraff squeezed through.

Tonight they were expecting Fergie, Gwen and Gavin, Justin, David and Posh, Kobe Bryant and his wife, Cate Blanchett, and the Duff sisters. Cammie had left explicit instructions that none of the following were to be allowed in: Paris, Lindsay, or Britney. They were overexposed. Toast. Yesterday. More buh-bye than Bye, Bye Love.

"That's Cammie Sheppard!" she heard a girl in line exclaim to her friend, pointing a fake nail in Cammie's direction. "Oh my God, she is so hot!"

"She certainly is," a male voice intoned from behind her. Cammie turned to see Parker Pinelli coming toward her, hand in hand with a beautiful girl with fabulous chestnut hair that fell like a waterfall around her face. Cammie remembered her from last night—Citron, his apparent new girlfriend. She was happy to see them. Parker added a hot quotient to any crowd, with his ghost-of-James-Dean chiseled good looks. He was currently shooting a Showtime original movie called *Boot,* about a group of young men brought together for Marine basic training at Camp Pendleton who kill the smallest guy in a prank gone wrong.

"Aren't you just the 'It' girl of the moment," Parker teased, kissing Cammie's tan cheek.

"Hey, I'm the girl of the millennium," Cammie corrected. Parker laughed and hugged her, and she realized all over again just how incredibly hot he was; he had been the only guy at Beverly Hills High who was, objectively speaking, probably better looking than Ben. Tonight he wore a distressed black T-shirt with angel wings on it, and even more distressed jeans—already rocking the uniform of the movie star he hoped to become. She extended a hand to Citron. "Hey, I'm Cammie. I'm sorry I didn't get to talk to you more last night. Let me buy you a drink later."

"That'd be grand," Citron replied, with a charming Southern accent. "I don't know too many people out here yet. Parker's been introducing me to some of his friends." She looked around, shaking her head. "This is out of control, huh?"

Cammie checked the girl out more closely. There were flecks of gold in her amber eyes. She wore a white Nina Ricci pencil skirt and layered white and cream tank tops that perfectly complimented her skin tone—hip, but not trying too hard. "So, what brought you to L.A.?" Cammie asked.

"She's a singer. Jazz. She's fantastic," Parker answered eagerly before Citron could get a word out. He smiled at her proudly.

"Jazz? That's unusual," Cammie commented. She stepped closer to the front door, motioning for Citron and Parker to follow. There were only ten minutes until the club opened up. The security and door people in their official Bye, Bye Love jackets would be taking up their positions any moment. "This town is all about rock and roll."

"My brother and I—we grew up on jazz," Citron explained. "I came out because he's here. He plays piano. I'm living with him in a guesthouse in Beverly Hills."

"Who's your brother?" Cammie asked idly, as the chief of club security—a beefy Latino guy with the nickname Chief—opened the door and came outside. There was a roar from the crowd that Chief acknowledged with a quick wave, and then groans as he closed the main door behind him again. Cammie, Parker, and Citron moved so he could pass. He gave Cammie a little thumbs-up, which Cammie acknowledged with a chuck of her chin. She was, after all, still working.

"Django Simms. He works for a guy named Jonathan Percy?"

Cammie's mind raced. "Anna Percy's father?" she asked, surprised.

"Bingo," Parker put in. "Small world and all that."

"I met Anna," Citron went on. "She's so nice! Did you know she was on that plane—?"

"Yeah, I heard." Cammie nodded coolly. Anna, Anna, Anna. Why did everything in Cammie's life seem to lead back to that freaking girl? She was glad she had survived and all, but take last night for example. Just when she was *finally* kissing Ben—which had taken weeks of work and some serious maneuvering on Cammie's part—in walked Anna to witness it. Actually, Cammie had enjoyed that part, but it had turned out to be the beginning of the end of a plan involving her and Ben very naked under high-thread-count imported sheets. Anna had probably engineered the LAX crash landing a few hours later just so she could foil the evening and be the center of attention again.

Okay. That was mean. She'd nearly died. But still.

Last night—actually, earlier today—she and Adam had stayed at the bar inside and watched the plane make its successful return to LAX. She'd found herself actually concerned that Anna would make it out okay, which was annoying. Then she couldn't help but be happy when everyone walked away from the stricken jet. That was even more annoying.

She and Adam watched the coverage until sunrise. They had little to say to each other, and that made things easier. It was like confirmation that their relationship was officially and completely over. Sitting at the bar, Adam had seemed distant, even cold. Whatever. She'd moved on to something hotter: Ben. They hadn't had the chance to hook up last night, but there was always tonight.

"Did you watch the coverage?" Citron asked.

"It was hard to avoid." Cammie heard the door behind her open again and a small group of security personnel took up positions in front of them. When the club opened, the last thing anyone wanted was a mad rush to enter.

"I was glued to the TV, man," Parker said. "It was like a movie."

"With a happy ending," Citron added, as Parker took her arm. Again, Cammie caught the faintest of drawls and wondered where she was from. Mississippi? Louisiana? She had to admit it was cute.

"I'm just so glad that Anna's all right," Citron breathed. "She's so lucky."

"Yeah, me too." Cammie craned her head around. Where was Ben? Already in the club?

As if Parker had been reading her mind, he asked, "What's up with Anna and the B-man?"

"Toast," Cammie declared with satisfaction.

Parker grinned. "Then I'd say *you're* the lucky one. Me too."

He looked like he had news. "Do tell."

"I just got a call for a new project." He punched the air. "You've heard of something called *Lifeboat?*"

"No shit?" Cammie was impressed.

"One of the leads," he said proudly.

She knew all about the movie. Her father, Clark, represented two of the producers. If Parker was cast in it, it would be a huge break, as he'd play one of seven people who had to abandon their yacht and drift at sea in a rubber lifeboat, hoping to be rescued. Kevin Bacon was directing. Rumor was everyone from Jack White from the White Stripes to Natalie Portman was signed. Whichever of those tiny blond twins was still acting—Cammie could never remember—couldn't even get a screen test.

"Well, congratulations. Go celebrate." Cammie reached into her Kooba Charlie silver-panel disco clutch and took out a few laminated cards that would be good for free drinks inside. "Take these." She pressed them into Citron's hand. "Drinks tonight are on me."

"Thanks!"

Citron's gratitude was genuine, and Cammie smiled. She got one of her door guys' attention and motioned for him to let Parker and Citron inside. The door opened, and they headed into the club to hoots and catcalls from the waiting masses. No. Not *the* club. *Her* club. Well, hers and Ben's. Theirs.

"Cammie! Over here!"

Cammie turned. Several photographers had moved into position, the better to snap pictures of clubgoers coming and going. Of course, the VIP entrance was around the back and no photographers were permitted in that area. But many celebrities liked to be photographed and chose to come in the front way.

Cammie struck a pose for the paparazzi as flashbulbs went off. A hand on her hip. A toss of her hair. She spun around and gave them a coquettish look over one shoulder. All of this came as naturally to her as breathing.

"So you're the teen queen who owns this place, right?" one guy with bleached spiky hair and an overeager smile called out.

"With my partner, Ben Birnbaum," Cammie answered, posing some more as people yelled, "Hey, Cammie!" and, "Over here!" She pursed her lips, cocked her head. Laughed. The photo op went on and on.

"Hey, Cammie, *Entertainment Tonight*! A few words before things get hopping tonight?" The body attached to the voice was surprisingly cute. He couldn't have been a day over twenty-five and looked like he'd just stepped out of a Ralph Lauren ad, with his close-cropped rusty gold hair and tennis player arms. A portly camera guy hovered behind him.

Entertainment Tonight was covering her club? Not that she ever watched *ET*—it was unbelievably cheesy, and she already knew everything they reported before they knew it. Still, having them there could only be a good thing.

"Hi, there," she purred, striking a pose with her left foot thrust forward.

"Hey. I'm Dashiell McCarthy." The reporter held a microphone close to Cammie's face. "Call me Dash. Your club opened last night and it's the hottest thing in town tonight. Did you know that the police are keeping spectators a block away so they don't disrupt traffic? How many people can your place hold? And how many do you expect to turn away?"

"How high can you count?" Cammie raised an eyebrow coyly.

Caught off guard by her boldness, Dash laughed and then moved on to his next question. "Why do you think your club is so successful?"

Cammie shrugged lightly. "Because it has the best of everything. We've got the best celebrity DJs. The best bartenders. The best mix. The best guest list. And the décor will be constantly changing, so anyone who can actually get in will never get tired of it. Everyone wants the best, right?"

Cammie stopped talking when she saw Ben step outside. He was dressed simply, in a pair of black True Religion jeans and a long-sleeved black button-down Calvin Klein shirt. He looked around, then saw her and beckoned.

"I have to go," Cammie told Dash as she smoothed her hair behind one shell-like ear.

"Just one more question," the reporter asked. "Everyone will want to know. Who are the hottest designers for clubwear right now? Whose clothes are you seeing the most of?"

"Martin Rittenhouse," Cammie replied, thinking fast. The rising young designer who created everything from high fashion to sportswear. Cammie had modeled for him at his LACMA show to benefit the New Visions program. "No doubt about it. Did you know he's launching a new line for petites? It's so hot. He's calling it Petite Couture by Rittenhouse, but what he's going to call it when it hits the runway is—"

She stopped for a brief moment. What would be a great name? Martin, petite, Rittenhouse, petite, Martin . . .

"Martinette. The face of Martinette is an amazing new model named Champagne. You heard it from me first. But you didn't hear it from me last."

Cammie nearly hugged herself. Damn, she was good. She had come up with that on the spot.

She gave Dash one last smoldering look just for practice, then moved off, as photographers continued to snap photos and other reporters called out questions. She smiled at her own quick thinking. She was Champagne's manager. They'd met when Cammie had helped out at a charity fashion show earlier in the summer.

When her interview aired on *ET*, there'd be buzz about Champagne even before anyone even saw her face. So what if Martin Rittenhouse hadn't officially named his new clothing line Martinette? It was a great fucking name. So what if the designer had merely verbally promised to feature Champagne in his fashion shows, and not yet said a word about making her the new face of Martinette—or whatever he decided to call it? When *ET* reported it, it would be a fait accompli. Just let Rittenhouse try to deny it.

It was a move worthy of her father, Clark Sheppard, the toughest agent in Hollywood. How many times had she heard it from him? Sell the sizzle, not the steak.

Cammie made her way to where Ben was waiting for her inside the front door. He smelled faintly of Acqua di Parma aftershave. "You ready for night two?"

They walked through the club together. Cammie still got a thrill every time she looked around *their* space. Playing on the fact that the club had once been an auto-body shop, antique car signage and license plates from around the world dotted the walls and ceiling, and interior upholstering from cars formed seating areas. An enormous slot-car track ran along the interior walls, and partiers could take their turns racing against their friends. Lights changed color and in turn changed the mood on the dance floor: sultry red, flirtatious pink, cool blue. They paused near the Cone of Silence, one of the add-ons they'd thought of at the last minute. Inside the cone, clubgoers could get a brief respite from the pounding music and throbbing beat.

"Two minutes to opening," he told her.

"Brilliant. You and me, baby." She effortlessly slipped a hand into his back pocket. To her satisfaction, he snaked one of his hands around her waist.

"You look great."

"Thanks."

She couldn't help herself. She waited a plausible five seconds to make it seem like it wasn't high on her conversation checklist, but she asked nonetheless.

"Have you talked to Anna?"

"I left her a message," he answered quickly.

Was she imagining it, or did the hand that was on her waist seem to stiffen as he shook his head? Was his skin paling slightly under his golden tan? Cammie shook out her curls. Forget Anna. "I was thinking maybe you and I would guest-DJ tonight for a while, so that everyone will know our faces. There's an open slot between Zac and Christina," she cooed.

"Great, let's do it," Ben agreed as his eyes locked with hers.

"Fantastic." She ran her fingers through the top of his straight brown hair. "We make such a perfect team." She gave him a dazzling smile, dropped her eyes to half-mast, and added, in what she knew to be her sexiest, most insinuating voice, "We really should do it more."

Heart to Heart

Saturday night, 11:54 p.m.

In the time it took her to plod down the spiral staircase from her bedroom to the living room, Anna realized that every part of her body hurt, ached, or throbbed. Her shoulders. Her knees. Her hips. Her neck. Her wrists. Joints that she didn't know existed were calling out to her for at least ibuprofen and possibly something a whole lot stronger.

She'd taken a shower before she'd finally fallen asleep at dawn. Nothing had felt sore then. Why so much pain now?

Adrenaline, she told herself, as she took the stairs with the caution of a septuagenarian, clinging to the iron railing. She'd been running on adrenaline all night long. There was a reason she'd been instructed to assume the brace position. Regardless of the pilot's considerable skill, landing on metal was a lot rougher than landing on wheels.

The living room was dark when she got to the bottom of the stairs. She flipped a light switch. Recessed overhead lighting lit the room. But her dad was nowhere in sight.

"Dad?"

Nothing. He had to be outside. Or maybe he'd gone out for the evening. Well, that was no surprise.

Logan had checked into a room at the Chateau Marmont in West Hollywood. He'd invited her to go with him, but she'd found that she needed the comfort of what had been her own room, her own bed, for the past few months. After a long hot shower and steam, and a few hours of lying in her antique four-poster bed, waiting for the adrenaline to wear off, she'd slept through the entire day.

Anna took a few steps toward the kitchen, the thick Berber carpeting caressing her bare feet. She thought again of being barefoot on the plane. Her conversation with Logan as they neared LAX came back to her. That line from the country song. She was no fan of country music—the last time she'd listened to it had been with Sam, when they'd found themselves in that mysterious villa on the Pacific coast of Mexico on the same trip where Sam had first met Eduardo. But the line that had come to her resonated.

Live like you were dying.

Today, it had a whole new meaning.

Anna had thought she'd come to Los Angeles to reinvent herself. In some ways, she'd succeeded. Certainly there had been more new experiences than she could imagine. But to live like she was dying? She hadn't. She'd lived like she was Anna Percy, on another coast where people didn't know her and couldn't or wouldn't report her to her mother. Even as she'd gotten on the plane to Bali—if she were to be honest with herself—she knew that in a corner of her mind she was already planning how to get back to the East Coast in time for the start of Yale. She probably wouldn't have stayed in Bali for more than a week.

"Dad?"

Still no answer. Maybe he was in the kitchen.

As she eased her way back toward the kitchen, she passed a wall full of the framed photographs that her father had recently started collecting. She'd passed them many times, but now she stopped to look. There were black-and-whites by Ansel Adams and Edward Clark. One of the Clark photos was of two migrant farm girls, their faces smudged with dirt, but with dainty bows in their hair. Anna nodded to them as if she'd just made a new acquaintance.

In the deserted kitchen she stared at the center-island cooking station with six burners and a convection oven. The marble kitchen table, the black refrigerator freezer large enough for a family of ten. On the granite countertop near the table, Anna saw a dinner tray and a full glass of fresh papaya, peach, and mango juice. Neatly folded to one side was a note with her name on it.

Anna,
I looked in on you sleeping before and didn't want to wake you up. It's been a madhouse here today, as you can imagine. Everyone called. I finally turned off the phone and forwarded everything to my cell so you wouldn't be disturbed. Your mother rang from Italy. Your sister from Massachusetts. Logan. He's still at the Chateau Marmont and said he'd wait for you to

call him, that he wasn't going to try to catch another plane to Bali for a couple of days. Can't say I blame him. Cyn from New York. Other New York friends. Sam, of course. Ben Birnbaum. Adam Flood. Parker and his girlfriend. Django stopped by. And reporters. If you ever wanted your fifteen minutes of fame, this would be your time.

The new cook, Mimi, made some of your favorite things—they're in the fridge if this little spread here isn't enough for you. I'm out back in the gazebo. I'll be there when you wake up, if you wake up before midnight. Otherwise, I'll see you in the a.m. If you're sore, there are two Advils on the tray. If you want to read about yourself, take a look at the Los Angeles Times *online. But you might not want to. I'm just so grateful you're okay.*

Love,
Dad

That was it. She hadn't shed even a tear last night, not in the worst of it, nor when she'd stepped into the international-arrivals terminal to be reunited with her father, Sam, and Eduardo. Crying in public was another banned activity in the *This Is How We Do Things* Big Book.

But now, reading her father's words, here alone in the kitchen, the tears came. And she let them. When she was finished, she wiped her cheeks with the backs of her hands, then rubbed her temples and took a deep breath.

Her dad had thought of everything, and thankfully there were tissues on the tray. The food that Mimi had left for her was simple: fresh fruit salad with diced mangoes and peaches, yogurt dotted with pistachio nuts, and herb-stuffed grape leaves. There was a miniature baguette fragrant with dill on the breadboard. She suddenly realized she was ravenous. She finished it all, slathering the bread with mounds of soft butter, relishing every bite and swallowing like it was her last meal on earth.

The midnight walk out to the gazebo had the same otherworldly quality. The fresh-cut grass smelled wonderful and tickled her bare feet. A few crickets chirped off toward the swimming pool, and an insomniac mockingbird sang in the branches of the eucalyptus tree. She took in everything. The gaslights that illuminated her path. The tennis court, the swimming pool, the hot tub, the shuffleboard court, and the barbecue pit. Her father's estate was one of the rare ones in Beverly Hills with lots of land around it—it was so easy to take that for granted, too.

"Anna." As promised, her father was waiting for her in the New England–style wooden gazebo, large enough to seat twenty. He wore a crisp white Lacoste polo and khakis. His feet were bare like hers. Shadows from the gaslights danced across his handsome, smiling face. Directly above them was an enormous eucalyptus tree.

"Good morning," she responded.

He laughed. "It's not morning, but it doesn't matter."

He patted the bench. She sat. He just stared at her. She knew why, but she still didn't know what to say.

"You saw my note?" She nodded slightly.

"You ate?"

"I ate."

"You're sore?"

"Worse than I've ever been in my life."

"There was Advil. That should help. . . ." He trailed off. "Someone once said that nothing focuses the mind like one's impending doom. I could say the same thing for the impending doom of your children. Did I ever tell you about your mother's and my experience in France? We were on a TGV from Paris to Lyon, and there was a bomb scare on our train. Very nerve-racking for most of the passengers, though the conductor just kept going, since the next station was just five kilometers away. Your mother simply raised a finger to summon a waiter into our stateroom and asked that the next martini be dry with an extra olive." He smiled at her. "But of course, nothing compares to what you went through. I could spend the next twenty-four hours just staring at your face."

Anna looked at her father in wonderment, still not quite sure what to say. This was another side of Jonathan Percy. Most of the time, he was an ambitious, driven businessman wearing Savile Row power suits and moving tens of millions of dollars of other people's money around. Off the clock, in his most private moments, he was a closet stoner with a three-day growth of beard and a Peter Pan "I never want to grow up" complex that Anna found more annoying than charming.

But now? In the aftermath of last night? He seemed like a different man entirely. A father.

"How did you happen to end up on a plane to Bali in the first place?" he asked as he ran his fingers through his spiky brown hair distractedly. "When Sam called to tell me you were on that plane—well, after she told me, I was so freaked that I pretty much didn't hear anything else."

How to explain? That she'd gone because of a wonderful boy she'd known since she was a kid but had only now rediscovered? That seeing Ben kissing Cammie at the club had made her want to flee as far as she could get, as fast as she could get there? Or the reason that sounded most ridiculous of all: she hadn't enjoyed the Yale freshman mixer back in New York.

"It sounds ridiculous now, but . . . I went with Logan on a whim."

"That's an awful long way to go on a whim," Jonathan noted, but he seemed more amused than angry. "When were you planning to come back? What about Yale?"

Ah, yes, what *about* Yale? She was due to report for freshman orientation in a week. She'd met her roommate, Contessa, a published poet and self-admitted sex addict from Horace Mann, who managed to be both stridently competitive and "I'm not part of your fascist power structure" at the same time. They had *not* clicked. But this wasn't the time to discuss that. Too much. Too fast.

"I'd have been back in time to go to school," she fibbed. "I just needed to get away for a while." She leaned back on the uncomfortable gazebo bench and stared out at the elegant house, built by her grandparents in the 1950s. It was massive, white stucco with red shutters, shaded by giant palm and eucalyptus trees. It was strange to think that after all these months of calling it home, from now on she might not see it more than once a year.

"I can understand that. So what now? Another, um, flight to Bali?"

"Would *you* be eager to jump on the next jet?" she asked, arching a blond eyebrow with a smile. "And can we put this discussion of Yale, trips, and the like off for twenty-four hours? All I want to do is breathe."

Her dad laughed, then reached down and scratched a bare ankle. "Consider it put off. Damn, I love being barefoot. It's hard to stay in the moment. Or at least it's always been hard for me. I always want the next thing and the next thing. And then it turns out the next thing I thought I wanted is never the thing I actually want."

She was curious. "So what is it you *do* want?"

It was very quiet in the yard. Anna thought she could hear the faint chirp of crickets. The moon glowed brightly above them.

"The summer I was twenty," her father finally said, "a buddy of mine took off on this tramp steamer to the South Seas. Fiji, or American Samoa, I don't exactly remember. He was going to do volunteer work in these native villages. Build a school. Teach English. This guy—Darren Chesterfield—his dad was a senior partner at Bear Stearns and owned about half of East Seventy-fourth street between Madison and Park Avenues. He could have done anything he wanted. He invited me along." Her father got a faraway look in his eyes, and he rubbed his chin thoughtfully. "I thought about it. The adventure. The feeling that I'd be doing something more important with my summer than smoking reefer and getting into trouble." His eyes flicked to her. "But I decided not to go."

"Where is Darren now?" Anna asked. She swatted at a couple of gnats that were circumnavigating her head.

"He ended up in Appalachia, in a town called Haggertsville, something like that. He's a teacher there. I hear from him now and then. He's really happy."

"Aren't you happy?" Anna asked, leaning forward on the gazebo bench and looking at her father intently.

He didn't answer right away. "I would like to matter," he finally responded. "I can't tell you how many times I've wondered what my life would have been like if I'd gone with Darren. I think I might have become a teacher too. But I didn't. I couldn't imagine telling my parents I was taking a leave of absence from college and doing something as déclassé as teaching high school." He shrugged.

"Why didn't you ever tell me that before?" Anna asked.

"Maybe because you were never in a plane crash before." He draped an arm around her shoulders. "Besides, if I had gone to be a schoolteacher, I would never have met your mother. Which means there'd be no Susan and no you."

"True." She turned her head from side to side. The Advil was finally kicking in, and she realized her range of motion had increased quite a bit. It still hurt, but it no longer felt like she'd been run over by a succession of heavy motor vehicles on the West Side Highway. "But except for the progeny part, you both would probably have been better off."

He smiled at her. "Ah, but the 'progeny' part trumps everything else. You'll see one day when you have kids."

Kids. Children. If she wasn't ready to talk about Yale,

she definitely wasn't ready for this conversation. In fact, she couldn't imagine why her dad had brought it up. "If being a parent was so important to you, why did you do so little of it?" Anna asked bluntly. It was something she would never have said even a day ago—too indiscreet, too direct. But if she was going to live like she was dying, there wasn't much utility in self-censorship. "When I came here at the end of December, I felt like I didn't know you at all."

Her father rubbed his chin. If he was offended by the question, he didn't show it. "I suppose wanting something and being good at it aren't necessarily the same thing."

Well, that was honest, at least, Anna thought.

"What about you, Anna Banana?" he asked, and she grinned. That had been her sister Susan's pet name for her when they were very young, and still part of something resembling an intact family. "Is there something you have a burning desire to do? Besides go to Yale?"

She said nothing, just shook her head. "Not now, Dad. Please. I need to think."

He nodded, pursing his lips. "Well, keep thinking. Here's how I see it. Right now, you're looking at the world with a special kind of clarity. That clarity fades, Anna. It doesn't last forever. Take advantage of it."

Anna stood.

"Heading back in?" he asked. "Going back to sleep?"

"Yes on the in, no on the sleep. I might read for a while. . . ."

"Say hi to *Don Quixote* for me. I may stay out here and have a smoke. It's been kind of stressful." Anna saw her father reach into his jeans pocket and take out the Altoid tin in which he kept his marijuana. He'd stopped hiding his penchant for it soon after she'd arrived. "Want to join me?" he asked.

"I'll pass. But enjoy." What else could she say? It *had* been kind of stressful.

"Wait a sec. Come here."

Her father stood too, and held his arms out to her. She went into them for the longest hug she could remember. Once again, she felt tears well up in her eyes. This time, she choked them back.

They parted wordlessly, and Anna made her way back toward the house, loving the feel of the cool night air on her skin and the grass again under her bare feet. It was well past midnight and she had every reason to go back to sleep. Or even draw herself a bubble bath to end all bubble baths in the white claw-foot tub in her bathroom. She had every accoutrement she needed. Candles. Vanilla bergamot bubble bath from Bliss. A white Egyptian-cotton robe from the Four Seasons gift shop. She could put on her iPod and relax or text back to the endless voice mails she was sure awaited her. Or at least call Logan. Thinking about him made her smile. That they had lived though a death-defying experience, in every sense of that word, made her feel so connected to him, even though they'd only reconnected just a few weeks ago. That he was so very *right* for her seemed miraculous. They were so much alike.

But. There was something else she needed, even before him, or the bubble bath, or more sleep. As she entered the house, her whole body tingled with an odd feeling of excitement. Purpose, even.

She stopped in the kitchen to make a container of French-press coffee. Black and strong, with fresh-ground beans from Costa Rica. She carried it up to her room, along with one white bone-china cup imported from Tunisia. Then she went straight to her rolltop desk, booted up her white iBook, and opened her draft screenplay—the autobiographical one, about the conservative Upper East Side high school senior who goes out to Los Angeles in the middle of her senior year.

Back in Manhattan, she'd written all of ten pages or so. Barely enough to establish her main character. Not nearly enough to get into the heart of the story.

Now she started to write. And write some more. Her fingers clicked at the keyboard, the coffee went untouched, and she didn't stop until noon the next day, so tired she could barely lift herself out of the chair. And the whole damn thing was done.

Wedding Bell Blues

Sunday afternoon, 12:38 p.m.

"**I**'ve decided I want a maid of honor. And I'd like it to be you. Cammie, you're my oldest friend. Good times and bad. Cool boyfriends and assholes. Dee, no offense," Sam concluded, turning from Cammie to Dee Young, who held the title of second-oldest friend.

Dee grinned back at Sam, blinking her huge, saucer-shaped blue eyes. "None taken. It should be Cammie. She deserves it," Dee affirmed in her girlish voice.

"I wouldn't go that far, Dee." Cammie said dryly. She looked down at the nail tech who was working busily on her pedicure. Sam and Dee were experiencing the same service on either side of her. "Easy on the cuticles," she cautioned.

It was Sunday morning—well, really early afternoon, since Sam didn't actually do Sunday mornings—and Sam was with Cammie and Dee in her bedroom, which was roughly the size of a small island nation, although better appointed. Each of them sprawled on a white silk chaise lounge brought up from the side of her father's heated swimming pool and arranged them in the center of Sam's floor. Three young women from Fab Feet on the Go provided foot soaks, reflexology massages, and pedicures.

It was a good thing, too. They had a Hollywood wedding to plan—one that would take place in just six days.

When Sam had woken up this morning, she'd felt a flutter of panic that had persisted all the way through her eucalyptus-scented steam shower and home-baked croissant with Kenyan mountain-grown coffee. Actually, it was more than a flutter. It was more like a flock of panicked birds wheeling in her pancreas. Had she really agreed to be married at the end of the week? Had she really agreed to think about skipping USC film school and moving to Paris with Eduardo instead? *Had she really let sixteen precious hours tick off the wedding-planning clock?*

The only way to possibly accomplish this affair was to enlist her best friends' help. But Cammie was totally and thoroughly booked. Overbooked, in fact, running Bye, Bye Love. That left Dee and Anna, in theory. But Anna was recovering from a near-death experience, and Sam hadn't even seen her since she'd crash-landed at LAX.

That left Dee. Dee was a lot of things. Petite. Cute. Amusing. Entertaining. From time to time a bit of a ditz. But a budding wedding planner wasn't one of the nouns or adjectives on the foregoing list.

In a crunch, Sam knew she could pull it off herself, if she had to. But the idea of being responsible for the planning of one's own wedding was humiliating. She glanced around the room, hoping for some jolt of inspiration.

Sam's room was as minimalist as the films she someday

wanted to make—focused around a few key details without too much clutter. The centerpiece was her California king bed, which had a clean, silver-poled, roofless canopy. The carpet was white, as were the walls. Adorning the walls were a collection of black-and-white framed movie posters, signed by the producer, the director, and the stars. Among these were *Au Revoir, Les Enfants; Amélie; Breakfast at Tiffany's;* and *Dominick and Eugene.* Her dad's action films were conspicuously absent. Sam caught Audrey Hepburn's eye, looking chic as ever in her black dress and diamond necklace. Holly Golightly, her character in *Tiffany's,* would never plan her own wedding, she was sure. But then again, she might be the type to get married with only a few days' notice.

"So what do you say, Cammie? Will you be Sam's maid of honor?" Dee prompted, jolting Sam out of her reverie. She realized that Cammie hadn't actually said okay.

Asking Cammie hadn't been an easy choice. Cammie could sometimes be a bigger bitch than just about anyone Sam had ever known. But they'd been best friends for so many years. Longevity counted, and so did loyalty. Especially in this town. She just hoped that neither Dee nor Anna would be insulted.

"Are you kidding?" Cammie downed a glassful of Taittinger champagne and set the empty glass on the carpet beside her. "Of course I'll do it."

"And you'll still be a bridesmaid," Sam added to Dee.

"Fantastic." Dee nodded her small blond head happily. Her bright blue eyes were shining. "I'm psyched. It's not every day that a girl gets to help plan her best friend's wedding *and* receive her high school diploma."

"It's too bad you didn't have a real graduation," Cammie pointed out.

"It was fine," Dee told her. "I finished my GED. After the year I had, I'm lucky to even be able to think straight."

Sam was glad that Dee had been able to finish all her GED requirements, given that she'd missed so much school when she had a medium-size nervous breakdown on a class trip to Las Vegas back in the spring. She'd ended up on the psychiatric floor at Cedars-Sinai, and then did a good long stay at the Ojai Institute near Santa Barbara, where the doctors figured out what was wrong with her brain chemistry—practically everything—and put her on a regimen of drugs designed to smooth out her manic depression.

Dee was a new person after Ojai. Kinder. Simpler. More coherent. But sometimes, Sam missed loopy, premeds Dee, who never met a countercultural or New Age fad she didn't fall in love with. EST. Kabbalah. Marianne Williamson. Whoever the guru of the moment happened to be. There was no doubt, however, that Dee was a far more stable and functional person after her treatment than before it. More boring, maybe. But more stable.

Sam studied her friends, who seemed to make up a living exercise in contrast.

Cammie could definitely pass as a bona fide Hollywood starlet, with her perfect (if artificially enhanced) breasts, mass of strawberry blond curls, and Pilates-toned figure. This morning, she wore a flirty little Zimmermann sundress and Jennifer Meyer chandelier earrings, even though the extent of their plans was to get pedicures, eat junk food, and maybe watch the *20 Most Extravagant Celebrity Weddings* countdown on E!

Next to Cammie, Dee looked almost mousy, though to call her plain would be a disservice. Her petite figure was *made* for skimpy L.A. fashion, and her shaggy, shoulder-length pale blond hair always looked rock-star perfect, with—near as Sam could tell—little to no effort. She'd come for her pedicure in a wild graphic print dress from Nicolas Ghesquière's new Balenciaga collection.

Sam herself wore a baby blue floral paisley Chloé shift dress, with a scoop neckline and oversize side-slash pockets that took the attention away from her oversize hips.

The nail tech tapped Sam's heel, a signal for her to switch feet. Her toenails had been painted a new dark brown shade called Vamp that was in the process of taking Hollywood by storm. Sam thought she could get away with wearing it one more time before she'd see it on girls from the San Fernando Valley and never be able to go near it again.

"So Dee, now that you're a high school graduate, what are you gonna do with your life?" Cammie had a knack for cutting right to the chase.

Dee smiled beatifically, not at all fazed by the question. "Plan Sam's wedding, duh. After that, who knows? Spend time with Jack."

"Isn't he going back to Princeton?" Sam asked.

Jack Walker, Dee's boyfriend, was a friend of Ben's from Princeton University, who had come out to Los Angeles for the summer to work in the reality TV department at Fox. Sam thought Jack could be a little condescending, but he seemed like a decent enough guy. At the very least, he made Dee happy.

Dee shrugged. "Oh, it'll work out, I'm sure. If we have to do long distance, we'll do long distance."

Cammie laughed as her nail tech went to work on some nonexistent calluses on her heel. "Long distance never works. Unless you're married. And even then, only for a few months at a time. It's why Sam has to decide to go to France, or Eduardo has to decide to stay here in Los Angeles. Not that anyone's listening to me," she added, pulling down on one of her chandelier earrings with a delicate finger.

Sam sighed and played with one of the pockets of her shift dress. Cammie had a point. She and Eduardo were getting married quickly so they'd be married when he went back to France. She didn't think she was ready to leave Los Angeles. But the idea of not being with her husband during their first year of marriage was even more abhorrent.

"They'll make it work. And so will we," Dee said pointedly. The early afternoon sunlight was streaming through the eight-foot plate glass windows. It gave her blond hair an angelic glow.

"Your optimism is refreshing," Cammie quipped. She brushed aside an errant curl as the nail tech switched files.

"I'm not optimistic," Dee said, shaking her shaggy head. "I'll make it work, like I'm making this wedding work. Tell her what I've done already, Sam."

Dee looked at Sam with her moon-shaped blue eyes for confirmation. "You're not going to believe it," Sam noted to Cammie. Dee had taken over as if she were a professional. Since yesterday, she had arranged for a half-dozen designers to send over an array of wedding dresses for Sam's perusal. That would happen later in the afternoon. Sam's dress would be custom-made, of course, but these would give her an idea of what looked good. (She'd considered using the designs that Eduardo had included in the portfolio, but then opted not to. That would mean that he'd seen her dress before she came down the aisle, and while Sam wasn't exactly superstitious, she did believe in making an entrance.)

After the wedding dress designer was chosen, the head seamstress would race with her staff to create her gown so it would be ready on Friday. Sam could only imagine the number of magical elves that would work round the clock. Dee had also made preliminary inquiries of florists, caterers, musicians, wedding cake bakers, and the like.

Sam sighed and watched as her nail tech buffed her new polish. Thinking about what Dee had accomplished on her behalf made her feel guilty. Cammie hadn't done shit, and she was going to be the maid of honor. How unfair was that?

"Hey, would you mind handing me that notebook? And the pen?" Dee asked her nail tech, who was applying a final topcoat of gold polish to her left big toe. She pointed to an open notebook on the white Persian rug.

"Sure." The nail tech, who sported spiky dark hair and thick eye makeup, handed over the simple black-and-white composition notebook and the gold Cross pen next to it.

"So, let's talk about these gowns," Dee said, opening the notebook to a dog-eared page and peering at what she'd scrawled. "You're trying a vintage lace Alvina Valenta, a fitted Lazaro with amazing beadwork, a Christos washed silk strapless, fitted under the bust, with an A-line skirt—very figure flattering—and an Ulla-Maija original: it's hand-draped silk satin with a twenty-foot cathedral train."

"Didn't your boyfriend mock up a bunch of drawings of you in custom-designed gowns?" Cammie asked.

"Fiancé, not boyfriend," Sam corrected.

"Ah. Yes." Cammie peered down at her toenails, which were now done in a vermilion shade called Shameless. "Fiancé. So?"

"The drawings were nice. But I don't want Eduardo to see my dress before the wedding. And the bitch Peruvian designer who drew them makes me nervous. I don't want her within three miles of my wedding." Sam was emphatic.

"Cool. Then go naked," Cammie quipped. "It's easier, it's hot, and you don't have to worry about anyone else copying you."

Sam shook her head with a smile. "You're the one who looks hot naked," she pointed out. "I'm the one who does the wild thing with the lights off. In fact, I'm happiest when there's a power failure and no candles or matches."

Cammie poured herself some more champagne as the nail tech buffed at another rough spot—how on earth had Cammie gotten a rough spot?—of skin on her opposite heel. "Oh, right. Well, then, you'll want to go with the A-line to hide those hips of yours. I'm just telling you as a friend."

"That was rude," Dee said in her breathy little voice.

"I know," Cammie agreed, sounding not at all bothered by Dee's remark. "It's a sickness. No cure. Oh well."

For the next ten minutes, the nail techs worked in

silence. Finally, the lead tech, who wore a white uniform—her assistants were in black—announced that they were done. All they had to do was pack their traveling valises. "Should we send the bill to the house?"

"Definitely. Add twenty percent for your tips."

"Thank you, Miss Sharpe. We'll find our way out."

Once the nail techs were gone, Cammie moved to a cluster of genuine 1950s TV dinner trays across the room near Sam's picture window. "How about some food?" A feast prepared by Jackson's weekend chef, the former tour caterer for Faith Hill and Tim McGraw, was set up on the tray tables. His name was Buck, and Buck had had clearly been in a Thai mood today. There was a huge platter of cold peanut noodles laced with slivers of spicy peppers and grilled chicken. Fresh pineapple salad with a savory cilantro and lime dressing. Cold shrimp spring rolls. A hot pot of yellow curry with potatoes—Sam still felt traumatized by Anna's near-crash, which in her mind justified a little carb indulgence—and braised beef. A bottle of Riesling nestled in an ice bucket, and fresh-squeezed orange juice filled a frosted-glass pitcher.

But Sam wasn't hungry. Maybe it was nerves over the wedding, or maybe it was nerves over having both her parents in the same city again. That would traumatize anyone. Jackson had taken Dina to brunch this morning at Shutters on the Beach, and Dina had been brought to the estate by limo before they drove off together in the Jensen. Sam had found them in the outdoor kitchen when she'd come down in her robe for coffee. They were chatting companionably and flipping through various sections of the *Los Angeles Times* before they departed—

for her mother, the book review; her father, the calendar section. Her father had been dressed in his tennis clothes from his regular early-Sunday-morning game at the Riviera Country Club. Her mother had been on the verge of fashionable, in black sandals, long black shorts, and a long-sleeved red T-shirt. She looked almost pretty. Neither had said a word about the wedding. Instead, they'd smiled thinly as they said good morning. There was no need for them to say more. Sam knew what they were thinking: *Call it off. Now.*

"Miss Sam?"

One of the new maids stuck her head inside the redwood door. She was petite and olive-skinned, with extraordinarily large dark eyes. "April Bloomfield is here to see you. She wants to know if you want to do the menu tasting down in the kitchen?"

Sam turned to Dee. "April Bloomfield?"

Dee smiled broadly. "One of your possible caterers. She just moved here from Chicago to open a restaurant in Santa Monica. *April Dawn?*"

Sam knew about April Dawn. You couldn't get a reservation at April Dawn less than a month in advance. Well, unless you were Jackson Sharpe's daughter.

"How'd you get April Bloomfield?" Cammie demanded. She was clearly impressed.

"I talked to my dad. He told her he'd do the record launch party for his next big CD at her restaurant. Anyway, we'll see what she can do. There are always other options."

It was Sam's turn to be impressed. Dee's father was a major music producer, responsible for dozens of platinum records and CDs over his storied career. Every year his clients won the top awards at the AMAs, VMAs, and every other acronymed music award show. In Hollywood terms, he was a player.

"Okay, Dee. You get the gold star for the day." Cammie beat her to the punch with the compliment. Dee beamed.

"The outdoor kitchen, thanks," Sam decided. Her father's soon-to-be ex-wife, Poppy Sinclair, had recently had an outdoor kitchen built adjacent to the indoor one, accessible via a sliding glass door. Sam liked the kitchen a lot better than she'd liked her dumb, cheating, not-much-older-than-Sam, soon-to-be-former stepmother. It was good to have her out of the house, but it would be better to read about the official divorce in *Variety*. Poppy and Jackson had decided to share custody of their baby, Ruby Hummingbird, and Poppy would get hefty child support.

"Wait. Let's just finish with this list before we go down," Dee suggested.

"Fair enough." Sam smiled at the maid. "Please ask her to wait."

"Fine, Miss Sam."

The housekeeper departed; Sam made a mental note to ask for her name next time, as Dee flipped a page in her notebook.

"Let me help," Cammie declared. She punctuated her announcement with a sip of the Riesling. "Here's what you need to cover. Hair."

Dee looked down her list. "Raymond. No other option. He's taking the day off from his new salon to do you. His treat. Enjoy."

"Venue?" Cammie asked. "It's short notice. You can always use Bye, Bye Love. First wedding ever there. Would get a ton of press. I'd close the club for you if you wanted. It's not my call alone, but I'm sure Ben would agree. "

"Tempting. Very tempting," Sam agreed. If she had her wedding there, it'd be on *Entertainment Tonight*. And in *People*.

"I thought of that. But decided against it. Too much chance that someone could sneak in." Dee shook her blond head, adamant.

"Are you crazy? We have great security." Cammie put a hand on her slender hip, obviously taking Dee's decision personally.

"One asshole and the whole night is ruined," Dee pronounced. "Besides, I've got the perfect location."

"What?" Cammie challenged, as she put down her wine and turned sharply toward Dee.

"A wedding at sea. That is, on the *Look Sharpe II*. Your dad just bought a new yacht, Sam. It's perfect. There's a helipad in the back to bring people to and from; we can charter some cigarette boats to shuttle people back and forth from the harbor at Malibu; and if the chop is bad— it won't be since it's August, but just in case—the captain can anchor by the Channel Islands."

Sam hadn't seen the new vessel, but it was supposed to be truly over the top. Jackson had bought it from Laurel Limoges, the cosmetics titan, who lived in Palm Beach, Florida. It had arrived with a full crew and had to be sailed from south Florida through the Panama Canal. Sam had overheard her father talking about it, but she hadn't had a chance to ride up to the yacht club in Malibu where it was anchored to get a firsthand look. Jackson claimed it was twice as large as the previous version of the *Look Sharpe*, and that vessel had handled seventy-five people with ease. This one could comfortably do a hundred and fifty. Dee had talked about a hundred guests, and a waitstaff of fifty. That would be the perfect size.

She nodded approvingly. "I like it. But my dad is against the wedding. My mom too."

"We'll work that out," Dee said easily. "Or shall I say, I'll work that out. He's a movie star. He has a public to please. He won't want bad press, so he'll cave."

"When did you find the time to do all this?" Cammie asked. She forked a chunk of pineapple salad into her mouth.

"It was a busy morning," Dee quipped.

"I think it's amazing. And I really, really appreciate it." Sam reached over to squeeze Dee's slender hand.

"I'm having a blast," Dee confided, snapping her notebook shut in a businesslike manner that was very un-Dee. "Planning your wedding. I always thought I'd be first. Not that I'm ready to get married now. But you know."

"Yeah." Sam twirled some caramel-streaked hair around one finger absentmindedly. Wedding. Her wedding. They were talking about *her wedding*. It all felt so unreal. Or surreal. Or something.

Everything was going really well, Sam thought, as she and her friends padded downstairs in their terry cloth pedicure sandals with the individual toe separators. In a matter of days, she'd be walking down the aisle in a beautiful white dress toward her beautiful, loving fiancé. She had everything she wanted. So why did she feel so jittery?

It must be cold feet, she reasoned with herself. Even terry cloth sandals couldn't fix that.

Champagne, Anyone?

Sunday night, 11:15 p.m.

Cammie slid gracefully up to Champagne and linked arms with her protégée as they stood near the barricades that separated the rest of Venice Boulevard from the area in front of Bye, Bye Love. The younger girl was wearing a black satin halter mini-dress with straps that crisscrossed in the front, wrapped around her neck, and tied in the back. She looked absolutely stunning. Her dress had been designed by Martin Rittenhouse, a prototype for his petite collection. Cammie reminded herself to tell Martin about the interview she'd done with *Entertainment Tonight*—and how on the spur of the moment she'd announced that the new line would be called Martinette.

"This is . . . amazing." Champagne was breathless. Her emerald eyes sparkled with admiration as she took in the crowd of A-list and almost-A-list celebrities who made up the clientele of the sizzling new club, in only its third night of operation.

"Amazing, remarkable, and very Champagne-friendly,"

Cammie agreed. "And whose inspired idea was it to make night three at Bye, Bye Love a street party? Mine."

It was later that night, and Bye, Bye Love was in full swing. She and Ben had decided that they'd be closed on just one night a week—Monday—during their first month, which meant a lot more work for both of them. But it was worth it.

For this night's theme, Cammie had the idea to take Bye, Bye Love outside. They'd scrambled to get the necessary permits from the city, and had been able to get Venice Boulevard closed in front of the club. A wooden stage had been erected at the south end of the closed-off street; in front of it was an expansive portable parquet dance floor. Drinks and food stations were set up directly in front of the club for easy access by the staff, and simple Costco-special plastic tables and chairs placed along the perimeter. The kicker was that Cammie had purchased three dozen superking Aero-style beds, had them inflated and then covered in brightly colored Indian silk blankets and oversize raw-silk pillows. Large potted palms had been placed around the beds, right in the middle of Venice Boulevard. Then Ben and Cammie had had the workers paint Moroccan-style tribal rugs on the asphalt, giving the party a mysterious casbah feel.

She'd dressed for it, too, in a sleeveless red silk Dior tent top and Miu Miu houndstooth skirt that barely cleared her lacy La Perla thong.

For a city as dominated by car culture as Los Angeles, the idea of a nighttime party in the middle of Venice Boulevard, a major thoroughfare, was intriguing. The execution of it, on a gloriously cool starry night, with a slight sea breeze coming in off the Pacific a few miles away, was even better.

Oh, there were block parties and street fairs all the time around the city. Cammie knew that. But those were open to the unwashed masses, who inevitably came en masse. Tonight was exclusive. No riffraff. Just fifteen thousand square feet of Venice Boulevard populated by the rich, the famous, the powerful, the beautiful, and the young—almost all of them a combination of at least three of the above. They'd messengered out five hundred invitations, scented with amber and jasmine, as befitted the Middle Eastern party theme, printed on fine gold parchment paper, rolled up and sealed in wax.

"Cammie! Cammie! Over here."

Cammie turned to see the rusty gold hair and grayish-blue eyes of Dash, the reporter from *Entertainment Tonight*, once again trailed by his cameraman. He was front and center of a gaggle of print and TV reporters. He was looking even hotter tonight than he had yesterday, wearing a gray Ralph Lauren Black Label cashmere T-shirt and worn Levi's, which were so out they were in. She waggled her fingers in his direction.

"Let him in," Cammie told one of the members of the club security force, an imposing young Russian named Igor, very blond with ice-blue eyes and the square jaw of an action hero. "And his cameraman."

"Will do," Igor told her. He had the cutest accent.

"Cammie?" Champagne reached for Cammie's arm and looked anxious. "Isn't that going to piss off the other reporters?"

"That's the whole point. We make Dash really happy,

he gives us what we want. That's how you play these suckers." She smiled impishly. "Besides, he's hot."

Cammie told Igor that they were going to the outdoor VIP area on the west side of the building, and to bring Dash and the camera guy over there. She led Champagne by the hand. "Just follow my lead and don't talk much."

"But—"

"Starting now would be good, 'kay?"

Five minutes later, she and Champagne were ensconced in the club's VIP area, which took the casbah theme a step further. Cammie and Ben had erected an outdoor tented pavilion with authentic tribal rugs placed over a floor that had been covered in sparkling white sand, and low antique tables imported from Tangier surrounded by silk pillows. There was a central circular bar with light blond wooden bar stools, and the bartenders were shirtless with full pants that gathered in around the ankle, complete with a sash and boots. The waitresses wore long, heavily embroidered jewel-tone dresses in the lightest of silk, slit up to the waist on either side. Of course, the notion of a VIP area was a bit of an oxymoron, because the only people allowed in Bye, Bye Love would be on VIP lists at any other place in town. But even here, there had to be some sense of hierarchy. L.A. clubs were nothing without it.

Cammie ordered a virgin Mary for Champagne and a pink Flirtini for herself. She was licking muddled raspberries from the finger she'd dipped into her drink when Dash and his portly cameraman arrived. The camera guy wore shorts—TV and movie tech guys always wore shorts, no matter what the weather—and an old Oakland Raiders T-shirt, which pooched out above the waistline.

Dash spoke sonorously into his mike. "We're here at night three of Bye, Bye Love, and the allure of this new Los Angeles hot spot just keeps growing. I'm seeing Jessica Alba, Jessica Simpson, and Jessica Biel to my right. It's Jessica heaven." He cocked his head at Cammie, then looked back into the camera. "And I'm here with the teen wunderkind who made this all possible—Cammie Sheppard, the club's co-owner. How's it going, Cammie, and who's your gorgeous friend?"

Camera Guy aimed the camera at Cammie and Champagne. Cammie was amazed at how quickly Champagne took the opportunity to pose and preen. Her shoulders went back, her chin up, radiant smile right into the camera. She was a natural.

Cammie had come to see Champagne as a protégée. Starting up the club had been incredibly fun. Starting up this girl's career as a petite model could be just as fun, and maybe even a bigger challenge. For the club, she had her father's showbiz connections. Those connections wouldn't be of much use in turning Champagne into a hot model. This she did on her own. That Champagne was dirt poor—well, that was a big-ass bonus. Cammie loved a good rags-to-riches story, especially when she was the one playing hot fairy godmother.

Cammie flashed her professionally whitened smile, giving the camera her best angle. "This lady goes by one name only: Champagne. Besides being exquisitely beautiful, she has an amazing story to tell."

Dash gave Champagne an admiring once-over and asked, "Exquisite beauty and an amazing story. Tell us more."

This was one time for the truth, Cammie decided. Embellished in the best Hollywood style, of course.

"Well, Champagne has overcome so many obstacles, obstacles that would've flattened an ordinary being. She grew up in the Valley, with a mother who was barely there and a father who was never there. She's just come through the New Visions program, and she'll be the first person in her family even to graduate from high school. That Martin Rittenhouse would choose her to model Martinette—the new petite fashion line he's launching— is a testament to both her inner beauty and her conquering attitude. And when you get to know her a little bit better, she might even talk to you about the time that she was homeless."

Two pink spots appeared on Champagne's high cheekbones. Well, if she was going to become famous, she was going to have to get over being self-conscious about her background. The trick was to make her past work for her in the present.

"I have a million questions," Dash began excitedly, looking like he'd just discovered a direct route to the Pulitzer.

Cammie handed a passing waiter her Flirtini and put a hand on Dash's. Now that she'd whetted his appetite, it was time to wrap this up. "I'd love to stay and chat, but I have a million things to do. This was fun. We'll talk again soon."

"How about you, Champagne? Stay a few more minutes and let the public get to know you," Dash coaxed, smiling at her flirtatiously like he was asking for a date rather than an interview.

Champagne opened her mouth, but Cammie smoothly stepped in before any sound came out. "There are a million people waiting to meet her," Cammie said apologetically. "Have a fab time tonight. Bye now!" Cammie quickly steered her client away from the *ET* crew, chattering as they walked. "And that, my dear, is called the spin. We give them just a little taste of you. Soon they'll be clamoring for more."

"Cammie?" Champagne looked up at her with her soulful green eyes.

"Yeah?"

"How did you know that I was homeless a few years ago?"

Cammie laughed. "I totally made that shit up. I was just embellishing. You really were?"

Champagne nodded. "But I don't want people to feel sorry for me. . . ."

Cammie took Champagne's slender hands. "Sweetie, listen to me. It's just hype. No one is going to feel sorry for a gorgeous girl who came from nothing and made it to the heights of something. They're going to be *happy* for you. And very soon, they're going to want to *be* you."

"Do I have to talk about that in interviews?"

Cammie edged away from the buffet stand so the cook could go back to making his couscous. "No. You don't have to. But you might want to. You have an amazing story. Tell it. You are Champagne, the model. People are going to care about you. Help them. Make them. Got it?"

"Got it," Champagne agreed. She squared her elegant shoulders, looking every bit the sensation-to-be that she was.

Cammie gave her a quick hug. Frankly, she respected Champagne for standing up to her. "This is for you and your career," Cammie said. "Now go out there and have fun. I'll catch up with you later. Is your cell on vibrate? I'll send you a text."

"Yeah, got it." Champagne smiled broadly, then headed off into the street party. It meant Cammie could move on to equally important matters.

Where was Ben?

Leaving the extravaganza of the street fair behind, she entered Bye, Bye Love. The club was deserted. The silence was a welcome relief, though Ben was nowhere to be found. She drifted toward one of the bar stools, remembering how packed this bar had been on opening night, and how surreal it had been to sit here with Adam and Ben, watching Anna's plane crash-land on TV. Remembering how cold Adam had been. How could he turn off his feelings for her so easily? When had he turned into such a heartless asshole? Maybe he just talked a good game like everyone else. Silly her, to think that he was different.

Well, whatever. She ran a petal-pink-polished nail in a circle of moisture on the bar. She wasn't one of those people who said, *Everything happens for a reason*. If she was, there would have to be some big cosmic reason for her mother doing a swan dive off a friend's boat, never to be seen or heard from again. That could not possibly have happened for a *reason*. But Cammie could say that everything had worked out for the best. She and Adam were officially over, the end, finis, have a pleasant life with some fat chick with an overbite in Michigan. Anna was alive. And she herself and Ben were . . . well, they *almost* were. That was the part of the story that needed fixing, and she was just the girl to fix it.

A door in the office area opened and Ben appeared. She watched with appreciation as he crossed the main floor of the club. He wore a black cotton T-shirt and black Costume National Homme jeans.

Stylish, sexy, and semi-mine, she thought. No time like the present to get rid of the *semi.*

"Hey, handsome," she said as he approached. She reached up to hug him, letting her strawberry blond curls brush seductively against his shoulder. "Whatcha been doing?"

"Paperwork. You?" He asked, sitting next to her on a bar stool. He half-turned his stool, playfully bumping his leg into hers.

There was an open bottle of Cristal on the table, and Cammie found a clean glass on the bar and poured herself three fingers' worth. "Pimping my protégée to the press."

"Champagne? The girl, I mean?"

"Yep."

"You sure you have time for her? This club is a demanding mistress."

"So am I," Cammie cooed, passing Ben the bottle of champagne. "I have time for all the important things. Work. Her. You. Here's to good karma, great parties, and even greater times to come."

She lifted her glass to him; he clinked the champagne bottle against it but didn't drink from it. "So. When can we move on to the good times? As in, pick up where we left off on Saturday morning at about 3 a.m.?"

He smiled, but ran a hand through his short brown hair. "I appreciate the sentiment. But there's a ton of work to do around here."

"That's why we have help," Cammie pointed out. "And why we're closed tomorrow. How about we drive up to the Santa Ynez Inn for a little R 'n' R? We deserve to chill for a day." As she set her glass down on the bar, she made sure that her forearm lightly brushed his.

"Love to, but I can't," Ben replied. "I'm meeting with our tax guy, our accountant, and with someone from the Department of Water who isn't happy with our sewer system. Unless you want to take that meeting?"

"I don't do sewers." She thrust the champagne bottle at him. "Drink up, party boy. The night is young."

"I'll pass," Ben replied easily. "Not getting happy while the club is open. There's too much to keep an eye on. Too much money going through this place. I need to stay—hold on." He whipped his Razr out of his back pocket and held it to his lips. "Yeah? This is Ben. Uh-huh. Uh-huh. Uh-huh."

Cammie zoned out as Ben launched into a conversation with the gatekeepers at the police barricades about a couple of purported members of Linkin Park who'd shown up unannounced and wanted to come in.

"Let 'em in," Cammie advised, even though she'd only heard Ben's half of the conversation.

"What if they're bullshitters? The door guy doesn't know their music. Gotta handle this myself," he told her, then told the door guy he'd be out in a minute.

He slid off his bar stool, leaving the champagne bottle on the bar. "Gotta run, beautiful." He kissed her on the cheek, then trotted toward the door.

Cammie pushed the Cristal away from her. She didn't feel like drinking anymore. There were priorities in life. Sure, running a club was one of them. But so was she. And right now, Ben didn't seem to be seeing it that way.

Love the One You're With

Monday morning, 12:19 a.m.

Anna sat at the best table at Bar Marmont, a banquette located in a cozy alcove with an open skylight cut into the ceiling, as she waited for Logan to come down from his room. The breeze, the black lacquered walls, and the red Chinese lanterns were a pleasant change of pace and a much-needed reprieve from the self-imposed solitary confinement of writing that she had thrown herself into for the past twenty-four hours.

Writing, writing, writing. It fulfilled her in a way she had never experienced before, and she wasn't about to share what she had been working on with anyone else—it just felt too personal, too raw, too intimate. She'd been in the oddest state while writing it; there, but not *there*. Off to some place inside her head, living the characters she was writing. She'd eaten nothing but fresh pistachio nuts and had drank nothing but spring water and black Sumatra coffee as she worked. What she had to show for that was eyes that burned, hands that shook, and acid swirling around in her empty stomach. But dammit, it was finished.

The first thing she'd done when her screenplay was finished was shower. Then she ate four containers of lemon chiffon yogurt and spooned tuna salad into her mouth while standing in front of the open refrigerator. After that, she called Logan. He was in his room at the hotel, reading García Lorca.

They hadn't seen each other, or even spoken, since the crash landing. Yet he was understanding of her need to be incommunicado. He'd been reliving the flight again and again himself. He'd love to see her. How about a drink at his hotel?

She'd searched her wardrobe for something elegant and sophisticated, considering several options before settling on a mocha Missoni sweater dress with a portrait neckline and three-quarter sleeves, delicate brown suede sandals she'd had forever and loved because they were so comfortable, and a beige Carolina Herrera cropped jacket. When she came downstairs, she found an envelope with her name on it by the Ming vase in the entryway. It was an invitation to a block party at Bye, Bye Love for that same night. She'd shoved it in her Prada bag—she had no intention of actually going—and been on her way.

A six-foot-tall, willowy, redheaded waitress with an Irish accent appeared wearing a uniform, if one could call hot pink short shorts paired with a vest sans shirt a uniform. Anna ordered a Black Velvet on the rocks. It felt like a very adult drink, and she was feeling very adult. She guessed Logan would want Belgian pale ale, as she remembered him drinking one in New York. Her order drew an approving smile from the waitress.

Anna had been to Chateau Marmont, a voguish 1920s-era hotel, which was modeled after an elegant Loire Valley castle, many times. Usually with Sam. Twice with Ben. Once with her dad. The gastropub at the Marmont was dimly lit, and an eclectic sound track—Anna thought it might be Billie Holiday—played as she felt a warm, strong hand on her shoulder.

She turned, and just looking into his deep blue eyes took her back to her fear on the plane, how he had held her hand, how he had tried so hard to be strong for her. She slid her arms around his neck and he held her close.

"I know," he whispered into her hair. And it didn't take any further explanation.

Anna felt tears sting her eyes, which made her laugh for some reason. "I'm sorry," she murmured, wiping them away with a forefinger. "I'm all . . . emotional."

He smiled and twined his fingers with hers. He looked so handsome, in khakis and a blue shirt with an Armani cashmere sports jacket. They sat. They drank. They talked about that night. Logan repeated that he was sticking around for a couple more days—he couldn't even get another flight to Bali until Tuesday.

Anna smiled sadly. "I have to stay here until next Saturday. My friend is getting married. Sam."

"No kidding." Logan raised his eyebrows. "Who gets married right out of high school?"

"Eduardo—you've met him—is wonderful, but . . ." Anna stopped herself before she said anything more, and shook her head. She was not going to judge Sam for her decision. Maybe Sam was just trying to live as if she were dying too.

"Well, how about after that? I could stick around. Bali isn't going anywhere."

Anna took a slow sip of her drink. The day after the wedding was the day she was supposed to go back east. Yet she still had no more idea about what she wanted, or what she was going to do, than she'd had before. "I can't answer that now."

To her surprise, Logan nodded. "Sometimes the best thing to do is to kick the can down the road. And sometimes the best thing to do is carpe diem."

"Seize the day," she agreed.

He reached into his pants pocket and pulled out an invitation. Anna recognized it. It was an invite to the Bye, Bye Love street party. "Sam had one of these sent to my room."

"I got one too." Anna fished hers out of her bag. She had no intention of going to the club. She wasn't all that keen on running into Cammie or Ben. And especially not into Cammie and Ben together.

"You up for it?" Logan asked. "It sounds like fun. We could use some fun, don't you think?"

True. Enough with life and death and the future. Why not? What was the worst that could happen? Certainly not worse than what had happened to her forty-six hours before.

"Seize the day?" she suggested. "I'd really love to see Sam."

"Consider it seized."

The ride was quiet. Logan had rented a black convertible Aston Martin, and he drove to Venice Boulevard with an arm around her. She snuggled against his shoulder, feeling the warm night air wash over them. It was so simple. So right. There was no awkwardness to the silence as they rode to the club.

When they arrived, they gave their car to the valet at the police barricade, flashed their invitations to the hulking doormen in matching tight black Gucci tees, and stepped past them and into the party.

Anna had been to any number of street festivals in New York—the San Gennaro one down in Little Italy in September was one of her favorites—but those outdoor gatherings had nothing on this block party. A rock band she didn't know was playing on a stage at the west end of the throng. Moorish belly dancers snaked through the crowd. Waiters and waitresses in sort of sexed-up versions of vaguely Middle Eastern attire passed hors d'oeuvres: fantail prawns and papaya, lobster and hummus, feta cheese with caviar. Water pipes had been set up at discrete intervals, circled by Hollywood glitterati putting them to good use. People were dancing; people were talking; people were cuddling intimately on jumbo-size mattresses. It was almost two in the morning, and the energy level was indescribably high.

Then she saw him. Them. They were talking with another couple whom Anna didn't recognize. She took Logan's arm. "That's Ben. And that's Cammie with him."

Logan peered across the crowd. "My comp, huh?"

"No," Anna said. "We're over. He's with Cammie." The words felt hollow to her.

"She's gorgeous," Logan decided, eyeing Cammie. "In an obvious L.A. plastic kind of way."

Anna nodded, glad he'd amended his statement, even if it was for her benefit.

Cammie noticed them from across the party and pulled on Ben's arm. He turned, and Anna thought she could see his jaw clench as he spotted her and Logan. Then, hand in hand, Anna watched Ben and Cammie make their way to them.

They stood as a foursome, Ben and Logan the same height, Cammie and Anna's eyes level. They did the usual Hollywood hug and air kiss, followed by the gushing "I'm so glad you guys are alive" that Anna had expected. Cammie actually seemed sincerely relieved. Ben simply said, "I'm glad you made it," rather soberly, locking eyes with Anna. She just nodded, not knowing what else to say.

"Your club is great," Logan put in, nodding appreciatively at the surroundings, clearly trying to make the meeting easier on everyone.

Ben flicked his eyes from Anna to Logan. "Thanks, man." He raised his voice a notch as the band cranked up the volume.

"All the proceeds of the first month are going to charity," Cammie boasted. One of the waiters passed by with a small tray of grape leaves stuffed with pistachio nuts and organic grains, and she plucked one from the tray.

Anna was impressed. "That's fantastic. You should be really proud of that. Both of you."

"We are." Cammie nuzzled even closer to Ben. Anna instinctively took Logan's hand.

"You guys need to go up to the stage," Ben advised. "We've brought in this fantastic street performance artist."

"His specialty is bubbles," Cammie added.

"Come on. Let's go check him out." Ben led them through the crowd to the stage, where the band had stopped playing and where the performance artist—Ben said his name was Fan Yang—was wowing the crowd by creating massive bubbles, bubbles within bubbles, even square bubbles.

"Ever see this guy before?" Ben asked.

Anna shook her head. She didn't particularly want to talk about bubbles, although she did have to admit that Fan Yang was amazing—at the moment he was creating enormous pear-shaped bubbles with smoke inside of them. As they watched, Fan invited Ben and Cammie up on the stage with him, to the delight of the crowd. There, he wrapped them in a huge oblong bubble and urged them to kiss. When they did—inside the translucent sphere—the crowd went nuts.

"A little heavy on the PDA," Logan noted. "But they seem to really be into each other."

"I guess." Anna found that she was gritting her teeth watching the display. Well, that was okay. The more times she saw the Traveling Ben and Cammie Show, the less it would bother her.

Suddenly, Anna felt herself thinking again. Overthinking, in her usual Anna Percy way. About Bali and Yale. About Logan and Ben. About her screenplay. About—

"Anna?"

She looked up at Logan.

"Relax. It'll all work out."

It was like he was reading her mind. "You think?"

His blue eyes were bright. "I'm going to say this one time. When you decided to get on that plane? You made a decision that was right. You chose in the moment, from your gut, your heart—someplace deep. You can do it again. Now," he said sternly, "enjoy the show." He stood behind her and wrapped his arms around her waist so that they could both watch Fan on stage. Now he was making a bubble large enough for a dozen people to stand inside.

She ordered her brain to turn off and leaned back into Logan. He kissed her temple. He was wonderful, terrific, smart, cute, kind, and all around better for her than Ben.

Fan Yang had moved into the crowd and was encapsulating other people in bubbles. With a giant swirl, he flashed one over Logan. Then over Anna. The bubble was clear, like glass, and she looked through it. The world sparkled, like some sort of fantasyland. It made her laugh with pure joy.

She was here. She was alive. She was with a guy she liked, could maybe even love. What could be better?

Being with him in Bali, perhaps?

Mommy Dearest

Monday, 11:21 a.m.

Anna awoke the next morning with a pounding head-ache. It could have been due to the fact that she had a hair consultation for Sam's wedding, and Sam had already gone off the stress scale—she'd left a rambling message for Anna the night before that was essentially one long run-on sentence that went something like: "Sorry I didn't come to Cammie's club there was too much planning to be done I hope you're having fun without me I can't fucking believe I'm getting married on Friday I have a zillion things to do I must be insane why am I doing this oh God I love Eduardo so much you have to be at my house tomorrow at four for a hair consultation with Raymond I'm thinking updos and according to his assistant you shouldn't wash it first because it's harder to put up clean hair and did I mention I'm getting fucking married?!"

Anna sat up in her antique four-poster bed and massaged her temples. Maybe it was knowing she had to have a talk with her father about her future that was stressing her out. She had to tell him about Yale, her feelings about going. Or not going, as the case might be. Not that she even knew. She just knew that after their heart-to-heart the other day, she owed him an honest conversation canvassing her doubts and fears. The story he'd told her about his teacher friend in Appalachia made her feel as if maybe, just maybe, he'd understand her confusion.

She showered quickly, threw on a white tank top and a pair of McQ-Alexander McQueen khakis she'd had forever, curled her wet hair into a bun, and went downstairs to find her dad. He'd mentioned that he'd be working at home today, so it was the perfect time to get him alone.

She found him on the phone in his home office. He lit up when he saw Anna and motioned for her to take a seat on the camel suede Bellini Clock sofa. Its two branches were designed to rotate around a circular coffee table like the hands of a clock. Anna slid onto the sofa and gazed out the picture window at the meticulously groomed English rose garden. It featured an abundance of rare flowers, like the Barbra Streisand, a fragrant mauve rose, and First Kiss, a wonderful landscape rose, given to Anna's dad from the Nixon Library's rose garden.

Her dad finished the call quickly. "Anna, sweetheart, I'm famished. Follow me," he said, hugging her. "Did you eat?"

"Not yet."

"Mimi will have some food outside," he noted, as he grabbed his navy Yale Class of '83 coffee mug and headed to the glass door that led to the back garden. Anna followed.

"How's your morning? I had an early game at the club," her father went on, his long legs loping so that she had to power-walk to keep up. "Took a tennis racket to the head—one of the guys I was playing doubles against lost control of it at the net."

"Ouch." Anna winced sympathetically. "Are you okay?"

"Oh yeah, sure. Zonked me out there for a minute, but I'm fine."

They emerged into the bright late-summer sunshine and Anna breathed deeply. She loved the back of her dad's house. Wrought-iron outdoor furniture graced the portico, which was covered with crimson bougainvillea. Beyond was a patio surrounded by greenery and a burst of flowering colors. A lush pathway of moss and stones meandered through the rose garden, which was organized like a museum—here a collection of all twenty-three varieties of the rare desert rose, there an exhibit of English tea roses. The vibrant colors were offset by elegant ivy-covered trellises that made the garden feel like a nineteenth-century romantic paradise. In the center of everything were the koi pond and gazebo where her father spent many an hour in "medicinal meditation," his euphemism for smoking weed.

On the patio, they sat down at the table set with Limoges fine bone china, as one of the household assistants, the very blond Tatyana, whose hair was wound on top of her head in two braids, served blueberry pancakes and omelets with basil, tomato, and goat cheese. The crystal French press in the center of the table gave off a heady aroma of roasting coffee that filled the air, mingling with the ever-present scent of roses and freshly cut grass.

Anna lifted her fork, then put it down again. "Dad, since the plane—"

"You've been doing a lot of thinking," he surmised.

She nodded and took a sip of coffee from her delicate china cup before continuing. "It's been . . ."

"Of course. You've been through a life-changing event." He poured himself more coffee, then held the French press toward her. She shook her head no, and he put the pot down again.

"True," Anna agreed, "but it's more than that. I'm feeling . . . confused. It's like, I know what I want to do." She thought of her screenplay. "And at the same time, I don't know what I want to do at all."

He put his fork down and wiped his mouth with the delicate cream-colored napkin. Clearly she had his undivided attention, so she pressed on. "About college, I mean. Yale has been the plan, the blueprint, the dream, *my* dream—"

"Since you were old enough to speak in full sentences, as I recall," her father said fondly.

"Right," she agreed, even though the acknowledgment was going to make this even harder. "Everything I've ever done was so wrapped up in the ultimate goal. But now . . ." Anna paused to consider the exact words, but couldn't find them.

"Honey, cut yourself some slack," Jonathan advised, and picked up his fork to stab a bite of blueberry pancake. "Anxiety is part of the deal when you're switching from one phase of your life to another." He washed the food down with a gulp of black coffee. "Mmm. How good are these pancakes?"

"Great," Anna agreed, even though she hadn't touched hers. He didn't notice.

Jonathan reached for a pinch of sea salt from the small gold seashell that held it and sprinkled it on his omelet. "Seriously, Anna," he continued, "you're going to have the best time. Yale is a Percy family tradition!" he exclaimed, brandishing his navy blue mug for emphasis. "The bulldog, the Shakespearean society, the yacht club—"

"Dad? I wouldn't go to Yale for any of that."

He drained his crystal goblet full of fresh-squeezed orange juice and smiled. He was still wearing the crisp white tennis clothes he'd had on from his early-morning match, and his tan arms were muscled and lean. "You're going for the education. That's okay. The bulldog can take care of itself." He took a huge forkful of tomato-basil omelet, pillowy white goat cheese falling onto the ivory plate. "This is just prefreshman jitters."

Anna bit into her pancakes thoughtfully. Was it? Was she totally overreacting? "It might be," she responded slowly. "But I don't think it's fair for me to take the spot of someone else who would kill, maim, or sell a body part to get off the waiting list and be accepted."

Her father put down his silver-plated fork and stared at her with something that looked like horror.

Anna forced herself to plunge on. "It's not fair for me to take that spot, Dad," she murmured, gulping hard. She winced, waiting for the axe to fall. Her father was quiet.

"I admire your selflessness," he finally said. "But I still think it's jitters. What would you do if you don't go? Go to Bali with Logan? Stay here and hang out with Sam? Go back to New York and work in a gallery?" He didn't seem mad. That was a relief. But he also didn't seem to understand the strength of her ambivalence.

"It doesn't surprise me, Anna," he continued, leaning back in the wrought-iron chair. "After what you went through—I couldn't imagine. You must have been sure you were going to die. But you didn't. Which to me says, Get on with your life. Let the jitters go."

For a split second, she wanted to tell him he was right, that it was only a little bit of precollege nerves. To talk about what it would be like in New Haven on early-morning walks across the quad, the smell of the leaves in the fall, the challenge and the fun and the lifelong relationships she'd forge.

But it simply didn't feel right.

The bright sunshine reflected off her father's crisp tennis whites, and Anna felt like she was staring into the sun. "I don't think it's jitters, Dad. Maybe the plane thing *is* affecting my thinking," she agreed. "But maybe that's a good thing. It's like . . ." She closed her eyes and felt the hot sun soak into her skin as she searched for the right words. "Like everything is stripped down to the barest essentials."

Her father was quiet for a little while. Finally he stood and stretched, then rubbed a spot on his left temple. "Damn racket. It hurts where it hit me."

She gave him a faint smile. "Did you win the point?"

"Lost the point, won the match." He shook his head a little, as if to clear it. "Don't put so much pressure on yourself. It will all work out in the end."

A cloud passed in front of the sun, casting a quick-moving shadow over the backyard. It passed, and summer sunlight washed over everything again.

"I appreciate your not blowing up over this," she told him.

"You're not a little girl anymore. You make your own decisions. But I do think it's a mistake not to go back to New York next Saturday and get yourself started at Yale."

"But—"

He held up a palm to interrupt her. "I'm asking you to keep your mind open for a little while longer. You still have a window—albeit an extremely small window—to make your decision." He came back to the glass-topped table and put a hand on hers. "Either way, you'll be okay, Anna."

She rose and wrapped her arms around his neck in a spontaneous hug, grateful that he wasn't ranting and raving. "Thanks, Dad."

"You're welcome."

For a moment she wondered what it would have been like to grow up with him, to have had the closeness that she felt with him at this very moment. But you couldn't move backward, only forward.

She left her father, went up to her room with a porcelain mug full of coffee, and sat down at her iBook. After checking her e-mail, she opened her screenplay and started adjusting scenes. Some needed to be lengthened. Some needed to be trimmed. One or two were superfluous, and she cut them with a couple of swift keystrokes. She was in the second act—at about page sixty—when the sound of her Razr chiming practically made her jump out of her skin.

She glanced at the clock. Four-fifteen. She was going to be late to Sam's. It was probably Sam calling, annoyed and crazed in her new Bridezilla way.

But when she checked the number, she saw it was her mom. Her mother was still in Italy, and it was probably 2 a.m. there. Anna smiled. It was thoughtful of her mom to check up on her. They didn't speak all that often. As much as she hadn't enjoyed her crash landing, some good things had come out of it.

"Hello?" Phone in hand, she moved to her oak canopy bed and plopped on the handmade silk tapestry quilt. The whole room was done in classic antique style: the hardwood floor gleamed beneath tapestry rugs with hand-knotted edges, an antique armoire scented with lavender sachet held her clothing, and there were fresh flowers in a crystal vase on a small table by the picture window, and an antique chaise lounge. And of course, an antique brown wood rolltop desk, on which she kept her laptop.

"Hello, darling," Jane began. "How are you? How do you feel? Have you recovered completely? What an ordeal!"

Anna smiled. "I'm good. I'm okay."

"Of course you're okay. You're a Percy," her mother intoned.

"Where are you, Mother?"

"Milan. The Intercontinental. There's a major art auction here tomorrow; I want to be a part of it. So tell me how things are going."

Her mother was uncharacteristically chatty. Anna talked a bit about Sam's wedding and about how she'd been doing a bit of writing. Her mother didn't inquire about what she was working on, and Anna didn't volunteer.

Anna glanced at the clock again. Four thirty-five. "Mom, I'm sorry, but I actually have to run to a hair thing at Sam's," she said. "I'm going to be late."

"Just a second, Anna, one last thing. There's someone in Los Angeles that you need to meet."

"Who?" Anna asked cautiously, leaning back against the fluffy white pillows.

"My dear friend Carlie Martin. I've known her forever. She's a Yale alum."

Anna sat up in bed like she'd been speared with a red-hot poker. So that was it. Her father, who had been so supportive at breakfast, had turned around and promptly called in the cavalry—namely, her mother. Jane Percy hadn't called at 2 a.m. to chat.

Instantly Anna curled her fingers into fists, feeling defensive. "Mother, please—"

"Anna, I won't hear another word. You owe it to yourself to speak with her before you make the biggest mistake of your life. She's in Los Angeles this very minute. I won't take no for an answer. You know who she is, of course?"

Of course Anna knew who Carlie Martin was—everyone in the western world knew. She was a triple threat actress/director/producer, who had to be around the same age as her parents. Jane's usual contacts were anti-Hollywood, and this was the first time Anna had heard that her mother even *knew* Carlie Martin. The whole thing was funny in some bitter way. Her parents, who could not get along for ten minutes without sniping at each other, could join forces so easily on what Anna now thought of as the Yale Problem. It reminded her of what she'd learned about Roosevelt and Stalin's collaboration during World War II, though who was Roosevelt and who was Stalin was up for grabs.

"Anna?" Jane prompted again.

Anna scuffed a bare foot into the tapestry throw rug. This was no time for a fight.

"Fine," she acquiesced. It wouldn't hurt to meet Carlie.

"Fantastic. I'll have her assistant call you to set a time?" Her mother said this as if it was a question because that was the polite thing to do, when in fact Anna knew it to be a parental decree.

"Yes, Mother." Anna played with a loose thread in her white Frette sheet, looking out the picture window toward the backyard, the gazebo in the distance. After her talk with her father, she'd felt like she won the point. Now it was clear that she'd lost the match.

They talked a few more moments, then Anna clicked off. She needed to get to Sam's. But there was one thing she needed to do first.

Live like you were dying, she told herself.

It was great to have a completed script. But it wasn't doing anyone any good on her iBook, and there was only one other person in the world she could send it to for an opinion. An honest opinion. She opened her Gmail and attached the script.

    Sam—tell me if this blows.

Without hesitation, she hit send.

Too Cool for School

Tuesday, 10:20 a.m.

"In Paris, you can become the next Truffaut," Eduardo murmured in Sam's ear as he came up behind her. He brushed her hair to the side so he could kiss the back of her neck.

Sam liked the kisses but wasn't sure about the concept.

"The whole French New Wave thing is highly overrated," she mused, turning to him. She fiddled with one citron starburst earring. She'd recently bought the pair at Fred Segal on a whim. "I mean, improvising lines and quick scene cuts might have been innovative in the fifties, but please—every kid in the 'burbs with a camcorder has been doing that for years now and calling himself an auteur."

Eduardo slipped his arms around her waist. He smiled at her attitude; clearly it didn't bother him in the least. They were in her room, alone in the massive house. Her father had taken her mother on an insiders' tour of the Paramount lot and then to lunch at the Ivy, and Eduardo had delayed going to his job at the Peruvian consulate so he could stop over to talk about wedding plans.

Of course, she hadn't revealed a thing. Part of it was because she wanted Friday night to be a surprise for him, and part of it was that Dee was still pulling together so many of the details. Sam was supposed to taste wedding cake samples later in the afternoon and then look at potential floral designs for the tables. There was so much to do—choosing a DJ, arranging the seating assignments, finalizing her color scheme—the list went on and on. At least she'd been able to check bridesmaid hairstyles off her list: Anna and Dee had come over yesterday for a consult with Raymond and had chosen their looks for the event—sweeping updos with the occasional cascading tendril, a yet-to-be-decided flower that would match the floral arrangements woven in.

"In that case you will be better than Truffaut," Eduardo decreed, gently brushing her just-moisturized skin with a tanned hand. That he was so proud of her talent was one of the many things she adored about him. "In Paris, you can be anything you want. Let me go downstairs and get you coffee so you won't be late." Sam smiled at his cute butt as he disappeared out the door, feeling like the luckiest girl in the world.

She turned back to the mirror on her vanity—which had a movie-quality lighting system that could be adjusted downward, in case of a bad body-image day—and shook her hair off her face. The citron earrings flashed in the morning light slanting through the open bay windows. She wore a black Yellow Dog jumper over black tights and chunky black suede Bruno Magli booties, thinking that the long black line would be flattering. She looked, she thought, rather cute. But then being with Eduardo, being *loved* by him, made her feel beautiful and brought out her self-confidence.

Funny how that worked.

A quick check of her Omega Constellation watch told her she had forty-five minutes to suck down some caffeine and get her ass downtown for the USC film school freshman orientation. The more she'd thought about it over the past few days, the less appealing of an option USC—and living halfway around the world from Eduardo—seemed to her. Sam was about 80 percent convinced that she wasn't going to go at all. After all, what could she possibly learn at film school that she didn't already know? She remembered taking an advanced filmmaking course at Stanford the summer after her freshman year and being bored out of her mind. And it wasn't like she needed contacts in the business. She *was* a contact in the business!

She loved the fact that Eduardo was being so supportive about her career, though. True, his parents had pressured her to go to France with him rather than having a long-distance marriage. But Eduardo himself had not. Other than the occasional Truffaut comment, of course. As for his folks, they'd gone back to their vacation and were going to return to Los Angeles on Thursday night for the rehearsal dinner, and then the ceremony on Fright out on the yacht. She was sort of glad they weren't around this week. It was easier to think and make decisions without Consuela, as well-meaning as she was, constantly pointing out where Sam's future ought to lie.

"Strong with extra sugar," Eduardo announced as he reappeared, bringing her a blue ceramic mug of coffee.

"Thanks." Sam blew on and then gingerly sipped the steaming-hot espresso. "You are the only person in the world who would willingly give me extra sugar."

"Ah, but sugar gives you energy," he teased, his warm brown eyes dancing. "And you'll need energy for all the things I'm going to do to you later." He then proceeded to whisper in her ear exactly what he intended to do to her later, in detail, until her cheeks were more red from his voice than from the steaming coffee.

He had to leave for the consulate soon, so they made plans to meet later for dinner. She had that wedding-cake tasting, and then a meeting with the DJ whom Dee had selected to go over music. Nothing could ruin a party faster than a DJ who played the wrong songs.

"Have fun at USC," he told her.

"I could probably teach half the courses myself," she replied, straightening the hem of her jumper.

"I know. Come to Paris, make a movie of your own, and they can study it in film school while you're in France with me. But go to this, so you can see for yourself."

"Okay, that sounds simple enough," Sam teased, setting the mug on her vanity to kiss him.

Two last sips of oh-so-sweet coffee, and they were out the door.

Sam took the Hummer to the USC campus near downtown, fighting traffic on Wilshire Boulevard all the way into the dicey neighborhood where USC was located. After having her name cleared by the security guard, Sam found a parking space and made her way toward the

Eileen L. Norris Theater Complex, an enormous white structure built only a few years back—she recalled that her father had made a high-six-figure donation to its construction. There were a number of bike racks outside the building, and Sam shuddered to think of four years spent biking around the campus. How . . . pedestrian.

Once inside, she joined a dozen or so others who were waiting for the elevator to take them to the Frank Sinatra Theater. The wide-eyed fellow students were all about her age, mostly dressed in shorts and T-shirts, an interesting mix of races and ethnicities, about half guys and half girls. She watched them eye the Sinatra memorabilia that lined the lobby, saw the reverence on their faces when they entered the refurbished 365-seat screening room. Sam had been at the party for the opening back in 2002, and all she remembered about it was that they had served chocolates in the shape of Frank's head, and Nancy Sinatra's daughter had eaten too many of them and barfed on her mother's mile-high red satin Jimmy Choo boots. Afterward Cammie had gone around singing, "These Boots Are Made for Puking."

She slid into a seat on the aisle. The guy next to her nodded coolly in her direction. He was pale and skinny and wore baggy jeans, a white T-shirt, and black-and-white plaid Converse high-tops. He had a wispy blond goatee and wore dark sunglasses. Sam gave a mental eye roll. He was already doing the affected, sunglasses-worn-indoors thing, and he hadn't even begun his freshman year. He was probably from somewhere in flyover country and had made some pretentious little film that got shown at his high school graduation, and everyone said he was *so* talented that he had to come to Hollywood and he was *so* going to be the next fill-in-the-blank hot young director of the moment, and he utterly, totally, and completely believed them. Undoubtedly he would use the words *my* and *vision* in close proximity in almost every sentence.

Sam shifted in the red cushioned auditorium seat and glanced around. Her eyes were drawn to a girl with spiky pink hair a few seats over. She wore a puffy zip-up vest from American Apparel and skintight black jeans that she was currently drawing designs on with a whiteout pen. The girl bobbed her head in time to music playing from the oversize headphones around her neck. Total hipster—she probably watched nothing but Japanese horror flicks and considered anything made after 1975 to be worthless commercial garbage.

And to think, these people would be Sam's classmates. She might actually have to spend time with them. Paris was looking better by the second.

The theater was packed, and there was a low rumble of excited, expectant voices as Elizabeth M. Daley, an attractive woman in her forties and dean of the USC film school, strode to the microphone on stage. She had a round, sweet face surrounded by short, choppy, chestnut brown hair similar to the color of Sam's if she hadn't had it highlighted. She wore a conservative taupe pants suit and didn't look very Hollywood at all.

"Thanks so much for coming today, and here's to the USC class of 2012!" The crowd roared in applause and Sam rolled her eyes. Film school spirit? "Don't worry, I don't have any grand speeches prepared," the dean continued, and Sam exhaled thankfully. "Instead of listening to me talk, what better way to convey what you're going to be experiencing for the next four years than with a film? That's why we're here after all, isn't it?" She backed away from the microphone as the overhead lights dimmed and an enormous screen was lowered from the ceiling.

A short documentary made in 2004 to honor the seventy-fifth anniversary of the film school came on. It told all about how USC was the first school in the country to offer a bachelor's degree in film, and how it had been founded by Hollywood legends Douglas S. Fairbanks, D. W. Griffith, and William C. DeMille. It boasted an awesome list of alumni, from Steven Spielberg to Will Ferrell. Sam found herself caught up in the history, both of the school and of L.A., her town. Sitting in the darkened theater, one part of Sam felt utterly jaded about what she was seeing. After all, just as many famous people had been to parties at her own home. But another part of her felt something she couldn't quite name, a kind of anticipation in the pit of her stomach at the idea of being part of all this, and not just for the usual reason that she was the daughter of Jackson Sharpe.

The film ended and the lights came back on, and Dean Daley took the stage again. "I hope you enjoyed the film. You're all invited to the lower lobby for a reception. A few dozen alumni will be there—directors, actors, agents, producers—here to mingle with you . . . and what's more Hollywood than that?" She paused as the crowd tittered excitedly. "Anyway, the people you meet today will be able to explain the USC film school experience better than any lecture, or even any film," she concluded.

Waste of my time, Sam thought, but she dutifully trudged down to the lower lobby with everyone else. Soon it was teeming with students and faculty. The usual cast of waiters in black pants and white shirts, all of whom looked like actor wannabes trying to make a connection with the various famous alumni, were sprinkled among the crowd and manning a sushi buffet. This year's Hollywood's culinary obsessions for party food were sushi, sashimi, and five varieties of mini burgers from In-N-Out Burger.

Just as Sam reached for a bottle of Fiji in a large sterling bowl of crushed ice, a voice near her right shoulder said, "You look familiar."

Sam turned, sweating water bottle in hand, to see Goatee Guy, still hidden behind those ridiculous knockoff Versace sunglasses.

"Probably because I was sitting next to you upstairs," Sam said dryly. She had zero interest in going through the *Hey, aren't you Jackson Sharpe's daughter?* conversation.

"No, that's not it." He two-fingered a piece of sashimi into his mouth and contemplated her. "I feel like I know you from somewhere else." He swallowed the raw fish, then stuck out his hand. Fortunately, it wasn't the sushi hand.

"Nars Muessen," he introduced himself. "And you're...?"

"Sam." She shook his hand, deliberately not giving her last name.

"I'm from Salt Lake City," Nars continued, as if Sam

was actually interested, as if she'd asked, which she most definitely hadn't. He went into a monologue about a student film he'd made a few months earlier, about a group of Mormon kids who hear a teen rock band and are so overwhelmed by their talent and their cool factor that they sell their souls to the devil in order to be in a similar band.

"Fresh," Sam commented. Like that hackneyed play on Mark Twain's "The Devil and Daniel Webster" hadn't already been told ad nauseam. Her eyes darted right and left, seeking an escape route.

"It's Nars, isn't it?"

Nars smiled, because the question had come from none other than George Petrus, who had sidled up next to them, water bottle in hand. His silver hair was swept back from his handsome face. He wore a black shirt tucked into black pants and was smiling at Goatee Guy. Petrus was one of the city's great directors. Lucas, Scorsese, and Petrus. Sam's father couldn't stand him, but no one ever argued with his talent.

"Great to see you again, Mr. Petrus," Nars exclaimed, shaking the famous director's hand as if it was a pump from which he was trying to coax water.

"I just wanted to tell you again how impressed I was with *Highway to Hell*," Petrus said. "One of the best student films I've ever seen."

Sam nearly inhaled her bottle of Fiji water. George Petrus knew Goatee's Guy's film? And thought it was great? Back when Petrus and Jackson were talking, he'd been a frequent dinner guest at the Sharpes'. But that had been back when Sam was still in middle school. He probably didn't even recognize her. Sam sort of wished she'd been nicer to Goatee Guy so that he'd bring her into the conversation. In Hollywood, people liked to corner talent and keep celebrities all to themselves.

Nars smiled so broadly that Sam thought his face might actually crack. "Oh, and this is Sam." He gestured politely at her, and George Petrus turned to take her in.

"Just Sam?" He shook her hand and smiled, amused.

"Just Sam." She smiled back. "I know you hear this all the time," Sam began, realizing she sounded a bit like a gushing teenager but not really caring. "But I'm a huge fan of *American Legion.*" The film was about four different teenagers coming of age in four different parts of the country, and then coming together at a Who concert in Denver one summer night. In fact, Sam had watched it again recently, one night when Eduardo was working late and she couldn't sleep.

"Actually, I don't," George said easily. "I usually hear about *Dark Star* and *Modesto,* so thanks. That one gets overlooked."

"How did you happen to see Nars's film?" Sam asked, truly curious.

"Connections," Nars admitted. "My dad went to USC. And then when I came to UCLA for my eye surgery a few months ago, I actually got to meet with Mr. Petrus." He fiddled with his dark glasses. "I keep growing these nasty tumors behind my eyeballs. Lots of surgery and lots of pairs of dark glasses."

Sam felt, simultaneously, like an idiot and a bitch. She had just assumed Nars's glasses were pretentious. But they weren't; they were functional. He had eye tumors, for God's sake.

Petrus spent a good fifteen minutes chatting with them about film, as if he was just some guy who happened to like cinema as much as they did. He would be doing a small freshman seminar on personal-journey movies, and invited both Sam and Nars to attend. Then he invited Nars to come in to his production office to talk about him interning the following summer. After that, he melted into the crowd.

"Great guy, huh?" Nars asked, turning to Sam with a smile. She noticed for the first time that he had world-class dimples.

"Amazing," Sam replied, quite honestly. "Why was he so nice?"

Nars's sparse eyebrows knit together over the top of his glasses. "I guess he knows we love film the way he loves film or we wouldn't be here. And . . ." He smiled. "I guess he liked my film. My parents maxed their credit cards for me to make it. But being a director is all I want to do."

Me too, Sam thought.

Just then, she heard her cell phone sound gently in her bag, and she fished it out. It was a text from Eduardo.

BORED MUCH? DREAMING OF PARIS?

She closed her cell without responding. Two hours ago, she would have responded, "Hell, yes." Now, she wasn't so sure.

She looked around the reception. All around she saw people engaged in conversations about film, not because they wanted to name-drop or show off, but because they were genuinely passionate and opinioned about cinema as an art form. Okay, maybe they wore ugly clothes and rode bikes around campus. Maybe they cheered like idiots at the sound of their graduation date. But maybe they were also her people, the people with whom she would connect and collaborate and exchange ideas as they journeyed together through the next four years of film school. Maybe Paris wasn't the right place for her, at least not right now.

The old saying, "Home is where the heart is," flew into her mind. Her heart was with Eduardo. And Eduardo was soon to be in Paris. Did that mean, though, that Paris had to be her home?

On the List

"**R**ight after this commercial break, comin' back atcha with a girl who just turned eighteen and— check it out—is owner of the most happenin' new club in L.A. Plus, she's managing the hottest new model in town. Stay tuned!"

The smile stayed on Kelly Clarkson's face until the camera blinked out. The kids gathered on pink and aqua faux-leather couches on the small Santa Monica MTV soundstage kept applauding and squealing as some mail-room graduate made twirling hand motions at them, which meant, *Keep it up.* Kelly was putting together her TV special, *Planet Kelly C.,* and pieces of what went on today would be spliced in.

And that was about as much as Cammie knew. Her dad had talked to Kelly's manager about getting Cammie on, and the deal had been struck late last night. Evidently, it hadn't been difficult. Kelly had already been to Bye, Bye Love twice to guest-DJ and loved the place. The national publicity, Cammie knew, was worth a mint.

"Okay, so, you ready?" an assistant asked Cammie, who stood just out of camera range. The girl squinted at Cammie. "You need a little pat-down for the shine." She craned her head around. "Where's Nattie with makeup? Damn. She's working on Kelly. Nattie! When you get a sec!"

"I do my own," Cammie said coolly, reaching for her kelly green quilted leather Chanel hobo bag to fish out her makeup case. She'd worn a Free People pink-and-aqua flounce-hemmed mini-dress, and strappy pink Jimmy Choo sandals with a suede wedge heel. Since she hadn't learned she'd be on national TV until last night, she'd found an eyelash-extension artist in the Valley who made house calls 24/7, and charged twenty dollars per lash. Cammie didn't care. As she powdered her nose and gazed at her Bambi-like eyes, she knew the five hundred dollars' worth of eyelash extensions had been worth it.

"Okay, don't be nervous, and don't look directly into the camera. Try to act like you and Kelly are just friends hanging out at home," an assistant director with greasy hair and a plaid collared shirt that belonged back in the nineties was blathering at Cammie.

"It's not a problem," Cammie assured him.

"People say that, but then the camera goes on and—"

Cammie held up a hand to interrupt. "Trust me." Her cell sounded. She plucked it from her pocket to answer.

"Oh my God, turn that off before we're back on air!" Another equally unkempt production assistant was on her immediately.

Cammie turned away and put it to her ear. "Hello?"

"Hi-hi."

Dee. Only one person in the world had a voice like

that. No amount of Prozac could change it, either. Cammie liked Dee's voice.

"Hey, what's up?" Cammie watched the makeup artist work on Kelly's mascara while the hairstylist swept the bangs to the side so that they looked artfully mussed, and then sprayed them into place.

"I'm at Tiffany, and you were supposed to meet me?" Dee reminded Cammie. "We're picking out the wedding party favors? Do we want to go with diamond studs for all the girls and diamond cuff links for the guys, or is that too old-fashioned?"

Cammie tried to remember ever telling Dee she'd help with this particular duty, and vaguely recalled a conversation that had taken place over the roar at the club late the night before. "Do whatever you want, Dee—I can't make it." Across the soundstage, the assistant director was giving the three-minute signal.

"But you're the maid of honor!" Dee protested. "This is what you're supposed to do. I'm just a bridesmaid!"

"I'm doing this television thing, Dee," Cammie explained quickly, gesturing to the hyperventilating production assistant that she was just wrapping it up. "And after that, I'm doing an interview for *Teen Vogue* at—"

"But we're supposed to meet Sam for coffee!"

Shit, she *had* said she'd meet them. But she'd also told Ben she'd meet him at the club to talk about the next round of designers they'd bring in, since they planned to change the interior décor every week. And she had a lot more interest in meeting with Ben than she did in planning Sam's wedding. Not that she didn't love Sam, because she did. But a wedding? The only people Cammie knew who actually got married at age eighteen were drunk bimbo celebs looking for cheap publicity by running off to Vegas with their high school boyfriends. And even then it was all a public relations stunt, and they planned to get divorced shortly thereafter.

But Sam was in love with a capital *l*. As in, always and forever. It was enough to make a girl upchuck the blackened mahimahi with pomegranate chutney she'd had for lunch at Kobe while being interviewed by *L.A. Weekly*. If Ben and Adam both proposed and threw in world peace, she'd still turn down the deal. Marriage. Cammie shuddered.

The assistant was holding up a one-minute finger. Cammie spoke quickly into the phone.

"Tell Sam I can't make it and I'll meet you guys later, sorry. I'll call you. Bye."

She hung up quickly before Dee could protest further. In some remote part of her brain, she thought maybe she was letting Sam down. But then again, Sam was just as ambitious as she was, so surely Sam would understand. In the long run—say, a week from Friday, after the wedding—Sam would have forgotten all about it.

Neighborhood coffee shops came and went, Sam mused, but Starbucks was ubiquitous, forever, and bred and multiplied like the obnoxious aliens from that *South Park* episode. Sam loathed Starbucks. It was the McDonald's of coffee shops. Fortunately, there were alternatives.

The Brighton Coffee Shop, located near North Camden, was one of them. Sam had come here with her friends and their accompanying nannies for years when they didn't feel like dealing with the tourists at the Beverly Hills Hotel. The home-cooked food was a big draw: meat loaf and mashed potatoes with gravy, warm chocolate chip cookies—the kind of thing their parents' chefs never prepared because it was either gauche, fattening, or both. "Home-cooked" had a varying definition at the Sharpe estate, since the "cook" who made said food in their "home" was almost always from another country and culture. Her father had gone through a Vietnamese phase, a Russian phase, and a Mexican phase as various cooks passed through her life. Plus, whatever food was "hot" at the time on the Los Angeles restaurant scene inevitably made it to her father's dinner table. She remembered eating Kobe beef skewers at least twice a week when she was in eighth grade.

Striding through the swinging glass doors, Sam saw that Cammie and Dee had already arrived and were at a red leather-backed booth. Cammie, looking even more made up than usual in a Free People number, leaned her head against the long mirror behind her as she chattered away to someone on her cell. She waggled fingers at Sam and kept talking as Sam slid into the booth next to Dee. Dee was wearing a brown-and-aqua polka-dotted Diane von Furstenberg wrap dress and a John Hardy twisted cuff bracelet. She already had her PowerBook open to SAM'S WEDDING FILE on the white Formica countertop, a cup of black coffee cooling next to it.

The new Interpol song was playing in the background, and Sam drummed her French-manicured nails in time with the music. This would be a great song for the opening credits of her first USC film, she mused, as visions of whirring dolly shots danced in her head. Not that she was sure she was even going. She hadn't even told Eduardo yet how impressed she'd been by the orientation, as if saying it aloud would be somehow betraying the Paris plan.

"Sam, gosh, we have so much to do," Dee exclaimed, interrupting her reverie. "We've got to finalize the guest list. The invites are printed, the messengers are standing by, but we have to tell the calligrapher the names we want." She blew her feathery bangs off her forehead, a nervous habit she'd had since she'd been four and they'd been in preschool together. "It's so great that you and Cammie both made it. We can get a ton of work done," Dee bubbled, kissing Sam's cheek.

"Hey, guys? Gimme a sec?" Cammie got up to take a few steps away to continue her phone call, but she was still loud enough for Sam to overhear. "No! I would rather have Bob Hope DJ than Avril Lavigne—I'm serious." There was a brief pause, and then Sam heard Cammie add, "Of course I know he's dead, that's the point!"

"What's up with her?" Sam asked. She couldn't help but be a bit miffed that Cammie, having been chosen as the one and only maid of honor Sam would ever have in her life, was treating the job as if it were the same priority level as a discretionary root canal.

"Something about the DJs at her club tonight," Dee explained, shrugging her small shoulders. She hit a few buttons on her PowerBook and a high-resolution slide show of diamond stud earrings appeared. "So, do you like this with the marquise cut? We could do heart or square, but I liked these better."

"Whatever you pick is fine." Sam said absentmindedly,

craning around. Even though it was 3 p.m. on a Tuesday, the coffee shop was bustling—Sam often wondered what percentage of Los Angelenos held actual nine-to-five jobs—with couples and groups clustered around the diner-style booths. Waitresses in old-school aprons strode briskly across the black-and-white checkered floor. Where was Cammie? Finally Sam spotted her—she'd actually stepped outside the coffee shop to continue the call. Sam could see her through the glass, laughing as she held her phone to her ear.

Dee rapped her knuckles on the countertop to get Sam's attention. "Sam, focus!""

Sam forced herself to turn around and planted a big smile on her face. "Yes. I'm focusing."

"Thank you." Dee peered at her laptop. "I just wanted to give you the rundown on what's been happening. Invites have already been engraved by Impressions Printing in Sherman Oaks. Best in the city. They'll be messengered all over town as soon as we approve the guest list. We'll have a hundred and fifty people on the vessel. That's coast guard limit—I checked. People can board the *Look Sharpe* three different ways. Either they can come aboard at the dock in Malibu, be shuttled by cigarette boat, or come by helicopter. Let's go over the guest list."

"Fine." Sam sneaked another look at Cammie. She really wished she had her maid of honor's input.

"I'm thinking all the usual suspects for our friends. Krishna, Blue, Parker, and Monte, of course," Dee suggested. "What about Adam Flood?"

"Of course," Sam replied. "What, you think I wouldn't invite him because he broke up with Cammie?"

"She broke up with him," Dee corrected.

"He's on the list," Sam decided. If Cammie didn't like it, too bad. It wasn't like she was showing any actually interest in planning what was only the most important day of Sam's life.

"Hi, ready to order?" A black-clad waitress with wavy dark hair and matte red lips interrupted Dee and stood beside their booth, pen poised over her order pad.

"Coffee and a raspberry Danish," Sam said distractedly, chewing the gloss off her lower lip.

The waitress took Dee's order—a bowl of strawberries with the whipped cream on the side—and moved off.

"You're upset," Dee concluded, eyeing Sam carefully.

"I'm about to get married, I'm supposed to freak." Sam shrugged. "Just on general principle."

"'Kay." Dee's round, blue eyes bore into Sam's. "Is that all?"

Sam considered confiding in Dee about her USC orientation. "Would you ever get married and not live where you husband lived?" she asked carefully.

"Gosh, no," Dee exclaimed. "I mean, what's the point of getting married then?" She inhaled sharply. "You mean you and Eduardo—?"

"It was a theoretical whatever," Sam said dismissively.

Dee tapped a fingernail against the white Formica tabletop. "You're still moving to Paris?"

"Yeah, of course."

Dee leaned closer. "You don't *want* to move to Paris?"

"I do, of course I do," Sam insisted. "Forget it." She didn't know why she was so reluctant to confide in anyone about the film school or Paris thing. Somehow, talking about it would, she just knew, make her even more anxious.

The coffee and Danish arrived. Sam lifted the large white mug and took a sip of coffee, followed by a bite of pastry, then turned to look outside at Cammie again. "She is totally blowing me off."

Dee didn't say a word.

"Well, she is," Sam insisted, as if Dee was arguing with her. Anger bubbled up inside her. "Soon as she gets her perky ass off the phone—"

Dee held up a hand of caution. "She's done. She's coming back in."

"Fine." Sam stared into her coffee until Cammie had slid back into the red leather booth, next to Dee and across from Sam.

"She's mad at you," Dee declared, as Cammie reached across the table for a sip of Sam's coffee.

"Why? I'm trying to run a business," Cammie defended herself. "This coffee is really good," she added, taking a sip.

"Careful, there's real sugar in that," Dee cautioned. "She's pissed because you're her maid of honor and you're blowing her off," she added, her enormous blue eyes fiercely protective.

"I can speak for myself, Dee," Sam said crossly. She cut her eyes at Cammie. "What she just said."

Cammie snorted dismissively. "You really need me to count napkins or choose cake frosting or whatever? *That's* what you think being maid of honor is about?"

"How the fuck would I know?" Sam railed. "I never had one before!" She was vaguely aware that she was upset about much more than Cammie, but chose not to examine that thought very closely.

"It's about friendship," Cammie enunciated, taking another sip of Sam's coffee.

"You don't give a shit about my wedding," Sam grumbled, as an apron-clad waitress came around with coffee refills. "We're working on the guest list, but you're not here to help."

"You're only saying that because you're in sugar shock," Cammie commented, eyeing the pastry.

"Put the bitch back in her box, because I am not in the mood," Sam snapped. "Dee is killing herself to put this wedding together practically overnight—"

"I've been busy. Bye, Bye Love is the hottest thing in town. I'm like a movie star when a movie first comes out. Who told you to have a wedding on Friday?" Cammie asked rhetorically, blinking her honey-colored eyes. Her lashes were thick and unimaginably long. "Most of the time, people plan ahead. Like, for at least two weeks."

The cute couple in the booth next to them interrupted their spit-swapping PDA to glare at them. They were trying very hard to look like they were important, she in her L.A.M.B. jumper and Posh Spice bob, he in his weathered leather jacket and fauxhawk.

"Let's not fight, you guys, okay?" Dee tried to make peace as Cammie smiled ingratiatingly at Sam. "Cammie, just give me a little help with this stuff. Okay?"

"Okay. Let's do the list. Okay, Sam?" Cammie put her coffee cup down and looked over Dee's shoulder at the names she'd started to type. But then her Razr sounded again. "Shit," she pronounced. "I gotta take this. I'll be back in a minute. Hang in there."

Sam was on her feet before Cammie was. She hadn't apologized. She hadn't acknowledged that thus far, she had been the world's suckiest maid of honor, and she hadn't promised to do better.

"Dee, you're my maid of honor," Sam decided. She tossed a twenty on the table. "Enjoy your call, Cammie. And enjoy your meal. It's on me. Leave the rest for the waitress. And if it's not too much trouble, I'd still like you to be a bridesmaid." With that, she turned on her Christian Louboutin peep-toe heel and walked away.

Bali High

"Anna?"

Anna looked up to see a tall, striking young woman just a few years older than herself, with thick dark hair that swung around her shoulders, crystalline blue eyes, and a tall, willowy figure smiling at her. She wore a nipped-waist jet black Givenchy jacket and trousers, and black patent leather booties. She wouldn't, Anna thought, have been out of place at a publishing house near Rockefeller Center.

"I'm Anna, yes." Anna was glad that she'd dressed similarly, in a simple gray cotton Ralph Lauren skirt that ended just above her knees, and a pale pink cashmere button-front cardigan. Her shoes were vintage Chanel cherry red suede peep-toe pumps her grandmother had given her after a shopping spree in Paris.

"I'm Caresse, Carlie Martin's assistant. Carlie's really looking forward to meeting you. Please follow me." The assistant's easy manner melted away any nervousness Anna still felt.

It was just past three-thirty in the afternoon; Anna's meeting with Carlie Martin had been scheduled for three fifteen. Fifteen minutes of waiting wasn't bad at all by Hollywood standards, especially for a woman as busy as Ms. Martin. Anna sat a simple waiting area: low-slung couches and a TV monitor tuned to whatever CBS show was on at the time—a talk show that Anna didn't recognize.

Carlie's office was in the Television City complex of CBS, located in the Fairfax District near the Grove shopping area and farmer's market. Anna had been to the Grove many times—there were great restaurants and a multiplex movie theater—but she'd never set foot inside the looming studio complex that was the home of CBS.

All that had changed this afternoon. She'd taken her Lexus through the white gate on Beverly Boulevard just east of Fairfax and checked in at the guard booth, where a man with a thick moustache and a friendly smile printed out a parking pass for her and a stick-on badge, and then directed her to the artists' entrance and visitors' parking. The CBS buildings loomed on her left as she made her way to the parking lot; they were low, white, and sprawling.

The guard had told her to go to the artists' entrance, just past the game-show entrance, where an endless line of tourists in funny getups, each wearing a number, were waiting to get in to *The Price Is Right* with its latest host, Drew Carey. One woman carried a sign that read MARRY ME, DREW!

"These are all the new shows," Caresse pointed out as they walked a long, poster-lined corridor; the posters featured actresses and actors from various CBS shows. Then they were on the studio floor, with Caresse explaining that the *Young and the Restless* soundstages were to the left, *The Price Is Right* was to the right, and that if Anna wanted to see either of these shows taping after her meeting, Caresse would be happy to play tour guide.

"Thanks, that's very nice of you, but it won't be necessary," Anna said politely as they walked east through the cavernous hall and then stopped at a small elevator. Anna didn't want to spend any more time than she had to at CBS, and was feeling resentful that she'd even agreed to waste an hour of her time. She was quite capable of making up her own mind about Yale. She didn't need, nor did she want, to be coerced into a decision about the next four years of her life.

The elevator doors opened and they got on. Caresse pressed the 1 button. "Carlie hasn't had lunch yet. It's kind of late, but she wondered if you'd meet her in the commissary?"

"Of course."

The elevator doors opened, and they stepped out onto a floor that looked very much like the one they'd just come from. There were lots of burly guys on this one, though, driving forklifts loaded with scenery, or moving costume racks from place to place. There was also the delicious aroma of frying onion rings and baking chicken. Anna realized she was actually hungry. She hoped that Carlie wasn't one of those dime-a-dozen Hollywood women for whom a pastrami sandwich held the same appeal as, say, an attack by a band of rabid Rottweilers.

The commissary was simple—just a counter that offered an array of sandwiches and a few daily specials, and a long, narrow eating area with wooden tables and orange banquettes along the sides.

Anna spotted Carlie immediately at one of the banquettes, with a pile of scripts spread out around her, reading glasses slipping down her elegant nose. In front of her was a clear plastic box with a cheeseburger and some of the onion rings that Anna had smelled cooking.

"Can I get you something to eat?" Caresse asked.

"I'll have what she's having."

"Good choice. Carlie?" Caresse approached her boss.

Carlie looked up. "Yes?"

"Anna Percy."

Carlie practically leaped to her feet. "Jane Cabot Percy's daughter? I should have known—you look so much like your mother. A hug. I demand a hug."

Her hair was several shades of delicate blond woven together, impeccably cut in a layered bob that framed her high-cheekboned, fortysomething face. Her eyes were honey colored, fringed with long lashes, her nose a touch too long, and her smile so huge it seemed to take up half her face. It was the smile that had lit up dozens of movies. And here she sat, comfortable and free of cosmetics or, it seemed to Anna, any sort of pretense. She was dressed for comfort, not speed, in black jeans and a blue work shirt, as if to say that she was so impressive that she didn't have to impress anyone. Yet when Carlie motioned to her for a hug, Anna felt hesitant.

Carlie laughed. A deep, booming, comfortable-in-her-own-skin laugh. "Oh yes," she chortled. "Your mother hates hugs in public too. In fact, your mother hates hugs in general. I do love to embarrass her that way. Well, sit down, sit down."

Anna sat, and Caresse moved away to the commissary counter.

Carlie tented her fingers and leaned toward Anna, elbows on the table. "Tell me, Anna, do you know why I'm here at CBS?"

Anna shook her head. "No clue."

"I'm here because the commissary makes the best cheeseburgers in the city."

She said this so emphatically, with such a straight face, that it took Anna a moment to realize she was joking. It was only after Carlie started to laugh, flashing that famous grin, that Anna laughed too.

"You had me there for a moment," Anna admitted.

Caresse showed up with Anna's burger and set it in front of her. Carlie sent her off to lunch. Then Anna bit into what was, as advertised, a truly superior cheeseburger. After eating in silence for a few moments, Carlie put down her burger and wiped her mouth with a thin paper napkin.

"Really, truly, the reason I'm at CBS," Carlie began, "is that this network is smart enough to realize that television doesn't have to always come in second to movies. I came in here with the goal of making a nighttime drama that has as much weight as *The Arrowhead*. You saw that film?"

Anna was still chewing, so she nodded. Carlie had done everything there was to do on the film, practically. Written it, directed it, produced it, and starred in it, as the mother of a boy who uncovered a single Indian arrowhead on a walk though Central Park, which took him into a pre-Columbian world of Manhattan Island before Europeans made it what it was. The film was everything a movie should be. Heartfelt. Magnificent to look at. Deeply moving. "I did. I loved it," Anna replied honestly.

"Thank you," Carlie said. "I love it too. There's no

reason that television can't be the same kind of viewing experience. In a movie, you live with the characters for ninety, maybe a hundred and twenty minutes. For TV, you can have them an hour a week, for twenty-two nights a year, for however many years that show should last. If anything, TV should, by nature, be more moving than film."

Anna looked at Carlie curiously. She'd never met anyone here in L.A. quite like her. She wondered if her equal even existed in the business.

They talked for an hour. Actually, Carlie mostly talked, and Anna mostly listened. As a rule, Anna grew impatient with people in love with the sounds of their own voices, and suspected that most big talkers fell into that category. Carlie, though, was different. It was as if while she talked she was listening, reacting to Anna's face by changing the subject or asking a few laserlike questions.

And then, finally, they got around to the real reason for their meeting. Carlie polished off her burger, the sleeves of her blue work shirt rolled almost to the elbows. "So, Anna. How long have you wanted to go to Yale?"

"As long as I can remember," Anna replied. "It's a family—"

"Legacy," Carlie filled in, nodding her delicate blond bobbed head. "Your mother told me. What do you want to study?"

"Literature," Anna replied, "and I have a feeling she told you that too."

Carlie held up a palm as if taking an oath. "Guilty as charged. Your mom is concerned that you're thinking about not going."

"I realize that," Anna said stiffly, removing her elbows from the orange banquette's table. She had known that the conversation would come down to this, so she had no idea why she was bristling now. It wasn't like anyone had forced her to come to this meeting. She could have said no. Of course, saying no to her mother was like saying no to the queen of England, except that her mother was much younger, and with much better taste in clothes.

"I know you mean well," Anna began. "And I know you and my mother are friends. But I don't think it's right for me to go to Yale just because everyone expects me to. People change. Their goals change—"

Carlie nodded, her honey-colored eyes taking Anna in. "True. So how have your goals changed?"

There was no way on God's green earth that Anna was going to tell Carlie Martin that she'd written a screenplay. First of all, it would sound as if what she really wanted was for Carlie to read it, when in fact that was the last thing Anna wanted. And second of all, Yale's theater department was world famous. So there was no reason that a wannabe screenwriter would find going there anathema to her future hopes and dreams.

"It seems to me," Anna began, idly touching the pearly buttons of her pink cashmere cardigan, "that if a person is going to go to Yale, she should be committed to it. And I just find . . . I can't explain why, exactly, but . . . I'm not."

"It has something to do with your plane nearly crashing?" Carlie ventured, sliding her reading glasses down the tip of her long nose.

Anna sighed. "My mother told you about that too?"

Carlie shrugged. "She wants the best for you."

Anna nearly laughed at that one. What Anna's mother wanted for Anna, and for Anna's sister, Susan, too, was what Jane wanted, what she considered the best. That her daughters might be utterly unlike her, and want different things, was simply not considered.

Carlie took an onion ring and chewed it carefully before she continued. "Just be careful, Anna, that you don't reject something wonderful simply because you are trying to define yourself."

"And the something wonderful is Yale," Anna filled in.

"Exactly. Yale will change you, Anna, as surely as your time here in California has changed you, and as surely as that horrible experience you had a few days ago has changed you. Not one of my classmates said to me at graduation, 'Damn, Carlie. I should have gone to Swarthmore.' Or, 'Damn, Carlie. I should have gone to an ashram.' There are people there from all over the world and all walks of life, doing some pretty amazing stuff. You could discover talents you never knew you had."

Anna sighed. Her skin felt prickly, her throat constricted. Because she knew that every single thing Carlie was telling her was true. "Or I could spend four years drinking beer and going to football games," Anna joked.

"Well, that's part of the fun of college, too," Carlie allowed. "But I have a feeling that majoring in beer is not your style."

Carlie took the stack of scripts sitting on the table and eased them into her black leather bag. She straightened to look again at Anna. "The thing is, there are a million paths you can take in life, but Yale's not a beginning, middle, and end. It's more like a preface. The things you'll learn, the people you'll meet, the experiences you'll have—they won't determine your life course, but they'll help shape it. In amazing and truly unpredictable ways. There's no place quite like it."

She stood. Anna did too. Then, Carlie extended her hand, more formal than the hug she'd offered at the beginning of their talk. "It's been great to meet you. Please stay in touch."

"I will," Anna agreed, because it was the right thing to say, and because she quite liked her mom's friend.

"Contact me toward the end of first semester about coming out here to intern in my office next summer," Carlie suggested.

"You think I'm still going to go to Yale."

"In the end, yes, I do," Carlie admitted. "And I think you'll be glad you did, too. Come on, I'll walk you out."

Carlie walked Anna back to the elevator, then escorted her past the ground-floor soundstages and back to the artists' entrance. As they walked, Anna saw how everyone on the floor, from the lowest gaffer to the chisel-jawed actors who had to be soap opera stars, to the interior security guards in their red CBS blazers, looked at Carlie with something approaching reverence.

This time, when Carlie held her arms out for a hug, Anna went into them.

A few moments later, Anna emerged in the CBS parking lot, the hot afternoon sunshine beating down on her. Los Angeles was experiencing one of its rare heat waves, but at least it wasn't the wet pressure cooker of a 95/95 New York City day in August, with 95 degree temps and 95 percent humidity.

As she made her way back to her car, her cell sounded with a text.

LOGAN HERE. ACTUALLY, NOT HERE. AT CANTER'S DELI IN
FAIRFAX. TWO MINUTES AWAY. COME MEET ME. GO NORTH ON
FAIRFAX, IT'S ON THE LEFT.

Anna smiled down at her phone. She'd told Logan
about this meeting, but she hadn't expected him to come
to the neighborhood. She texted back that she'd be there
in five minutes.

Canter's, a Los Angeles landmark, was the only deli
Anna had ever been to—and growing up in New York
City, she'd been to her fair share—that was also a hot
music venue. Adjacent to the main dining room was the
Kibitz Room, a lounge with a full bar where some of the
best local bands performed nightly. Anna had been there
recently with Sam and Dee to see Dead Pink, an up-and-
coming indie rock group that Dee's father managed.

By day, however, it was just a typical deli, with long
white counters and shiny green vinyl booths. Logan was
inside, in jeans and a white tennis shirt, his short blond
hair slightly spiky.

"How'd it go?" He stood gallantly as she approached,
motioning her into the booth across from him. "I ordered
coffee. I think it's the most like on the Upper East Side
you'll ever find."

She smiled at their shared history. "It was . . . interesting." She actually didn't feel much like talking about her
meeting. She wanted to think about it. Process it.

"This should be interesting too." He plopped a thick
white envelope on the table between them. Anna could
tell immediately what it was.

"Tickets. To Bali," she guessed.

"Live like you were dying." He grinned hugely, his

pearly teeth startlingly white against his tanned skin. "Go to Sam's wedding, go to the airport, get on a plane. Actually, same flight as the one we took, minus the drama. Early Saturday morning from LAX, just a week later. Just like riding a horse." He reached across the table for her hand. "You get tossed, you climb right back in the saddle."

"I don't know, Logan." Anna sipped her coffee—he was right, it tasted just like the coffee in New York. It was strange how far away she felt from her old life on the Upper East Side.

He smiled again, his blue eyes bright. "Of course you don't. That's why I'm here. To help you see the light."

The bright late-afternoon sunshine filtered through the diner's plate glass windows, slanting across the countertop in front of them. The plane tickets, nestled in their envelope, lay untouched. Part of Anna wanted to tear the envelope open and hold the tickets in her hands, to feel how very real the trip in less than one week's time could be. But part of her felt frozen, her arms glued to her sides.

Before she could move a muscle, her cell sounded, and she checked the number. Unfamiliar, with a 310 area code.

"Excuse me," she said, and took the call, grateful for the distraction. It was probably regarding a wedding crisis, which was what you got when you planned an elaborate ceremony in mere days.

"Hello?" she answered.

"Miss Percy? This is Dr. Adrienne Miller at Cedars-Sinai Medical Center."

Cedars-Sinai? Anna suddenly felt nauseated. Why were they calling her? "We have your father here," the doctor continued. "I think you should come right away."

Ex Marks the Spot

Tuesday evening, 6:07 p.m.

"Dr. Miller, Dr. Adrienne Miller to the emergency room nursing station. Dr. Miller, Dr. Adrienne Miller. To the nursing station."

The short, rather squat nurse named Alma spoke into the white paging telephone. "She'll be here in a moment," she told Anna, as she hung up and motioned toward several rows of hard white plastic chairs to the left of the nursing station. They were directly under a bank of harsh fluorescent lights. "Please sit."

Anna didn't move. "But how is my father?"

"This is our procedure. There's nothing I can tell you. Please wait for Dr. Miller." Alma scurried off toward three other nurses at the far end of the nurse's station.

With no one available to give her any information—she didn't know if her father was in a coma or conscious, in terrible pain or no pain at all, or even what had happened—Anna found an empty seat in the waiting area. An hour before, she'd been in the CBS commissary with one of the most famous producers in the country. Now she was in the emergency room at Cedars-Sinai, fearing the worst. The doctor who had called her at Canter's had offered nothing except to say that her father was stable. For the moment. That had been twenty minutes ago. Thank God the hospital was close to the Fairfax District, a short drive due west on Beverly Boulevard. It was good she hadn't had to turn left or right, as Anna still felt as though she were sleepwalking.

Logan had offered to come with her. She'd been almost too numb to respond, but something inside her told her to say no. This was too personal. What decisions would she have to make? What might she see? How would she react? She told him she'd rather go alone. There'd been a momentary flash of hurt in his eyes, but he'd said he understood. He'd have his cell with him at all times, he promised. The moment she knew something definitive, she'd call him.

The emergency room was crowded. To her right sat an Indian mother in a red sari, cradling a whimpering infant in her arms. To her left was a burly construction worker, grimacing with pain from a serious cut on his forearm that had been hastily wrapped in bandages. Behind her was a family whose elderly grandmother had an oxygen tank and a walker.

"Anna Percy? Are you Anna Percy?"

Anna hadn't even seen the woman in the green surgical scrubs slide into the empty seat next to her.

Anna nodded. "I'm Anna."

"I'm Dr. Miller. Adrienne Miller. I'm taking care of your father."

Dr. Miller was medium height, with curly brown hair, brown eyes, and thick glasses.

"How is he?" Even as she spoke, she felt like a character in one of the doctor TV shows she almost never watched. They all seemed the same, with brilliant physicians making crucial diagnoses or emergency room saves that revived a dying patient. In real life, it was different. She'd read how those electric-shock paddles they used with heart attack victims only worked a small percentage of the time. And they never, ever talked about strokes. What if her father had had one of those?

"He'll live."

Anna sighed deeply and felt her shoulders relax.

"But that doesn't mean he's doing well," the doctor continued. "Because he isn't."

Those same shoulders snapped back into high-tension mode.

"How bad is it?" Anna asked. "What is it?"

"He's not conscious, because we've sedated him. He's undergoing some scans right now, and I'll have the results for you as soon as we get them."

"Scans for what?" Anna could barely get the words out. She knew she was whispering, but couldn't help it.

"Something in his brain. Once we know what's going on, we can talk more. Now if you'll excuse me, I have other patients to see. If you stay here, I'll come back as soon as I can."

She started away, but Anna called to her. "Doctor! Wait!"

Dr. Miller turned around. "Yes, Miss Percy?"

"I want to know everything. What happened? Who

brought him here? How did you find my name? What do you think is going on with him?"

The doctor pursed her lips and then sat again, ignoring a quick buzz from her beeper. "From what I understand, there was a response to a 911 call from his residence. He didn't make it, a housekeeper did. She saw him acting strangely, slurring his words, knocking into things, problems with balance. By the time he was brought in, he had little control of his limbs. Clearly some kind of brain problem, once we ruled out drugs or alcohol. Is he a chronic abuser?"

This was no time for Anna to be coy, and she knew it. "He smokes marijuana. A fair amount."

"That wouldn't do it."

She felt a moment of relief. Not that it helped the situation anyway.

"How about alcohol abuse?" Dr. Miller pressed.

"He drinks. But not excessively."

Dr. Miller shook her head. "I don't think that's it."

"What do you . . ."

Anna's voice trailed off as she had a sudden memory, all the way back from when she'd first arrived in Los Angeles. She remembered how she'd found her father out in the gazebo behind the mansion, smoking some high-quality reefer. He'd complained about headaches, then. Serious ones, which had no apparent cause. Was it possible that . . . ?

"He had headaches. Bad ones."

Dr. Miller snapped to attention. "When? What kind of headaches? When did he have his last one?" The questions came rapid-fire.

"It was months ago. They seemed to get better." She felt like kicking herself. She should have insisted that he go to a doctor then. She should have taken him there herself. Maybe straight to this hospital. He should have been looked at immediately.

"It's possible," Dr. Miller admitted. "But also possibly not. Please, wait here. It shouldn't be long. I'll check in with you as soon as I know something."

Anna didn't want to wait. "Can I see him?"

"Please wait," the doctor said again.

Anna waited. And waited. She realized that doctor Miller's concept of "it shouldn't be long" and her own concept of the same phrase were quite different from each other, since an ugly black numeral wall clock directly across the hallway was there to keep her company. An hour ticked off. An hour and a half. The Indian woman's baby, the grandmother, and the construction worker were all treated and released. Just for something to do, she walked over to the nurses' station to check in with Alma, but the nurse said that Dr. Miller had not forgotten about her, that her father was still undergoing tests, and that the best thing Anna could do was to be patient.

She returned to the orange plastic chair and eyed the new cast of characters that had taken the place of the others. If they weren't suffering themselves, they had the same nervous look of expectation, as if they were steeling themselves for the worst news possible. A middle-aged woman seated a few chairs over was wringing her hands and muttering to herself in Spanish. Nearby, a couple of teenagers with skateboards huddled together in sober silence. Meanwhile, the nurses blithely went about their business—making phone calls, filing paperwork, chatting casually about their plans for the weekend.

She had been in emergency rooms back in New York. Parties where friends had had too much to drink. Once, after the taxicab she was riding in with her mother north on Park Avenue had stopped for a light at Seventy-second Street, they'd been rear-ended, and her mother had insisted on both of them being taken to Lenox Hill Hospital for precautionary X-rays.

Her mother—she needed to be called. Also her sister. But Anna couldn't bring herself to dial their numbers when she didn't know anything.

Instead, she called Sam, and caught her in her Hummer, on the way home from a meeting with a DJ.

"Sam?"

"What's wrong, Anna? Spill. I can hear it in your voice."

"My father's in the hospital."

Sam's voice was reassuringly calm. "Which one?"

"Cedars-Sinai," Anna reported.

"I'm in my car and on my way. Who else knows?"

Anna shifted her body around. The hard-backed plastic chair was incredibly uncomfortable. "Just you and me. And Logan. I was with him when I got the call."

"Anna, you need to call your family. They'll want to know. Keep your cell on. I'm at Sunset and Crescent Heights. I'll be there in fifteen minutes."

She thanked Sam, clicked off, and started to make the painful calls. She reached her sister, Susan, at the Kripalu Yoga Institute in the Berkshires of western Massachusetts. Susan had moved there after getting out of rehab, and so far the simple life of the center—she worked as a kitchen assistant—was keeping her clean and sober.

Her sister took the news without hysteria, once she heard that their father was stable, and reported that their mother was still in Italy if Anna wanted to call her there. Anna said she would, even though it was after midnight in Milan. Susan made Anna swear to check in every two hours. If she needed to come to California, she'd get on a plane. All Anna had to do was give the word.

Next Anna called their mother. When she answered the phone at the Hotel Intercontinental in Milan, Jane Cabot Percy was impressively cool. She didn't even sound sleepy. "He's stable, you say, Anna?"

"Yes, Mother. He's stable."

"It's not his heart?"

"Something in his brain, they think."

Her mother barked a short laugh. "Well, your dad has extra in that department, even if he got shortchanged when it came to judgment, the poor thing. You call me as soon as you know anything. Okay, Anna? I mean it. I want to hear from you in the morning my time, no matter what."

A foursome of noisy orderlies went past, pushing a couple of gurneys. Anna waited until they were out of sight to answer. "I will," she agreed.

"My thoughts are with you both." Anna's mother clicked off.

Anna snapped the phone shut and slouched back in the hard plastic waiting room chair. It had been a long couple of hours.

"Anna!"

She turned. Sam was hurrying into the waiting area, a Gucci bag in one hand and a takeout bag from Jerry's Delicatessen, which was right across the street from the hospital, in the other. She wore black boot-cut jeans with a slinky black silk top.

"What do you know?" Sam demanded, her voice worried. "What's the latest?"

Anna felt a surge of fear as she considered the possibilities.

"Anna? I've got some information."

Coming from the other direction was Dr. Miller. She looked more tired than she had just a few hours ago.

"We've brought your father into surgery. He has a subdural hematoma."

"What's that?" Sam asked.

"And who are you?" Dr. Miller asked sharply, her brown eyes taking Sam in questioningly.

"My good friend. This is Sam Sharpe. Go on, Dr. Miller," Anna insisted, as another gurney was pushed by them. "Did it have anything to do with those headaches I told you about?"

"Doubtful. Very doubtful, I'd say."

Even as the doctor said the words, Anna felt marginally better. At least there wasn't anything that could have been done.

"So what is this subdural thingie?" Sam prompted.

Dr. Miller took out a small pad and a pen, and quickly sketched a rough picture. "There are blood vessels between the outer part of the brain, called the *dura*, and the brain itself. One of his bled out. Right here."

She pointed to her own head, a little above her left ear. "That's what caused all the symptoms."

"Is it treatable?" Anna queried.

"Yes. Your father is in surgery now. They're drilling into his skull to let the blood drain and relieve the pressure. He wasn't in a major accident, as far as we can tell, so it wasn't caused by a major trauma. That's good. I understand the hematoma is quite substantial, which isn't so good."

Anna shivered. "When can I see him?"

"He'll be out in another hour. Then we'll bring him up to intensive care. It's on the fifth floor. He'll still be sedated. But you and your friend should be free to go up there now and wait. I'll try to check in with you as the surgery progresses.

"Thank you," Anna said dully.

Two hours later, she and Sam sat together in the intensive care waiting room, which was as different from the emergency room waiting area as two locations in the same hospital could be. While the emergency room was crowded, the intensive care area was empty save for the two of them. The room itself was spacious and white-walled, with a huge picture window facing north toward the Hollywood hills. There were plush gray fabric couches, a flat-screen TV on the wall, all the latest sports and fashion magazines, and low, calm lighting.

Anna had called Susan and texted her mother with the latest word from Dr. Miller, and she and Sam were making their way through knishes Sam had brought from the deli. They sipped cups of coffee from the coffeemaker on a side table.

"Anna?" Dr. Miller appeared in the doorway. She

smiled broadly. Anna and Sam were on her immediately, but the doctor started in before they could even get their knishes out of their hands. "We're done," she reported. "The surgery was a success. He's in a room here. We'll keep him here for forty-eight hours, then move him to a private room downstairs. Or he might be able to be released even more quickly than that."

"That's great!" Anna exclaimed, her heart lifting. "He'll be fine?"

Dr. Miller shook her head. "I won't go that far. We need to evaluate him. Seventy-five percent of patients with his kind of injury make a good or complete recovery. But this isn't like a sprained ankle. This is serious business."

"Can I see him?" Anna asked.

"Absolutely, if you don't mind that he's asleep. Come with me. One at a time, please," she added, glancing at Sam.

"I'll wait for you—however long you're in there," Sam promised.

Anna tried to steel herself for what she was about to see as she stepped through the doorway into the austere hospital room. She'd thought she was prepared, but when she caught sight of her strong father unconscious in an intensive care bed, hooked up to every kind of monitor in the history of medicine, with one side of his head shaved for the surgery and bandaged to catch any drainage from the wound, she felt as nervous and emotional as she had when she was certain her plane was headed for disaster. She willed herself not to cry. Instead, she went to her father's bedside and put her hand atop one of his. "I'm here. I'll be here. I'll be here until you wake up. I love you, Dad."

That was it. That was all that she could take. She stumbled out of the room and trudged back to the waiting area. He was alive. That was good. But to see him that way was simply too much for her.

The waiting room was empty. Anna figured that Sam had gone down to the cafeteria. That was good. She could use a break. Maybe while she was gone Anna would take the opportunity to rest for a little while herself, to not talk to anyone, to try not to even think. She moved toward one of the couches, thinking she might even put her feet up.

"Anna?"

The male voice behind her was barely perceptible. Logan. How thoughtful. He'd come anyway. She turned. Standing at the entrance to the ICU waiting room in jeans, sneakers, and a blue button-down shirt, was Ben.

"If you want me to go, I will," he said quickly. "But Sam called me. She thought I'd want to know. I hope you're not angry I came."

He looked tired and unshaven, his brown hair tousled, slight lines creasing the corners of his blue eyes. Maybe running the club was harder than she'd imagined. Maybe he was upset to be in this place. Or both.

"No. I'm glad."

She didn't move toward him. But she didn't move away, either.

"I'm sorry about your father."

"He's alive," she said simply, tucking a wisp of blond hair behind her ear. "The surgery went okay. That's what the doctor said. Where's Sam?" She glanced around the empty waiting area.

"She went downstairs to call Dee. Something about the wedding caterer. She'll be back."

The gray fabric couches sat invitingly empty, with their view of the Hollywood Hills, but neither made any motion to sit. That would imply a friendship. An intimacy. The only sound was the plasma television's low hum and an audible *drip, drip* from the coffeemaker in the corner.

"I mostly came to show support." Ben shoved his hands into the pockets of his faded jeans. "I know I have no business being here. But I came anyway."

"Ben?"

"Yeah?"

"I'm glad you did."

He smiled wanly and leaned against the white wall by the ICU door. "Really? Because I'm sorry how weird things have gotten between us."

"I am too," Anna agreed. She was still in her business outfit from meeting Carlie Martin, and wished she'd thought to ask Sam to bring her some more comfortable clothing. Who knew how long she'd be here? Her vintage suede pumps had not been designed with hospital waiting in mind.

"I hope that will change," Ben offered.

Anna gave him a small smile. "You know what I think? Maybe it just did."

Ben smiled back, his blue eyes warm. In an instant, his face went from tired to encouraging, and she felt strangely reassured, even with her father unconscious and his prognosis uncertain. She was glad to have Ben here, she realized. It changed everything.

And in that same moment, she realized she still hadn't called Logan.

Faking It

"Cammie, here's what our readers want to know. In a week, you've become L.A.'s teen queen. What can you tell our readers about the view from the top?"

Cammie brushed a lock of strawberry-blond hair behind her left ear, cocked her head at the *People* magazine reporter, and pretended to give the question a lot of thought. But the truth was, she'd already thought about this question today, and she'd already answered it. Twice. These promotional interviews for her club were starting to get awfully repetitious.

She and the reporter—what was his name? Chuck? Buck?—were seated on a pair of black gunmetal chairs at one of the black tables near Bye, Bye Love's main bar. It was still an hour before opening, and the venue was silent save for the grunts and mutterings of the laborers who were wheeling in bales of hay and a bucking-bronco machine for that night's theme: Ride 'Em, Cowboy.

The concept had been Cammie's idea—she'd gotten it when she'd read about Willie Nelson playing a concert later in the week at the Hollywood Bowl—and they were going all out. They'd borrowed several life-size cowboy statues from the Saddle Ranch Chop House on the Sunset Strip and placed them strategically outside by Venice Boulevard to set the mood as guests waited in line. As for the interior, everything was Western, from the cowboy waiters who would carry trays of hors d'oeuvres—miniature flap jacks, biscuits and gravy, bite-size steaks—to the specialty drink list, which included cocktails like the Midwestern Margarita, Texan Tequila Sunrise, and Ranch-Lover's Rum & Coke. There was even an authentic lasso near the bar, which would be put to use at hourly intervals. Anyone who managed to rope either Ben or Cammie on the first attempt would drink free for the rest of the night.

Out back, in the alley behind the club, they had transformed the smokers' patio into a campfire area, with a dug-in-the-ground stone barbecue pit, where tired club-goers could take a break from riding the electric bull to roast their own s'mores, eat baked beans à la *Blazing Saddles,* and listen to a Montana cowboy musician who'd once been part of the legendary Chris Ledoux's band play old Western songs.

Ever since the theme had been announced this morning, the office phone had been ringing nonstop with celebs and their entourages clamoring to get on the night's guest list. Willie Nelson's tour bus had pulled into town early, and he'd been invited. Someone had even called from the national campaign headquarters of a presidential candidate interested in making a guest DJ appearance. Cammie had turned the offer down. Not because she didn't like the candidate, but because she wasn't a fan of Fleetwood Mac.

The word was out. Cammie and Ben's club was *it*.

Which was great. Except that being *it* meant instead of free time, Cammie now had interview time; interview after interview after interview. She felt like a movie star doing a junket for a film that wasn't particularly interesting.

The *People* reporter had ears that stuck out and a distracting gap-toothed smile. He wore khakis and a crumpled Hawaiian shirt from Old Navy. He had a nice voice and a pleasant manner, and the chat wouldn't have been so bad but for the fact that this was her sixth interview of the day. She'd started with the *Star* at lunch. On to *In Touch* at two. *New Woman*—that baffled her, until she decided that the reporter wanted to be comped, so she gave her one just to be nice—at three-thirty. And so forth. The questions ranged from repetitious to dumb. *New Woman* had asked where she would be interested in retiring someday. Cammie just smiled and said, "Next question."

"What's it like to be the queen?" Cammie repeated. "Oh, it's great being queen, especially since my partner and co-owner is Ben. As in Ben Birnbaum. The king. My king." Cammie oozed sincerity as she watched Ben out of the corner of her eye. He was just now arriving at the club—he'd called and said he'd be late—crossing from the front door of the club to the office. That figured. He hated doing interviews, and left that part of the job of running the club to Cammie. She was fine with it. Except when there were six of them in one day.

"What made the queen want to join forces with the

king?" the reporter asked, playing along. "And why rule this kingdom? The clubbing industry, that is."

"Simple," she explained, knowing Buck-Chuck would lap up whatever spilled from her mouth. "We're kindred spirits. Life is short; you have to take risks—big risks, big gains. That's what it's all about. Life is a party and there's nothing I'd rather be doing, so why not make a business out of what I love?"

Cammie flipped her strawberry-blond curls playfully. Her smile and exuberance were automatic and perfectly timed.

But for reasons she couldn't fathom, what Adam would say if he were here right now flew into her mind: *It's not like you cured cancer, Cam. Is this really how you want to spend all your time?*

"And it's not all about money. I love that we're giving so much to charity," Cammie added, for imaginary Adam's benefit.

"Do you have a favorite cause?" Buck-Chuck queried.

"New Visions." She glanced at the bartender, a beautiful Cuban woman named Alita with long, lustrous hair, who doubled as a model. She was doing her prep for the evening, wiping the bar down with a wet cloth. "It's a program that helps teen girls who get into trouble find a different path. The fashion and beauty industries are really involved in helping these girls. When you look great, you feel great, and that's a start."

Buck-Chuck eyed her dress. "And who are you wearing? My readers will want to know."

"Pucci," she replied. Her bubble dress was pink-and-brown paisley. It had been sent over by her personal

shopper at Fred Segal. "Thanks so much for the interview, but we're going to open soon, and there's a lot to
do. But it was great to meet you . . . Ch-buck."

She kind of mumbled that last part into her hand as
she stood, knowing that reporters loved it when you
remembered their names. At least she had 75 percent of
this guy's name under control.

"Mind if I hang around and watch the action?" Ch-buck
asked.

"Enjoy. Here, take these."

She pressed a couple of drink coupons on him, which
he gallantly refused—something about ethics—and then
bid him goodbye as she moved off toward the rear of
the club, dodging more workers wheelbarrowing in more
hay. She stopped to check her watch. Was there time to
call Sam? She hadn't spoken to her since Sam had fired
her as maid of honor.

Truth was, Cammie *did* feel guilty that she'd neglected
Sam's wedding. If she had to be honest with herself, she
was not ecstatic that Sam was thinking about leaving her
life in Los Angeles for Paris with Eduardo. No matter
how much they fought, Sam was still her best friend; more
like a sister than that bitch of a half-sister, Mia, who, no
matter how many times Cammie warned her, simply did
not know the meaning of the simple five-word sentence
"Stay out of my closet."

Call her, she told herself. *She'll forgive you.*

Cammie decided she'd call Sam after she checked in
with Ben. Usually at this time of the night he was in the
club office, double-checking the guest list and making
sure that everyone who was supposed to report to work

was actually on the premises. People in the nightclub business were notoriously flaky.

Cammie decided to lend him a helping hand. Or maybe two. Sex in the office didn't appeal to her. However, appetizers were always appropriate before the main course. Sometimes even hours before.

She found Ben in the office, hunched over a spreadsheet. He wore Diesel jeans and a blue James Perse button-up, the sleeves rolled up to his elbows. He was focused so intently he didn't even hear her come in.

"Hello, there, hard worker."

He looked up, and a slow smile spread over his face. "I'm in here doing the grunt work, you're out there doing the glamour work. Tell me what's fair about that."

"Sounds fair to me. Where were you before?"

He looked away. "Out. Had an errand."

She moved toward him a step. "Let me make it up to you," she said coyly. "Maybe you'll be convinced to come to the club on time next time."

There was a knock, and Ben's eyes looked behind Cammie toward the office door behind her. "Can you get that?" he asked.

"Sure." Awful timing, whoever it was. Cammie opened the door to find the photographer from *People* who'd come along with Buck-Chuck, a tall, blond, long-haired Swede named Sven. A portrait camera was slung around his neck, and he wore a white Marc Jacobs T-shirt with Seven jeans

"Sorry to bother you guys. Ready for your close-up? I thought one shot of the two of you in here, where all the behind-the-scenes action happens, would be something different." Sven's English was impeccable, and he exuded confidence in a way that Buck-Chuck never could.

"Sure," Ben agreed. "You good with that, Cammie?"

"Of course."

She offered Sven a radiant smile as Ben sidled up next to her and wrapped an arm around her shoulders. She leaned into him. They looked darling, this much she knew. Because they'd struck this pose for all the other press photographers and they'd looked darling in every photo she'd seen.

"Give me something fresh," Sven urged them. Oops. Maybe he'd seen the earlier photos.

"How's this?" Cammie said. She turned to Ben and wrapped both arms around his neck, then kissed him on the cheek.

"Love it!" Sven cried as he snapped away. "More, more, more!"

Cammie moved this way and that—in front of Ben with his arms around her from behind, back-to-back, whatever. As she draped herself over him in various positions, Cammie kept thinking about how great they looked together. They acted like a couple. They seemed like a couple. They worked together the way most couples could only dream. So why was it that they weren't together again as a couple for real?

"Maybe we can wrap up with this photographer," she told Ben under her breath, so Sven couldn't hear.

"Nah. We need the press. Let him do his thing," Ben replied, not breaking his camera-ready smile.

She let Sven do his thing, and he stuck around for five more minutes, shooting them from various angles.

"These are great," he noted of a shot of Ben leaning on the desk, holding Cammie in his arms. "You're the king and queen of the nightclub scene," he added. Cammie knew Sven was just trying to get a good picture out of them—the confident, radiant smiles you always saw in magazines had less to do with the subject and more with the photographer's smooth prodding. "You're a publicist's dream."

How right you are, Cammie thought. Publicists cared about how things looked, not how they were in reality.

Ben squeezed Cammie in close, leaning in to give her a delicate kiss on top of her mountain of strawberry-blond curls. "Perfect!" Sven cried.

But Ben and Cammie's happy, coupley photograph was starting to feel staged, and awfully convenient. Cammie couldn't help but wonder if, in real life, the same wasn't true of their relationship.

Pitch This

"Just have a seat, Sam. Marty will be with you in a moment."

"Sure thing, Clarice."

"You look great. How's your father? How's the family? Is it true you're getting married?"

"Thank you, good, good, and yes," Sam replied. She'd worn a pair of DKNY black slacks and a black Chloé long-sleeved cotton blouse with puffy sleeves to this meeting, counting on the "wear black, it's slimming" effect.

"Congrats on that. I'll be sure to send something over. Now, there's coffee in the waiting area outside Marty's cubicle. Marty will be right with you."

"Thanks."

Sam drifted over to a somewhat improvised collection of gray fabric chairs, a single black couch, and a coffee table covered with back issues of the industry trades, plus *Entertainment Weekly, Premiere,* and *Cahiers du Cinéma,* the French movie magazine. She picked up *Premiere* and idly flipped through it as she waited for Marty to see her.

Marty Martinsen, the chief executive of mini major Transnational Pictures, had come to the faltering studio in the late 1980s and made it solvent via a string of shrewd acquisitions of horror and slasher films like *The Nail Clipper* (about a homicidal owner of a pedicure salon). He'd hit pay dirt in the early 1990s with a low-budget teen comedy called *I Call Shotgun*, about a not-too-good-looking guy and his drop-dead-gorgeous male best friend. The underdog wound up getting the hot girl, the hot car, and about a million dollars' worth of hot diamonds that landed in his lap after being tossed out of a helicopter during a chase sequence. The box office for *I Call Shotgun* set low-budget-feature records, as did its sequels and spin-off Xbox and PlayStation games, and the franchise had established Transnational as a Hollywood player for the next fifteen years.

Though studio execs were legendary in their battles for corner offices and imported furniture, Marty had held on to the very first gray-fabric cubicle he'd occupied, when he came to the company to work in the finance department. He had a regular, snazzy office, too, for when he had to impress an agent or the international press. But mostly, he liked to work in his cubicle. He said it kept him humble.

"How've you been, Sam?" Clarice sipped coffee from an oversize mug with the *I Call Shotgun 3* logo on it. Marty supposedly paid Clarice—a no-nonsense woman in her fifties with a short graying pageboy bob and gleaming white teeth—a salary that was equal to that of his chief financial officer.

"I've been good," Sam replied. Because that's just what

you did. When people asked how you were, they didn't really want to know. The truth was, she was freaking out. She was getting married in less than fifty hours. She still had not made a decision about going to film school or to Paris. Nor had she mentioned that indecision to her soon-to-be groom.

"I just wanted to say that it was fun, the way you had your wedding invitations delivered by messenger. We got ours just this morning." Clarice smiled like she herself had been invited, when actually the invite had gone to Marty and his wife.

That was fine, Sam thought. If Clarice wanted to bask in just being in the know about her wedding, more power to her. One of the great advantages of being married on a yacht far out to sea was that there was no risk of wedding crashers.

"Can I get you anything? Coffee? Pellegrino? Juice?"

"Nothing, I'm good."

Clarice glanced left and right, as if someone might overhear. "He's on with Cruise/Wagner Productions," she said confidentially. "This could take a while. You're here because . . . ?"

"Script," Sam said laconically.

"Any good?"

"I wouldn't be here two days before my wedding if I didn't think so."

Sam looked down at the three-hole-punched script she'd brought with her, and which was currently residing in her too-large-by-her-own-measure lap—the script that Anna had sent over to her the night before with a self-deprecating message. Anna had titled it *The Big*

Palm, which Sam figured was a play on words on New York City as the Big Apple and L.A.'s own horticultural mascot.

When Sam had finally stretched out last night after midnight to read it—she'd fortified herself with a small glass of Baileys—she'd been oh so skeptical. Mostly, she was tackling the script as a favor to her friend, as a way to boost her spirits with her dad in the hospital. She'd talked to Anna first thing that morning—her dad had regained consciousness but was still very woozy—and she wanted to do something to help. But it was hard to write a good movie. Everyone in town, plus their plumber, BMW mechanic, and astrologer had a spec script in their back pocket. But the truth was, 99 percent of them were senseless deaths of trees. That is, not even fit for toilet paper.

As Sam had opened Anna's script to read the first page, she had already been thinking of how to let Anna down nicely without being mean.

[FADE IN]

INT. FIRST-CLASS CABIN—JUMBO JET—DAY

A tall, blond girl whose mother probably trained her from birth to maintain the perfect posture she displays steps into the first-class cabin of the plane.

She's dressed like the East Coast old-money girl she is, right down to her heirloom understated-but-worth-a-fortune diamond stud earrings.

First class is full, except for a single seat next to a middle-aged hipster who you just know is bald under his Dodgers baseball cap. And you also know he's hoping—praying!—that someone cute and young will slide in next to him.

Meet Emma, age 18. And Richie, 16 in the gonads and 48 on the calendar.

> RICHIE
>
> Yo! You looking for your seat?

> EMMA
>
> Four-E. That's me.

Richie caresses the empty seat next to him as he eyes Emma's ass. She looks for an escape route. Short of skydiving, it's unlikely. So she sits next to Richie.

> RICHIE
>
> Damn. This is gonna be an awesome freaking flight!

Emma keeps a smile on her face—she'd smile during her own beheading just to be polite—and closes her eyes. As she does, we flash back to . . .

EXT. VEST POCKET PARK—MANHATTAN PRIVATE SCHOOL—
DAY

. . . and see Emma during the previous autumn. Leaves falling, October ochre light slanting;

*you can almost taste the changing of the season.
She's alone on a park bench reading Turgenev's*
Fathers and Sons. *Every once in a while she
glances up. Across the park is a cute guy writing on a laptop.*

*She knows this guy. She longs for him. But
she's never talked to him. Never ever.*

*Emma screws up her courage and gives a shy
wave. And . . . he waves back. And smiles!*

*Should she walk over there? Every inch of her
body longs to. She begins to rise . . .*

*And then, an incredibly beautiful girl sneaks
up on the guy from behind. Hands go over his
eyes; lip-lockage ensues. Emma buries her head
in her hands.*

And we're out *of flashback* and back . . .

INT. FIRST-CLASS CABIN—JUMBO JET—DAY

*On the plane, now in flight. Richie ponti-
ficates unbidden.*

                    RICHIE
I'm a hyphenate.

                    EMMA
Excuse me?

                    RICHIE
Producer-musician-writer-director-impresario.
Do 'em all, do 'em all well.

Richie adores his own insinuation as he checks
out her chest without shame.

                    RICHIE
I do lots of things well. You want a drink or
three?

Emma keeps smiling. Checks her watch surrepti-
tiously as Richie prattles on. She's the kind
of girl who doesn't want to hurt the feelings
of even a boor like him.

Only five hours and twenty-one minutes to Los
Angeles. What fun.

Just when jumping begins to look like a good
alternative, a guy a few seats away stands. He
pulls his Princeton sweatshirt over his head,
revealing the kind of lean but muscled male
perfection girls dream of.

Emma is enjoying the view when he turns and
smiles at her.

This is Alex. And this is the start of Emma
and Alex.

    Sam stayed up past 2 a.m. reading. She was hooked.
Oh, Anna's screenplay wasn't perfect. Some of it was over-

written, and she could use a little work punching up her dialogue. And of course, it was shamelessly autobiographical.

But it was also funny. Touching. Parts of it made Sam cry. She didn't even mind that there was a Sam character in the script named Krystal, the daughter of America's most famous movie star, with fat ankles that no amount of plastic surgery could fix. This Krystal was thinner than the actual Sam, which was as good a sign as any that she and Anna would be friends for life.

After she'd reread the script a second time, she'd made a decision. She wasn't above using her family clout to get Anna's script read. The problem was, this kind of movie was mainstream. It was a summer teen-themed dramedy. It wasn't edgy enough, quirky enough, racy enough, or esoteric enough to be an indie. Which meant that her production options were limited. Columbia TriStar, Paramount, Universal, Fox, Warners, maybe New Line if they could keep it PG-13. Plus Transnational.

She decided to start with Marty, figuring he owed her dad one. Maybe this could be payback in a mutually beneficial way.

"Sam Sharpe! Come here!"

Marty's voice boomed out over the bullpen of cubicles. He was known in town for his aggressively casual style at the office—it took a lot for him to put on a jacket for a social function like a movie wrap party—and today was no exception: he sported two days' growth of beard in addition to his gray goatee, his bushy eyebrows were sorely in need of a trim, and he wore khaki pants and a vintage long-sleeved black Rolling Stones T-shirt with the red tongue on it.

He hugged her—hugs were standard-issue Holly-wood, even among enemies. Then he asked quickly about her father and about her wedding plans. "Problem for me is, what do you get the girl who has everything? Are you registered at Fred Segal?" He raised his eyebrows to show that he was joking.

Actually, Sam and Eduardo had talked about wedding presents. They'd decided that they wanted their guests to make donations to Kidsave, a Los Angeles–based charity that brought adoptable older children from Russia, Kazakhstan, and Colombia to America for a summer experience that might well end in adoption. Her closest friends, she thought, would still bring presents. But really, she was a girl who had everything. Crystal bowls, tea sets, and Wedgwood dishes seemed superfluous for a couple that always ate out. What more could she want?

"It's all in the invite," she told him.

"The messenger delivered it. What brings you here? You want a job? You want a job, I got a job for you."

"No job. Pitch." She motioned with the script in her right hand.

Marty grinned. "Well, why didn't you say so? Let's go to the conference room. You'll have my undivided atten-tion."

The Transnational executive conference room was on the same floor as Marty's cubicle, just a short walk past a small army of assistants, script readers, line producers, number crunchers, and all the other people who did the mundane business of a studio that turned out eight or ten movies a year.

As they walked, Sam noticed a harried-looking female intern wearing gray Armani slacks and a white-collared Stella McCartney shirt delivering coffee to a handsome development assistant with a buzz cut who was simultaneously answering e-mails and working his way through a monumental pile of scripts, all the while listening in on his boss's phone calls via headset. After she dropped off the coffee, the intern was promptly handed a messy stack of receipts, which she would presumably be labeling and organizing for some kind of expense report. Sam shuddered at the thought of spending her days individually taping receipts to sheets of paper and mentally thanked the gods of nepotism for making Jackson Sharpe her father.

The conference room was in the southwest corner of the building. There was a large picture window that looked out on the production lot. This morning, the studio was filming an eighteenth-century drama, judging from the costumed extras and horse-drawn carriages on a dirt-covered street. Sam hated costume dramas. They were so often vanity projects for the actors involved.

The other walls of the room featured posters of Transnational films past and present. *I Call Shotgun* and her father's upcoming *Ben-Hur* were both prominently placed. Sam had heard of studios that switched the movie posters depending on which big star was coming in, so the visiting star could labor under the misconception that his or her films were the most important pictures that the studio had ever made. Since she'd arrived at Transnational with only an hour's notice, she doubted that Marty had done the framed poster switcheroo.

That was a good sign. Her dad was this studio's main man.

"So, Sam." Marty settled back into a black leather chair and put his Converse-clad feet up on the blindingly white conference table. "Tell me your movie. Who's the writer? What's it about? Why should I care?"

"The writer? Just someone I know," Sam said carefully.

No sense prejudicing Marty out of the chute. No studio exec would care about a script by an unseasoned recent high school graduate. A wunderkind like Harmony Korine, who wrote the screenplay for *Kids* at age nineteen, didn't come along more than once a decade, and he barely had one good film in him. If you needed proof, try to watch *Gummo*.

"The story?" Marty uncrossed his feet.

"Coming-of-age, fish-out-of-water, about a rich girl from New York who moves to Beverly Hills for her senior year of high school. Think *Mean Girls* meets *The Great Gatsby*."

Marty was smiling. He wagged a finger at her. "You practiced that."

"Of course. I'm my father's daughter."

"Go on. What's the market?"

"This film captures your entire teen demo. Plus women in their twenties and thirties will see it as a chick flick. But it's not some tossed-off gross-out comedy, and it's not some dark and moody indie thing, either. We've got some core adult characters, and there's plenty of romance and sex. The girl loses her virginity at the end of the first act. Repeatedly."

Marty laughed. "I like it. I'm seeing a good box shot. Let's hear the plot."

Sam grinned. The "box shot" to which Marty was referring was the inevitable picture of the scantily clad female lead that ended up on the DVD box. "You want the minute, five-minute, or full version?"

"Gimme the five-minute. I'm getting a little hungry."

This was a little disappointing, though Sam knew better than to let it show in her eyes. Any Hollywood producer worth his or her laser-printer cartridges knew to come to a pitch meeting with three different versions of their pitch. The one-minute pitch was the one to give if you were walking an exec to his or her BMW. The full version was the one that told the whole story, with any boring parts left out. That was what you wanted them to ask for. That was the best sell for your movie.

The five-minute pitch request was always ambiguous. It could mean that Marty didn't have interest and was just being polite. It could mean his stomach was honestly growling for a triple-decker pastrami sandwich from Canter's. There was no way to know. And for God's sake, you had to be a blooming idiot to ask.

She pitched. He looked appropriately interested, and even asked a couple of questions about opportunities for music and skin, in that order. As five minutes stretched to six, Sam hit the last beat of the story.

"So Emma, who met this guy Brogan on her trip to New York, comes back to L.A. for her last week of the summer. He follows her there and puts the question to her: Him or me? She chooses him. And they fly off into the sunset together. Literally. On a plane to the Far East.

She says fuck you to Alex, fuck you to Yale, fuck you to what's expected of her, fuck you to everything except what her heart wants."

Marty nodded thoughtfully, then stood and stretched his arms as if doing a warm-up in aerobics class. "Got it. Thanks for coming in."

Sam stood. Damn, damn, damn. The "thanks for coming in" kiss of death.

"Thanks for listening," Sam told him, as she edged around the conference table.

"Leave the script behind," he added.

That was the moral equivalent of putting her on life support, as opposed to just smothering her with a pillow. Or maybe he was just being nice, because she was, after all, Jackson Sharpe's daughter.

She hugged him, her heart deflating. She was glad she hadn't told Anna she was coming here. Anna was in a bad enough place right now. Imagine how she'd feel if she had to deal with Marty Martinsen rejecting her movie without even reading it.

"Thanks again, Marty. I can't wait to see you at the wedding."

Born to Run

I t was mortifying, verging on humiliating. It was an outcome that Sam wouldn't have wished on Lindsay Lohan. But it was the truth, and she had to accept it.

She'd be wearing a gown designed by that bitch Gisella to her own wedding.

There was a simple reason for it: Gisella's designs were incredible, and all the other wedding gowns she'd tried on blew chunks in comparison. Which was why she and Dee were standing on wooden blocks in Gisella's atelier in West Hollywood, with the Peruvian designer and her two male assistants bustling around them, draping exquisite fabric over their bodies and sticking pins into it at every conceivable angle.

The workshop, on the corner of Melrose and Robertson, was in a second-floor loft and looked like it could have been transported straight from SoHo. The enormous rectangular room had a two-story-high ceiling with exposed HVAC pipes that were painted all the shades of the rainbow. Racks of finished ensembles were scattered haphazardly around the room, while two or three dozen mannequins held the works in progress. The huge window that would ordinarily look out over Melrose was largely obscured by six-foot-tall sketches of designs that Gisella had drawn for her newest collection. The vibe was intense—assistants were scuttling about rolling fabric, boxing prototypes, and making notes on identical clipboards. Occasionally one would approach Gisella and whisper a question in her ear before returning to the task at hand.

Sam had been at Gisella's atelier since early afternoon, and the only things that were making this experience bearable were the skill with which Gisella and her staff were doing their work, the sushi-and-champagne buffet that Dee had ordered in from Sushi Mac, and the gorgeous, fawnlike model type with impossibly long legs and impossibly blue eyes who had stopped by for a half hour and followed Gisella around like a puppy. Not that Sam normally got excited about female models; in fact, she had been known to leave a room simply when one entered rather than risk the unflattering comparison. However, from the way said blue-eyed model was looking at Gisella, and the way Gisella was looking at the model, Sam suspected that both were part of the West Hollywood gay mafia.

Call it stupid. Call it petty. Call it amazingly reassuring.

"Just a few minutes more. Your dress is going to be gorgeous," Gisella assured Sam. "And you will be gorgeous as well."

"You know, I used to hate your guts," Sam confessed. Lipstick lesbian or not, it was still hard to be friendly with her.

"Only because you're protective of your man. This is a good quality. I imagine that your friend Dee is also protective of her man." *Snip, snip, snip* went Gisella's scissors. "True?"

"I guess that's true," Dee agreed, nodding. One of the assistants, a diminutive Brazilian girl named Samanta, with some of the most beautiful dark hair that Sam had ever seen, pushed Dee's hip slightly to one side so she could better pin a piece of fabric in place. "But I think if you hold a guy too close, that's going to make him want to run away. I had that problem in the past, remember?" She turned toward Sam, and the assistant working at the hem of her bridesmaid dress coughed politely, reminding her not to move.

Sam definitely remembered. Dee had been the queen of short-lived relationships, and she was never the one who ended it. Before the advent of Jack, her boyfriends had always been the ones to dump her. Then they went gay.

"So now," Dee continued, careful to stay in position, "I give Jack a lot of freedom, and he circles around me like I'm the earth and he's the sun."

Sam had to bite her lower lip to keep herself from correcting Dee's faulty take on the solar system. So what if science wasn't her strong suit? She was turning out to be a hell of an impromptu wedding planner.

"Samanta?" Gisella motioned for her assistant to pin Sam's right shoulder seam tighter. "Thank you. Sam, you met Eduardo's family in Peru?"

Sam nodded. During their trip after graduation, four aunts and uncles had come to an enormous Sunday dinner at his parents' estate in the hills overlooking Lima.

There had to have been thirty or forty cousins as well. The feast had gone well into the night.

"All those aunts and uncles," Gisella began. "They are all married to their original husbands or wives. Can you imagine?" Gisella clucked as she delicately pinned the waist of Sam's gown-to-be. "Peru is not like America, where people change partners like they change outfits, on a whim. I hope that you will be willing to do it the Peruvian way, not the American way. Otherwise, Eduardo will be very disappointed." She studied Sam, then nodded. "Yes. Now have a look."

Gisella turned Sam around. There was a three-quarter-round mirror directly behind her, and Sam gasped with joy when she saw herself. The wedding gown was off-white and off the shoulders, with bands of sheer, pearl-encrusted chiffon falling gracefully over each upper arm. It was fitted through the bust, and then fell in folds of chiffon and silk dotted with hand-sewn pearls and actual diamonds to the floor.

"Omigod," Sam breathed.

"You like?" There was genuine concern in Gisella's voice.

"I—"

For the first time in a long time, Sam Sharpe found herself speechless. Finally, the words came. "Gisella, I don't think there's a girl in the world who doesn't imagine what she'll look like in her wedding gown. But this . . . this . . . this is better than I ever dreamed." Sam gulped hard. "I'm *pretty*."

"No, you're beautiful." The designer's dark eyes shone. "You are smart that your maid of honor and bridesmaids dresses are pink, and simpler. All the attention will be on you."

"And that's the way it should be," Dee chimed in, straining to get a good look at Sam in her gown without causing more work on her own. "Besides, I love my dress," she said, admiring the pink sheath draped over her body.

Gisella's dresses for Dee, Cammie, and Anna were indeed far simpler than her own. Dee's maid-of-honor dress was a strapless pale pink sheath. The bridesmaids' dresses were a deeper shade of pink, with halter tops. All of them fell just below the knee, so that Sam wouldn't have to feel like someone else's legs—well, all of her friends' legs—were easier on the eyes than her own. If that fact was true, it was still worth denying on one's wedding day.

Gisella's cell rang; she excused herself to take the phone call. Sam turned to Dee. "What do you think? She's gone now—you can be brutal."

"I think it rocks."

"Good. Has Cammie been in for her fitting?"

"Negative," Dee answered. "Too busy at the club, probably. If worse comes to worst, Gisella will bring her shop to Cammie. Same thing with Anna. It's all on my checklist."

"You are amazingly organized."

"The right meds changed my life," Dee said solemnly, her blue eyes intense. "I think of everything now. I meant to tell you: We'll have a backup bridal gown out on the yacht just in case there's an accident with this one."

"That is a horrifying thought," Sam shuddered. She

turned around in front of the two-hundred-and-seventy-degree mirror, taking in her reflection from every possible angle. If anything, the dress looked even better from the sides and the back than it did from the front.

Dee got off her wooden block to join her, retrieving her composition notebook on the way. Sam saw that Dee had hand-printed SAM'S WEDDING on the front in girlish black Magic Marker letters. "My motto is, Be prepared," she said as she saw Sam looking. "You'd be amazed how many brides barf while they're waiting to walk down the aisle—I read that on Bridezilla.com. Also, I'll have super-glue for your shoes in case you break a heel. And there's a full cosmetics kit in the stateroom bathroom, in case you hate what the makeup artist does. But she worked on the new Cate Blanchett movie, so I'd be confident if I were you."

"You are really good at this," Sam marveled.

"That's my job," Dee said with an easy shrug, scribbling something down in the notebook. She moved to stand behind Sam. "I want to take all the stress of the wedding day off your shoulders."

Sam smiled at her friend in the mirror. "You know what's funny?"

"What?"

"You make me feel calmer than my so-called therapist, Dr. Fred." She turned to face Dee. "Do you ever watch his TV show? He's pimping this whole new magic plan for weight loss. Meanwhile, he lives on Dunkin' Donuts and shops at Rochester Big & Tall. It'll probably be another best-seller."

"You've complained about him for years," Dee pointed

out, running a hand through her shaggy haircut. "Why don't you just stop seeing him? Have you even talked to him about getting married?"

"No. And I don't plan to."

"Then call the guy and end it," Dee counseled. "You didn't send him an invitation."

Sam ran her hands gently down the bodice of her dress as she realized that Dee was right. She didn't need Dr. Fred anymore. She was happy, and she doubted that the television therapist was the reason why.

Sam's Razr sounded. She'd left it on a small coffee table to the left of the mirrors. "Hello?"

"Hey, it's Anna. How's the fitting going?"

"I look so hot, I would do me," Sam quipped, winking at Dee.

Anna laughed. "Glad to hear that. Sorry I couldn't make it—I wanted to spend some more time with my dad. He's been sleeping a lot, which is a good thing, according to his doctor. But I just kind of want to be here when he wakes up and can talk."

Sam could understand that. How would she feel if something happened to her own father? She couldn't imagine, since she was so used to thinking of him as ten feet tall and bulletproof; exactly the way America saw him.

"Is her dad doing better?" Dee asked, scribbling another note.

Sam nodded. "Much."

"That's great. That's really great."

Sam ended the call and watched Dee flip through her wedding book. "The photographer," Dee explained. "I want to know who's going to do it if he gets sick."

"You actually have a future in this, Dee."

Dee looked up from under her fringe of bangs. "What, as a wedding planner?"

"You're good at it."

"Yes, she is." Gisella stepped over to them, closing her own Razr as she did. She wore a short blue shift dress, one of her own designs, and looked beautiful, but Sam was surprised to find she didn't feel jealous anymore.

"You have a talent and a passion, Dee," the designer went on, as she repinned the shoulder seam on Sam's gown. "Always choose to do with your life something for which you have a passion. I've done it. You should do it. Eduardo has a passion for Sam. That's why he's marrying her."

Sam looked around again at the bustling, light-filled studio. Sketches and material covered every surface, and the loft was near bursting with the creative energy of Gisella working out her own passions. Sam hoped she would have a space like this someday. She'd always dreamed of an editing room to call her own, where she'd cut and splice the films she'd always wanted to make. Maybe it could be in Malibu, she mused, so that if difficult cutting-room-floor decisions were getting to her, she could zip outside for a mind-clearing walk on the beach.

But no, Sam realized. If she moved to Paris with Eduardo, who knew when they'd come back? It could be years before the California coast was her home again. It could be never. They could end up in Lima, for God's sake.

Dee bit her lower lip. "A wedding planner. I never thought about that."

"You should," Sam insisted, brought back into the

present. She turned and gazed over her shoulder for one last rear view. Damn. Her butt did not look like the state of Texas after all. The dress was amazing. Dee was amazing. In fact, Sam's entire life had become amazing.

But when she looked down at her left hand—at the immense diamond engagement ring on it—she had the strangest feeling. Like she wanted to take that ring off her finger, fling it out into La Cienega Boulevard, and then get on with the life she was supposed to have. The joy of being eighteen and starting at USC film school with her whole life before her, full of possibility.

But when she thought about *not* marrying Eduardo, she felt sick to her stomach. The idea of not marrying him made her even more anxious than the idea of marrying him. She loved him, adored him, would never find another guy like him. You simply did not let such a wonderful guy get away because he had not shown up on your schedule.

"What's next on the agenda, Dee?" Sam tried to keep her voice casual.

"I'm going to get my eyebrows done at Valerie's— your appointment is tomorrow morning."

"I'll come with," Sam offered. She really did not feel like being alone with her thoughts and doubts and anxieties.

"But you're supposed to stay here, remember?" Dee said, closing her notebook and sticking her pen inside her Kate Spade hobo bag. "Your mom is coming for a fitting."

"Oh shit. I totally forgot."

Dina had told her and Dee that she wasn't happy with

the dress she'd brought—a plain blue sleeveless number with buttons down the front—because she feared
it wouldn't be elegant enough for the event. Dee hadn't
hesitated. She'd made the appointment for Dina to be
fitted with one of Gisella's creations.

"Have you talked to your mom and dad any more
about the wedding?" Dee asked.

"Not really," Sam admitted. "But they've been hanging out."

"Hanging out, or hanging *out*?"

Sam shuddered. "The former. I'm just impressed that
my dad would be such a gentleman to her."

"Hey, someone has to set an example in this town.
Well, I'm out of here," Dee announced.

Gisella, who'd moved off to one side to consult with
one of her minions, came back to kiss Dee first on one
cheek and then on the other. "You are doing a wonderful
job for your friend," she said warmly.

Dee smiled—Sam could see how much the compliment delighted her. She waggled her fingers at Sam. "I'll
check in later."

When Dee was gone, Gisella motioned to Sam. "Go
get changed. *Ahora*. I don't want your mother to see you
in your dress almost as much as I don't want Eduardo to
see you in it. Let it be a surprise for both of them. And
your father, too." Gisella pointed the way to three small
changing rooms in her workshop. "Marcia, would you
help Sam, please?"

Marcia, a British girl with multicolored hair and snapping dark eyes, was Gisella's senior assistant. "Come
along, Sam. Follow me."

When Sam reemerged in the all-black outfit she'd worn to Transnational Pictures for her unsuccessful pitch to Marty Martinsen, she found her mother chatting amiably with Gisella by the sushi spread.

"Hi, Dina," she said stiffly. She tried to muster more enthusiasm, but it was difficult. It was as if her mother's presence made everything more real. Besides, what kind of mom skipped out on her daughter's life and then showed up to play the dewy-eyed mother of the bride?

Gisella politely said she had something to attend to in her office, which was an obvious maneuver to leave Sam alone with her mother.

"She's lovely," Dina commented. She was dressed in typical Dina clothes: too-baggy blue pants and a style-free beige blouse. Fashion was not Sam's mother's long suit. Thank God it wasn't an inherited trait.

"She is," Sam agreed, feeling generous after having met Gisella's possible lesbian lover.

They stood in silence for a few moments, Sam unwilling to make the effort of small talk. Her mother scanned the sushi spread.

"So, which of these do you recommend? I'm afraid we don't get much sushi in western North Carolina. Catfish is better fried," she added with a smile.

Sam had never tasted catfish, fried or otherwise, and didn't feel like chatting about raw fish.

"The ahi is pretty good," Sam finally said, her tone flat. "The California sea urchin rolls are okay. As for the house special fire rolls—those are the ones with the orange stuff dripped on top—unless you want your tongue to go radioactive, I'd stay away."

Dina went right for the house special fire rolls, which were tuna wrapped in rice wrapped in seaweed with the ultrahot topping. She ate two, and chased them with half a glassful of Taittinger champagne.

"Fabulous," she pronounced. "Not fabulous enough to move back here tomorrow, but still very fabulous. I've missed it. This place." She put down her champagne glass to look at her daughter. "You."

Sam bristled. She started to reach for the champagne bottle to pour herself a glass, but then realized she didn't need the calories. "What a crock. You haven't stayed in touch. You haven't even tried."

"Samantha," Dina said slowly, swirling her champagne in her glass, "I know this may be strange for you to hear, but just because I've been out of touch doesn't mean I haven't been thinking about you, following your life. Do you want to know how many Google hits you'll come up with if you search the words *Sam Sharpe* in quotes? Thirty-seven thousand, five hundred. A year ago? Sixteen thousand, three hundred. Nine years ago, when everyone used AltaVista? Three thousand. And I think I've read every one of the links."

Sam raised her eyebrows. This was unexpected. Was her mom making this shit up?

Dina seemed to sense Sam's skepticism. She wiped her lips with a white cloth napkin. "When you were in fifth grade, Sam," she continued, "there was an article about you and Camilla in *Los Angeles* magazine. It was about how savvy showbiz kids are. They put you two in a movie trivia contest against a pair of entertainment reporters. You and Cammie crushed them."

"That's right," Sam said slowly. She remembered that contest. She hadn't thought about that in years. There'd been some crazy talk afterward about putting her and Cammie on a TV game show, which, now that Sam thought about it, was pretty funny when you thought about the success of *Are You Smarter Than a Fifth Grader?*

"You've always been smart," Dina continued. "And you've always known what you want and how you feel." She took another sip of champagne. "Which is why I think you know how you really feel about this wedding."

Heat came to Sam's face. "I don't know what you're talking about," she snapped.

Dina stepped over to the window and looked out at West Hollywood, peering between two newsprint sheets of Gisella's personal designs. "Some things change, Samantha. Some things don't. When you were a girl—this was in nursery school—and you were upset or agitated about something, you'd scuff your toes against the floor. Look at your shoes."

Sam scuffed her black suede Jimmy Choo platform pumps against the floor just for something to do. The toes on both were a mess. It was better to focus on the shoes than on whether her mom was right. "You talk about what I did in nursery school like you're the doting mother who was always there," she said hotly. "But you weren't. You were a missing-in-action joke."

Her mother nodded, turning back from the window to face her daughter. "You're right. As a mother, I've been terrible."

Sam folded her arms. "At least you're being honest."

"Do you want to know why?" Dina asked.

Sam did want to know. Desperately. But she wasn't about to admit it to the woman who had abandoned her. She sipped her champagne and eyed her mother coolly over the rim of her crystal flute. "Does it matter?"

"Maybe not, but I'll tell you anyway," Dina said. "It doesn't paint a very pretty portrait of me, but at least you'll know the truth." She twirled the stem of the champagne flute between her fingers nervously. "When your dad and I got married, I was so in love with him, I couldn't see straight. He was a struggling actor. I was a struggling writer."

"Can we fast-forward this?" Sam said. It came out more harshly than she intended, but these memories were painful to hear.

"Fine," Dina agreed, fingering one of the buttons on her frumpy beige blouse. "The short version. Your dad got very successful very fast. Our lives were utterly changed by Hollywood in the fast lane. It wasn't a world where I felt comfortable. I didn't like it, and I didn't want it. In fact, I hated it."

"Oh, I see. So it's all Dad's fault for getting success-ful." As if hating Hollywood and money and success had given her mother the right to chuck it all. "That makes *so* much sense."

Dina plunged on. "When we split up, I was running away from everything. Your father, Hollywood, a certain kind of lifestyle, and you," she admitted. "I was going to reinvent myself in New York and pursue my writing. It was selfish and wrong, but I was young and stupid and probably much more self-centered than I want to admit even now."

Her eyes flicked to Sam, then back to her flute, as if, Sam thought, holding her gaze was too painful. She brushed a speck of lint from her ugly trousers.

Sam watched a diminutive woman with a choppy bob start to clean up the material and pins and fabric tape that Gisella had discarded while fitting Sam's gown. Her gaze went back to her mother.

"If you're waiting for me to encourage you to continue, you'll be waiting a long time," Sam said flatly.

Dina nodded. "Fair enough. After a while, when I hadn't spoken to you, it became harder and harder to reach out. We lived in different worlds. I told myself you were better off without me. And . . . I suppose I told myself that so many times that I even started to believe it."

Silence. That was it? That was the big maternal confession? Sam tugged angrily at the hem of her black blouse. She didn't know what to say. To think that her mother had left because she simply didn't like the way her life had turned out? It was mind-boggling. It was . . .

It was the kind of thing Sam would do. Maybe not abandon a child, but Sam could *see* herself doing whatever it took to get away from a suffocating life.

"I don't expect you to forgive me, Sam," Dina went on. "But I hope you'll give me a chance to get to you know again, at least. To be your friend."

Sam didn't need a friend. But over the years, she'd needed a mother desperately. One part of her wanted to hurl her champagne flute against the three-quarter mirror, watch it shatter into a thousand shards, and tell her mother to go to hell. But another part of her wanted to bury her face in her mother's arms.

The needy part of her won out.

Sam didn't trust herself to speak. So she just nodded. Then her eyes landed on Dina's cheap brown flats. Target. Wal-Mart. Someplace like that. They made her laugh.

Dina's eyes looked a little hurt. "I was going for profound."

"Look at your toes."

Dina looked down. She was scuffing the toe of her right foot against the toe of her left foot. She smiled. "I guess it's genetic."

Now Sam and her mother shared a smile. The *same* smile, Sam realized. Could it be that she and her mother were—gasp—sharing a *moment*?

"Hey, you two!"

Sam and Dina both turned. America's Best-Loved Action Star had just stepped into Gisella's studio. He wore faded jeans, an old white button-down dress shirt with the sleeves rolled up, and Adidas tennis shoes. But as he crossed the floor, dodging mannequins and racks of clothes, it was as if a tsunami of charisma preceded him, clearing the way. Sam had seen the Jackson Sharpe effect in action many times. That it would work on others was a given. That it still affected her was astonishing.

"How's the mother and daughter?" The charisma got more intense the closer he came.

"Eating and talking, not fitting," Dina admitted. Her eyes shone, a dead giveaway that she was not immune to the Jackson charisma wave either, even if she'd divorced him years before.

Jackson cupped his hands in the direction of Gisella's

office. "Hello! Madame Designer? Come out and do your thing for the mother of the bride who's against the wedding! And by the way, so is the father!"

Under ordinary circumstances, Sam would have been irritated. But her dad's voice was so good-natured, and she was so wrung out from her talk with her mother, that she couldn't muster up any annoyance.

"Thank you *so* much for your support," she quipped, which made her mother and father both laugh.

Gisella came back out of her office. Sam and Jackson talked easily and ate more sushi as the designer measured Dina, then cut fabric and pinned it and measured some more, finally promising that she'd have Dina's gown ready the next morning. What would it look like? Gisella would only smile and say that Dina had to trust her. As for Jackson, he'd be wearing a tux by Ted Lapidus, his favorite designer.

"How'd you get here?" he asked Dina, when Gisella was finally finished.

"Cab," she admitted.

"Sam, you've got the Hummer?"

"Yep."

"Well, I've got the Jensen. How about we send my assistant, Kiki, to pick the Hummer up later, and I drive us all home?" Jackson took the keys from his pocket and tossed them lightly in the air.

There was every reason to say no. They were against the wedding. They weren't a real family. She'd wanted to go for a massage at the Century City Athletic Club, because Olga from Moldova was working this afternoon.

Sam said yes.

Twisted Sister

Thursday morning, 11:00 a.m.

Anna's father looked pale under his tan. "Scared the hell out of you, huh, sweetheart?"

Actually, there weren't any words for how scared she'd been. The mental tug-of-war that had been her relationship with her dad ever since she'd moved west had been based on the assumption that he would always be there. She was too young to think about the mortality of her parents. And yet it happened all the time; people dying young, in an accident, or just out of nowhere. It had almost happened to her in a plane crash, just a few days ago.

She shuddered, not wanting to share any of her morbid thoughts with her dad. Instead she smiled. "You could say that."

He laughed, gingerly touching the bandage that circled his head. "Scared the hell out of myself."

It was two days after Jonathan had been rushed to Cedars-Sinai for emergency brain surgery. Anna was happy to find her father had been moved to a luxury private room on the fourth floor and was in the midst of making a rapid recovery. She hadn't talked to Dr. Miller—she was scheduled to stop in sometime during the next half hour—but from her conversation with her father, the way his eyes followed her around the room as she moved, his lucidity, and even his sense of humor, she'd have been surprised if his subdural hematoma had any severe aftereffects.

There was a plush dove gray easy chair to the left of his hospital bed—a bed that looked more like it had been imported from a French château than the kind of bed Anna was used to seeing in a hospital. Anna plopped into it. Her dad's breakfast had just been served, and clearly he already had an appetite, because he was forking scrambled eggs with capers and creamed cheese into his mouth with gusto. Cedars-Sinai was the preferred hospital of Hollywood's rich, famous, and infamous, and had recently been experimenting with the idea of luxury hospital accommodations and care for their many patients to whom money was no object.

Jonathan's present suite—Anna couldn't bring herself to call it a hospital room, because it was much closer to a luxury hotel room than to typical hospital accommodations—was one of these experiments. Painted in soft sky blue, with framed photographs on the walls that Anna recognized as having been taken by Ansel Adams and Alfred Stieglitz, a wall-mounted fifty-inch HD flat-screen television monitor, a state-of-the art sound system with an eight-gig iPod on the nightstand plus connections for the patient's own iPod, high-speed wireless Internet, a small refrigerator fully stocked by the hospital's dietician, and the aforesaid bed, easy chair, and matching couch, and soft lighting that could be adjusted by the same remote that worked the electronics, it was a place to be sick in style.

"Want some of this?" her father offered, gesturing to the tray of food. "It's damn good."

"I'm not that hungry." Something about this was still making Anna anxious.

"Are you sure this is from tennis?"

"Of course I'm sure! I was playing doubles at the Riviera Country Club with a couple of Sony execs in from Tokyo. I was at the net, and one of these Sony guys lost his grip on his racquet while he was hitting an overhead; the racquet caught me on the side of the head. I didn't think a thing of it at the time, just thought I had a bump."

Anna shivered. It was so, so random. Her dad was lucky that he had been at home when the symptoms had hit. What if he'd been driving? He could have crashed and killed himself. Or what if he hadn't been Jonathan Percy, but had just been your average Los Angeleno who didn't have full-time household help to call for an ambulance? The thought made her weak in the knees because it was so real. She could so easily have been at a funeral this morning instead of in her father's plush hospital room.

"But you're having a complete physical and everything?" Anna asked, because she still needed reassurance. "Just in case those headaches—"

"Anna. I'm fine. Really." He took a sip of melon juice. "So what have you been doing since yesterday?" He pushed a button on the remote; a moment later a young woman with jet black hair in a shaggy bob, clad in a fitted navy Armani blazer, and sporting a name tag that read BETH WILLIAMS, GUEST SERVICES, as if this were a hotel rather than a hospital, came in to remove the breakfast tray.

"Besides worrying about you?" Anna asked, after the young woman left. "I had a fitting for my bridesmaid dress for Sam's wedding last night; the rehearsal dinner is tonight and the wedding is tomorrow."

Jonathan shook his head. "Better her than you."

Anna actually agreed with that sentiment. She couldn't see herself marrying for a long, long time. But Sam, on the other hand, seemed so happy. And Anna only wanted the best for her friend, so . . .

"There's a time for weddings and a time to stay single," her father went on. "Don't rush."

Anna was about to say she had no intention of rushing when her father's bedside phone rang. He answered with his customary "Jonathan Percy" and then launched into a detailed conversation about hedge funds and stock index futures, which was both excruciatingly boring and further confirmation that his mental faculties seemed unimpaired. It gave her a moment to check her own appointment list for the day, which she'd scribbled on a sticky note just to keep it all straight. At noon, she was supposed to meet Dee for a final wedding-cake tasting. Dee had tracked down the best baker in the city, a young woman named Joy Wilson, whose Web site was a thing of beauty—her cakes really were a work of art—and whose cupcakes Dee had devoured at the CD launch party for Jordin Sparks. Joy was going to do the actual baking this evening, a cake for seventy-five people, but they still had to decide whether it would be vanilla-coconut or Belgian chocolate. Sam had left the decision in Dee's hands.

Then they'd go to the Beverly Hills Hotel for the wedding rehearsal and rehearsal dinner. Dee had already consulted her on the menu and wine list, which she'd narrowed down with the help of the hotel's head chef and sommelier. Dee had hired Django to play and Citron to sing at the rehearsal dinner, and the jazz singer Diana Krall would perform at the wedding itself.

Dee's overall notion for the wedding was simple: "Elegant, elegant, elegant," as she put it. "Very Old Hollywood. Glamour and glitz as befits the daughter of Jackson Sharpe, with some Peruvian touches for Eduardo and his family."

It was good that Dee was so on top of things, because with her father in the hospital, Anna had barely been able to concentrate enough to turn the switch of the Braun coffeemaker this morning. And Cammie, who should have been helping out, was missing in action. Anna felt bad on Sam's behalf. Cammie was supposed to be Sam's oldest and closest friend, yet, per usual, she was taking the selfish way out.

Logan was being so sweet about everything. He'd stopped by the house yesterday with a takeout lunch from Spago, given her a supportive hug, and asked that she stay in touch. Being with him was so easy—as if she'd known him forever. Maybe because she had. Anna had invited him to the rehearsal dinner and the wedding, and she smiled just thinking about sharing the evening with him.

But she couldn't help wonder, every now and then, if she shouldn't be thinking about him more. Was it normal to have days go by and not think about a guy when a relationship was brand-new? When she'd been with Ben, she'd thought about him all the time. But she certainly didn't miss the drama, anxiety, and insecurity that had come with the relationship. Anna decided this was how it was supposed to be if a romance was healthy.

Honestly, though . . . sometimes she *still* thought about Ben. His family had sent a massive flower arrangement. And Ben had made a personal delivery of a box of DVDs from Vidiots in Santa Monica that would supplement the hospital's already-large collection. Or at least, so she'd been told—she'd been off talking to the doctor when he'd stopped by, and he'd only stayed long enough to check in on Jonathan and deliver the DVDs. He hadn't called Anna since he'd surprised her in the intensive care waiting room, and she hadn't called him. That part of her life was over. She had accepted it and was ready to move on.

But the question was . . . move on to what? She was either off to Yale, or to Bali with Logan. And she still didn't know which choice was right.

About the only thing that would take her mind off her father's health, or her own indecision about the future, was writing. Part of her was nervous and uncertain. She'd uploaded her screenplay for *The Big Palm* to Sam a few nights before, and every time she talked to her friend she expected a reply. A comment. Something. But all she got was a big nothing. Anna could only conclude that Sam had hated it, and that by being silent, she was being kind. She didn't want to out-and-out lie to Anna about the awfulness of her writing, so she figured silence was the best alternative.

A creative writing teacher had once told Anna that you couldn't write to try and impress anyone, or you would end up impressing no one. That finally, you had to write for yourself. Ironically, Anna had not impressed that particular teacher with her writing. Although she'd aced the class, just as she aced every class, she had not been thought of as the star, the talent. There had been two other students who got all the attention.

So maybe she was crazy to keep writing, but now she found it an unexpected lifeline. With one screenplay done, she started on another one. This one was about a rich girl who got hooked on heroin and had to hide it from everyone. In the first twelve pages the girl went to a MoMA fund-raiser looking skinny and ethereal and perfect. She wore couture, and was adorned with hundreds of thousands of dollars' worth of jewelry, but her long gloves hid the track marks on her arms, and she passed out in a toilet stall, blood dripping across her pale pink evening gown.

When Anna finished twelve pages, she reread it. It wasn't entirely dreadful. Too dramatic, maybe bordering on melodramatic? But Anna had known girls like this; her own sister, in fact, had passed out in some of the best ladies' rooms in New York. But good? Anna had no idea if it was good.

"I'm telling you, Malcolm, this is a great deal and you should get in on it," her father insisted, switching the phone to his other ear. The business call droned on.

"He's making a quick recovery." Anna heard the steady voice of Dr. Miller growing louder as she approached the room. "He'll need to take it easy for a couple of weeks. No driving, lots of rest, and his wound will need some care. But I'm starting to think that your father is the poster boy for subdural hematomas."

Anna stood up from the dove gray chair slowly. Who was Dr. Miller talking to? She'd said "your father." That could only mean . . .

Anna's sister, Susan, bounded into the room, followed

by Dr. Miller, in her customary green scrubs. Susan wore faded jeans and a white Kripalu Center T-shirt from the yoga retreat where she worked, red flip-flops on her feet. Her hair was stuck in a haphazard ponytail and she wore no makeup. Seeing Susan au naturel—she was known for her over-the-top sex queen outfits—was almost as shocking as seeing her sister at all. Susan was grinning, clearly enjoying the shock value of showing up out of nowhere. Anna had kept her apprised by phone about how her father was progressing; Susan had called twice today, in fact. But Anna had never expected her sister, who was not big on family obligations, just to walk blithely into her dad's hospital room.

"Surprise," Susan said, her blue eyes clear and bright.

Her father stabbed a happy finger in Susan's direction, as if to say, *You trickster!* and quickly wound up his phone call.

"Susan!" Her father hung up the phone. "Both my girls!"

"Shut up and hug me!" Susan demanded, and Jonathan did. Then Susan hugged Anna, and Anna found herself hugging back, hard. No one in the world could understand how terrible it had been to watch her dad go through this but her sister.

"This is . . . this is unbelievable. I never expected . . ." Jonathan's voice became choked with emotion. Dr. Miller slipped discreetly out of the room.

"What? That I'd come? I had to," Susan said lightly, running a hand through her short blond hair. "Besides, who else would take over the second shift?"

"Excuse me?" Anna asked, confused.

"I'm replacing you. So someone can be here with Dad when you leave for Yale. When do you fly out?"

Anna was so surprised she could hardly speak. "Oh—I—Saturday at noon," Anna sputtered.

That was when she was *supposed* to fly out, at least, though whether or not Anna would be on that flight was unclear. It was the craziest thing. Every time she thought seriously about Yale, Bali looked like a better option. Every time she thought seriously about Bali, she'd hear Carlie Martin's voice and feel herself drawn to New Haven and Yale. She'd been almost grateful, strange as it sounded, for the distraction of her father in the hospital, once she knew that his life wasn't in danger. It gave her less time to think.

"Saturday at noon," Susan nodded. "That's what I thought. Good thing I have a flexible schedule. And caretaking experience," she added, gesturing to her Kripalu T-shirt.

"I can hire a nurse!" Jonathan protested, sitting up in his hospital bed.

"Yes, you can. But you're not going to. Because I'm moving in, and I'll do what Anna's doing right now. Only better, because I'm older and smarter and more treacherous." Susan grinned wickedly, refilling Jonathan's glass of melon juice with the jug on his meal tray.

"Susan, I—I don't really know what to say. Are you sure you want to do this?" Jonathan asked.

"Of course. You're my father," Susan replied. "You only get one, you know. So even if I do think that you've been something of a butthole for many years of my life, I have not exactly been a model daughter either, and anyway, all of that is beside the point." Her eyes softened. "I want to be with you, Dad. If you'll let me."

Anna felt a lump in her throat. Evidently tragedy was bringing out the best in her sister, who had harbored bad feelings toward her parents for years, ever since they'd played a part in breaking up her relationship with a druggie boyfriend back in college. "But what about your job?" she asked.

"It'll be there when I'm finished here. Or maybe I'll stay. I don't know. All I know is, this is where I need to be right now." She shrugged easily and adjusted the covers over their dad's pajama-clad legs.

Anna actually found herself envying her sister for the ease with which she'd been able to change her life course, when Anna herself was caught in such a tangle about her own future.

Dr. Miller stuck her brunette head into the room again. "Excuse me, Mr. Percy, we'll need to take you for another PET scan now." She looked at Anna and Susan. "He'll be done in around forty-five minutes. And there's no pain involved."

"Works for me," Jonathan quipped. His eyes went from Anna to Susan and back to Anna again. "If it took a subdural hematoma to get you girls together like this—"

"What, you're going to do it on a regular basis?" Susan said, hands on hips. "I don't freaking *think* so! I don't cuss anymore, either," she added serenely.

Jonathan laughed.

"I'm so glad you're here," Anna blurted out. She hadn't realized how alone she'd felt until just this minute. "You want to go get some coffee while dad's having his test?"

Susan slung an arm around Anna's shoulders. "Absolutely, little sis. We've got a lot to talk about."

Dream Lover

Thursday night, 8:47 p.m.

Cammie checked her antique silver windup watch with the emerald face—it had been a prop on her father's TV show, *Hermosa Beach*, and when Cammie had admired it, the wardrobe person had simply handed it to her. Cammie knew this had nothing to do with kindness and everything to do with sucking up to the daughter of the big guy, but whatever—she loved the watch. She was counting the hours until Sam, her best and oldest friend, would be actually, really, truly married. Less than twenty-four. Married. Sam. Shit.

Cammie took a sip of her Flirtini. She was at the bar in the Polo Lounge, which was closed to the public for Sam's rehearsal dinner. Even though the Polo Lounge was as familiar to Cammie as her own bedroom, Dee had transformed the place overnight into a festive yet elegant venue befitting the Sharpe wedding extravaganza. Thousands of twinkling lights adorned the large oak trees on the outdoor patio, making it feel like a magical fairy garden. Inside, roses and bouquets of hibiscuses on every table gave off a pleasantly sweet aroma. Dee had also ordered the staff to sprinkle white rose petals on every available surface. Every single detail had been accounted for, right down to the cream-colored cocktail napkins encircled with Swarovski crystal napkin rings, which were custom made by Kate's Paperie and had SAM & EDUARDO printed in small, elegant cursive in the upper-left-hand corner. Cammie felt a twinge of guilt when she thought about how many of these decisions she had been involved in—none, to be exact.

A year ago, if someone had told her that Sam would get married right after they graduated from high school, Cammie would have asked what drugs they were on. And now . . . well, now everything had changed. She was happy that Sam was happy. But also, if Cammie was going to be brutally honest with herself, it felt very weird. As if she, Cammie, was losing something.

"How's it going?"

Adam sidled up to the bar. He wore a black T-shirt that said THINK and under that, in small letters: IT'S NOT ILLEGAL YET. A deconstructed black cotton blazer, jeans, and black Vans completed the outfit. His hair was short again; the star tattoo behind his ear showed. He was altogether understated and comfortable in his own skin.

Adam. *Her* Adam.

But no. That was then, this was now.

Cammie wondered how she looked to him, in her sleek gold sheath dress that ended six inches above the knee. She had a strange desire for him to still find her attractive, even though she knew that of all the guys she'd ever been with, he was the one to whom looks mattered least.

"I'm good. The club's going great, so I've been busy," she said, nodding quickly. "I'm . . ." She drained her Flirtini. "Well, actually, I'm having a hard time believing that Sam is really getting married," Cammie said honestly.

"Me too," Adam agreed. He sipped his Heineken and set an elbow on the bar, brushing aside some of the white rose petals that had been scattered over its surface. "But Eduardo's a great guy, so if it's what she wants . . ."

"Yeah, that's what I was just thinking," Cammie agreed.

It was strange to be here with Adam, talking easily, as if nothing had ever happened. As if they hadn't been insanely in love with each other. As if he hadn't decided to move to Michigan, as if they hadn't crashed and burned.

Adam set his green beer bottle on the bar. "So, the club's going well?"

"Very well. But I'm going to be less involved in it from now on," Cammie replied.

Adam's eyebrows shot up. "Why?"

She shrugged. "It's Ben's thing, not mine. I mean, it was fun getting it started. I enjoyed the challenge. But it's like a twenty-hour-a-day, seven-days-a-week job to keep it going, keep it hot. . . ." Her voice trailed off as she played with her antique silver watch.

Adam contemplated her. "So you're on to the next?"

"I'm going to spend more time promoting Champagne," Cammie explained, looking up to face him. "You know, the petite model I'm managing?"

"Right." Adam nodded. "Watch it, though," he teased, the corners of his mouth curling upward. "The next thing you know, your father will take you on as an agent at Apex, and you'll be his Mini-Me."

"I don't think so," Cammie mused, shaking her strawberry-blond curls. "I don't want to work for anyone else."

Adam took a sip of his beer and ran a finger around the rim. "Well, Cam, if anyone can make Champagne into a supermodel, it's you."

Cammie looked at him hopefully. "You think?"

"I know," Adam insisted, his brown eyes adamant. "When you set your mind to something, nothing can stop you." He glanced around at the dozens of people mingling before dinner was served. "Ben here?"

Cammie brushed the curls out of her eyes. "Yeah. Why?"

"Just wondering," Adam said. He hesitated for a moment. "You know I want you to be happy, right?"

"Right," Cammie agreed softly. She did know that. With Adam, she'd never doubted it for a second. He was such a great guy. And she had dropped him like a Prada knockoff. "So what about you?" she wondered. "Are you excited about Michigan?"

Adam scratched behind his ear, something, Cammie knew, he tended to do when he was nervous. "Hey, next year real life starts, right?" He grinned and drained his beer. "And Beverly Hills High will be nothing but the people I hung out with in high school."

Cammie felt a pang somewhere near her heart. She supposed he was right. You left high school behind like childhood and moved on, and never looked back except to laugh at how crucial it all seemed to you at the time.

"Hey, I see a friend of mine," Adam said. "You take

care, okay?" He gave Cammie a quick peck on the cheek, and then he was gone.

Cammie looked after him. And it felt as if she was leaving behind more than high school memories. She was leaving behind the very best of herself.

Anna watched Pedro Munoz raise his champagne glass as he finished a toast to Sam and his son.

"No matter how much you beg me, Samantha, I won't recount for all the guests my son's most embarrassing moments growing up. Although I do remember this one occasion when he was playing soccer for his elementary school—"

"*Por favor, no, Papa! Hay mas buenos cuentos!*" Eduardo raised a hand in protest, though he was smiling. All the guests at Sam's rehearsal dinner who were under the age of thirty sat at a horseshoe-shaped table at the front of the Polo Lounge in the Beverly Hills Hotel. For the first time since President Kennedy and his wife had visited in 1962, the lounge was closed to regular hotel guests in favor of a private party: Sam and Eduardo's wedding rehearsal dinner. Anna was impressed that Jackson Sharpe had such clout. Or maybe it was Pedro Munoz, who might have threatened that no president or prime minister in the Organization of American States would ever stay at the hotel unless it made this accommodation.

"Go on, Pedro!" Cammie urged. "I can tell some of Sam's embarrassing stories too!"

Everyone laughed, Sam buried her head in her hands, and Pedro went on. "I will leave it to my son to recount. Suffice it to say that it involved Eduardo, in a very important game, dribbling a football—you call it a soccer ball—the length of the field and scoring a goal . . . without realizing it was his own team's net that he was shooting at!"

He held the champagne out to his son. Veuve-Clicquot 1977. The rehearsal dinner party had already consumed a case of it. "Eduardo, my son, you may have not been the most successful football player, but your aim is true in the most important things. You have chosen a wonderful girl. We will be proud to have her in the family. To my son and to Samantha!"

"To Eduardo! To Sam!"

All around the room, people picked up the cry, raising a toast to the soon-to-be newlyweds and shouting their names. Anna looked at Sam. Her friend was smiling, but she seemed a bit pale. Had to be nerves, Anna decided.

Not that Anna was immune to nerves. Luckily, her father was no longer a source of worry—she'd left him happily watching DVDs at the hospital, in Susan's capable hands. But tomorrow night, her life was going to change. She'd either go back East, or go to Bali.

Jackson, who was the master of ceremonies for the evening, took the microphone from Eduardo's dad. He wore black razor-pressed trousers and a yellow silk shirt under an unvented Ralph Lauren Black Label sport coat, and looked like the movie star he was. "It's been a great evening so far," he pronounced. "And fortunately, Pedro's English is a helluva lot better than my Spanish!"

Pedro called out, "You will learn, Jackson! Just pray that I am not your teacher!"

Jackson waited for the thirty or so assembled guests to stop laughing.

"I would just like to say to my little girl . . ." He looked over at Sam. "I had my doubts about this wedding." There were murmurs in the crowd, and Anna saw anxiety flit across Sam's face. "But now that I've gotten to know Eduardo and his wonderful family, I'll be honored, as of tomorrow, to start calling them *our* family."

The crowd gave a collective "awww."

"Tonight," Jackson continued, "the lovely Citron Simms will entertain us, with her brother, Django, on the piano. Eat and drink, everyone. And have fun!"

With that, Jackson put down the handheld mic, and Citron, looking beautiful in a white silk skirt and black silk capris, sang the opening notes of "My Funny Valentine," which made sense, because Sam had once mentioned that it was her father's favorite song. Django did some amazing flourishes on the piano. He'd dressed formally, in a dark charcoal Yves Saint Laurent suit, white shirt, and gray tie. As Anna watched and listened, she couldn't believe someone so talented had been living in her father's guesthouse this whole time. Funny how the most amazing things sometimes turned out to be right under your nose.

The rehearsal dinner had been a stunning affair, as lavish as some people's weddings. A friend of Jackson's—a former teen megastar who had gone to law school when he'd outgrown his cuteness, and had then gone on to become a justice on the California Supreme Court—would perform the wedding itself. The members of the wedding, which included Sam, Dee, Anna, and

Cammie, plus Eduardo, and the parents on both sides, were asked to come early. Eduardo's older brother, Paco, who owned one of the premier soccer teams in Lima and the largest television station, would serve as best man. He was here with his wife, a lovely blond Russian woman named Alina, whom he'd met at Harvard. She worked with him both at the television station and with the soccer team.

All the female members of the wedding party had dressed in style. Anna had on a miniskirt by Alaïa, black stockings by Juicy Couture, and a black blouse from Givenchy. Dee wore a tailored Bebe suit, with a Coach clutch and their newest signature jewelry, while Cammie was absolutely dazzling in a gold mini Dolce & Gabbana. As for Sam, she'd come in a calf-length lavender skirt from Dior with a black off-the-shoulder cashmere tee by Ralph Lauren. The guys had been asked to wear sport coats and jeans—casual Los Angeles chic. What was under the sport coats ranged from a black T-shirt (Logan) to a white dress shirt (Jack) to a plain white T-shirt (Parker Pinelli). Ben was nowhere to be seen; Anna assumed he was busy with the club and would make it late (not that she cared).

The eating and drinking had been exquisite. In addition to the champagne, there was sauvignon blanc and delicious, slightly biting burgundy from Jackson's favorite cellar in Beaune. They'd started with a cold lobster bisque, moved on to a diced mushroom and cucumber salad with truffles and fresh croutons, then had a choice of either Jamaican jerk chicken fresh from a pit that had been dug especially for this meal, or pan-seared halibut with wilted endive and capers. As a kind gesture to Eduardo and his family, there was a potato cart that featured many different varieties of the Peruvian staple, including a small red baking potato that tasted like a cross between a conventional potato and a macadamia nut. Anna ate three of them, dripping with clarified butter. Dessert was to be fresh-picked strawberries shipped in from a farm in New Mexico, dipped in melted Belgian chocolate.

"Are you having a good time?" Dee asked, as she sidled up to Anna with her arm through Jack's. "I hope everyone likes the food and the decorations. Do you think I did okay?"

"Here's my answer: Jack, whatever you do, do not lose this girl," Anna advised, to which Dee grinned happily

"I'm not planning to," Jack declared. "When you find a good thing, you hang on to it."

"When do you head to Princeton?" Anna asked, buttering a roll.

"I go back next Wednesday. Going to be weird without Ben, though. He's staying here to run the club, at least for the year. I'll miss him."

Anna nodded noncommittally. So Ben was sticking around. Back when they'd been dating, she'd thought about how convenient it might have been once she headed to Yale, since Princeton was only a few hours' drive. But none of that mattered now.

"But I'll still have great company," Jack finished with a grin, kissing Dee on her pink cheek as he pulled her onto his lap.

"You're going too?" Anna asked, surprised.

"Yeah, I just decided the other day. And I'm going

to college, too," Dee chirped, as Jack smoothed a wisp of her angelic, shaggy blond hair. "Maybe just community college at first. But I've decided I want to become a wedding planner!"

"That's fantastic news. Bravo for you guys," Anna declared, raising her glass of champagne in a toast. It seemed like everything was really coming together for Dee, and she was truly happy for her.

"Thanks." Dee took a sip of her own champagne, then pushed her chin toward the door that led to the outdoor patio. "Anna, Logan's looking for you."

Anna looked. Logan was standing on the other side of the enormous dining area. He caught her eye and motioned for her to come to over. "Excuse me," she said to Dee and Jack, and made her way toward him.

He was sitting at one of the rose-petal-covered circular tables. He rose when she approached.

"Anna Percy." He was deliberately and amusingly formal.

"Logan Cresswell," she countered. "I remember when you ate nothing but cherry Popsicles for two weeks when we were in kindergarten. You mother was not happy."

"My mother was rarely happy," he observed. "And as I recall, the same could be said of yours." He sat and patted the soft cushion of the seat next to him. She sat too, and he entwined his fingers with hers. That was when she noticed the envelope on the white tablecloth in front of them; the envelope that held the plane tickets to Bali, the flight that left the day after tomorrow.

Logan looked at her meaningfully, waiting for her to take hers.

Anna's eyes immediately swept around the room, as if to take in all that she'd be leaving behind. She saw Sam and Eduardo kissing, his eyes laughing down into hers. Cammie was flirting with an actor who had been in Jackson's last movie—Anna couldn't remember his name—as he gave her a sip of the champagne from his flute. Sam's parents and Eduardo's parents were in intense conversation, with Jackson's arm slung around the back of his ex-wife's chair. Citron was singing "The Way We Were," which even Anna, who really did not know movies very well at all, knew was from a tearjerker about lost love.

And at that moment, Ben walked in.

Light from the chandelier bounced off his face so that he seemed to glow. Images tumbled through her mind. How he had made her laugh on the plane that day they'd met, by pretending to be her old friend so that she could escape from the boor seated next to her. The time they'd gone to Hustler, the sex superstore, and Anna had found the nerve to model a pair of red plastic pants that zipped all the way around, which had them dying of laughter. The time they'd made love on his boat, the only noise the gentle crashing of the waves outside.

She looked back to Logan. He was still holding her hand. Her eyes focused on the plane tickets.

Here he was, this wonderful guy, offering a dream, an escape, or maybe just a pause in her life so that she could catch her breath. In her mind's eye she saw herself in Bali, on the beach, in a bikini, letting the ocean do all the worrying. And in her fantasy, she turned and smiled at the boy next to her, and it was . . .

Not Logan.

It could only have been a millisecond, but it felt like two years, because she didn't know what to say. And she didn't know what do, not in any big way. But suddenly, she knew what she should *not* do.

"I can't go with you," Anna said quietly.

Logan's blue eyes bore into hers, waiting for more of an explanation.

"I know going to Bali is the right thing for you, Logan," Anna continued. "But it's not the right thing for me."

Citron's voice soared. Something about how it was the laughter they would remember, this couple who had loved and lost each other.

"I can't say I'm not disappointed," Logan remarked, letting go of her hand. "So you're going to Yale, then."

"I . . . There's something I need to do first." It was a lame explanation, but it was true. "You're really amazing, Logan. Maybe that sounds flimsy—I don't know—but I mean it. I've loved every single moment I spent with you."

He leaned in and kissed her cheek. "I wish you the best, Anna Percy. Always." With that he stood, gave her a sad half-smile, and wound his way through the guests until she could no longer see him. He was gone.

She Did *Not* Say That

Thursday night, 9:51 p.m.

Sam had three thoughts as she finished her seventh strawberry dipped in Belgian chocolate. One, this dessert was so good that she could eat it for breakfast, lunch, dinner, and postclubbing snack. Two, she didn't know how regular brides planned a wedding that was seven or ten or fifteen months away, and thus had hundreds of days to obsess and worry, even if they had a professional wedding planner like Fleur Abra instead of a supremely talented amateur like Dee Young. And three, it better not rain tomorrow night when they were out on the boat. Rainstorms were rare in Los Angeles in August, but it wasn't impossible. What a mess that would be.

"Open, please." Eduardo dunked another strawberry into the little silver basin of chocolate on the table in front of them and moved it toward Sam's Stila-glossed lips.

"I've had enough, I think," Sam demurred, pushing back from the circular white table. She couldn't help but imagine her couture wedding dress splitting a seam twenty-four hours from now.

"Are you concerned about your figure? Because you know I think it's magnificent." Eduardo whispered huskily in her ear as he put the strawberry back on the plate.

"Are you ever not a gentleman?" Sam leaned in and gave him a strawberry-and-chocolate-flavored kiss.

"It's a Peruvian tradition. Nice as can be until the ring is on the finger, and then a jerk for the rest of your life," Eduardo teased as he lovingly brushed a strand of auburn hair off of her face. "Forever and ever."

Sam felt the smile on her face falter, and was glad Eduardo was burying his head in her neck. *Until the ring is on the finger. Forever and ever.* To have her own fate tied to the fate of someone else.

Women had been doing it ever since men graduated from the cave and club to more sophisticated mating rituals. It was natural. It was normal. But was it natural and normal at age eighteen?

"How is the happy couple?" Mrs. Munoz came up behind her son and Sam, and put a gentle hand on each of their shoulders. She was elegantly attired in a tan Versace suit, cut simply enough to showcase the stunning strand of diamonds draped around her neck, just below the collarbone. But no piece of jewelry could rival the radiant expression on the proud face of the mother of the groom.

"We're doing great, Mama," Eduardo answered, putting his hand over Sam's on the table.

"You too, Sam? This should be the happiest night of your life," Mrs. Munoz rhapsodized.

"I'm fine. I'm good," Sam nodded.

"Excellent." She leaned down toward Sam's ear to

whisper, so her son couldn't hear. "And if you wanted to give Eduardo's father and me a little surprise nine months from tomorrow night, I can tell you for a fact that he wouldn't mind at all. Neither would I." She pulled away from Sam's ear and beamed at the couple.

"Giving her advice on how to keep me happy?" Eduardo teased.

"How to keep us all happy," his mother replied, smiling.

Standing over them, Mrs. Munoz obscured their view of the party, and Sam felt as if she'd been blockaded in. Suddenly, she needed some fresh air. A wedding, that was okay. Being a mother? She was several years away from that. Maybe more than several years. Maybe a couple of decades. "Excuse me, Consuela. I'm going to walk back toward the tennis courts," she told Eduardo. "Wanna come?"

He shook his head. "I'll hang out here with my parents. They're so excited about this—it's like they're getting married all over again. Come back soon?"

"Very."

His dark eyes flashed. "Good."

She gave him a radiant grin, nodded politely at his mother, and got up from her table just as one of the black-clad waiters poured her and Eduardo more champagne. On stage, Citron was starting another song. The girl was tireless. She was also outstanding. Couples were swaying to the music. Eduardo's brother and his wife. Jack and Dee. Ben and Cammie. Anna and Parker were dancing together, and Sam wondered where Logan had gone.

The rear entrance to the Polo Lounge opened onto the expansive, immaculately manicured grounds of the hotel.

The bungalows were back that way, as well as one of the most famous hotel tennis facilities in the world, where champions like Pancho Gonzales and Alex Olmedo had trained when they were juniors, and where stars like the Williams sisters and Maria Sharapova liked to play when they were in town.

It was a cool, cloudless night, and a bright full moon shone overhead as she walked down the asphalt path toward the tennis courts. Well, no rain tomorrow. Maybe even no clouds. That was nice; there'd be a full moon for the wedding. Out at sea, a full moon shining. How romantic. As romantic as you could get for a wedding. And Paris was about as romantic as you could get for your time as a newlywed.

But would they even still go to Paris? That was what Eduardo expected. How could it be the night before her wedding and she *still* hadn't told him about her doubts? Nor had he even asked. It was like he expected her to come with him. Yet the film program at USC was so much more impressive than she'd expected it to be. As much as she had been jaded by Hollywood at times— she was still miffed that Marty Martinsen was blowing her off about Anna's screenplay—it was, after all, her home.

She could hear the thwack-thwack of players on the tennis courts playing late-night matches as she followed the asphalt path to the facility. About a hundred feet from the white clubhouse, she stopped dead in her tracks.

No. Please, God. She prayed her eyes were deceiving her.

It was her father, America's Favorite Action Hero. He

was doing what he seemed to do best, which was to engage in a serious lip-lock with an unexpected lip-lockee.

Her mother.

Sam stood rooted to the spot. They were divorced. What was wrong with him? What was wrong with her mom? *What did this mean?* All roads led to a definitive *yuck*.

She fled back the way she'd come, back to the Polo Lounge. Eduardo saw her immediately, and she knew she must be looking as ill as she felt from the words he shouted at her. "Samantha! What's wrong? Are you sick?

"Sick, yes. But—"

Eduardo motioned toward the maître d'hôtel, an elegant African-American gentleman named Richard whom Sam had known since middle school, when she'd started coming here. "Call the house doctor! Samantha is not feeling well!"

Richard went straight for his walkie-talkie, but Sam cut him off. "I'm not that kind of sick. I just—"

She opened her mouth to speak, to tell him that it wasn't the shellfish, it was the sight of her parents together.

"I just can't do this! I can't get married tomorrow!"

The words tumbled out before she could stop them.

Django stopped playing. Citron stopped singing. People stopped dancing and talking. The waiters stopped serving and cleaning up. Time stopped. Sam looked from face to face. Anna. Cammie. Dee. Parker. And then finally, at Eduardo, who was now ringed by his family. Pedro's face was a mask of pure anger. Consuela's tight-knit brows and open mouth betrayed both fury and disbelief. Eduardo was simply ashen.

"It's okay, Samantha." His voice was calm as ever, but his hand quavered as he took hers. "You've just got—how do you say it in English?—you've just got prewedding jitters."

It was the strangest thing. She knew what she'd said was shocking. Utterly inappropriate. Guaranteed to make a scene. Which, judging from the circle of friends and family around her, she had done. Yet at the moment she'd said the words—or rather, they'd decided to come out of her lips—she'd felt an incredible sense of relief wash over her. She hadn't felt this way since she'd seen Anna's plane land safely at LAX nearly a week ago.

Consuela Munoz forced a smile. She smoothed her dark bun with her left hand, her enormous wedding ring sparkling in the light. "Yes, of course. Why didn't I think of that? The night before Pedro and I married in Lima, I was so mad at him, I didn't speak to him for the entire evening. Do you remember that, Pedro?"

"Of course I do!" Pedro was upbeat, and his broad shoulders seemed to relax under his perfectly cut tuxedo. "I don't even remember what the argument was about. Do you, Consuela?"

"I don't. No, Pedro, I don't." She shook her head, smiling.

"What's going on here?"

Sam turned around. Jackson and Dina had just stepped back into the Polo Lounge, arm in arm. Her parents, so long estranged, had reunited—at least for the moment. She nearly laughed at the irony.

"Your daughter is having an attack of the jitters." Pedro laughed nervously.

"It's okay, Mr. Sharpe," Eduardo assured. "It's taken care of. Samantha, why don't we go for that walk to the tennis courts," he said, squeezing her hand. His hand felt warm and confident in hers, and Sam wanted to go with him. But she knew she couldn't.

"No, I really mean it." Sam looked at him pleadingly. "I can't get married tomorrow," she said softly. "Or any other day."

Eduardo looked the way she felt: utterly heartbroken. He couldn't even muster a sentence.

Consuela edged closer to Jackson. "It is typical of young brides," she continued loudly. "I was just telling your daughter, I was a young bride myself. Mr. Sharpe, if you would just take some time with Samantha, I am sure we can bring this lovely dinner to the happy conclusion it deserves. Sam, how do they say it in the movie business? Can we take it from the top? So we will have a wonderful story to tell at your twenty-fifth-anniversary party?"

Everyone laughed at Consuela's attempt at a joke, and Sam felt herself weaken. Maybe it was just nerves. Maybe it was the shock of seeing her parents playing tonsil hockey. Whatever was happening with Paris and film school, she wanted to be with Eduardo, and to be with him meant being married to him. "Yes, I'm sorry," Sam began meekly.

Suddenly, Cammie's voice boomed out over everything. "What the fuck do you people think you're doing?"

Her strawberry-blond hair swished around her head as she surveyed the stunned crowd, the light from the candles playing off her shimmery gold sheath dress. "I haven't been the best friend to my friend Sam these last few weeks. I've been a little busy with a number of other things, for which I am really, deeply, truly sorry." She met Sam's brown eyes with her own, and kept them on Sam as she continued. "But I'm still here, and I still have ears, and I heard what Sam had to say loud and clear. *She does not want to get married tomorrow.* She changed her mind. When a girl says yes and then she says no, the no *always* takes priority." Cammie walked to where Sam was standing and took her hand. "Sam? Yes or no?"

Sam looked at her friend thankfully and made a decision.

"No," she told Cammie.

Cammie held her hands out wide. "Then I'd say it's time for everyone to go home. Have a pleasant evening. Robert Cray is at the House of Blues—you might want to check him out. And if you come to Bye, Bye Love afterward, drinks are on me," she added. "Sam, come with me."

Sam felt Cammie's arm go around her, and she followed blindly as Cammie led her out of the Polo Lounge and into the pink-hued lobby of the hotel, to the registration desk. There, they sat in low-slung chairs near a large group of young Eurotrash female models, each with a skirt shorter than the next. She nearly collapsed into her friend's embrace, inhaling the scent of her Narciso Rodríguez perfume and remembering all over again why she loved Cammie.

"Thank you." She could barely get the words out.

"Anytime. Want to go get a drink somewhere?"

"That sounds perfect. But there's something I need to do first."

*   *   *

The longest walk that Sam had ever taken was across the hotel lobby and back into the Polo Lounge. There, she found Eduardo still standing where she'd left him. His parents moved to him when they saw Sam, but he shooed them away. To his credit, he didn't back away when she approached.

"I'm sorry," she told him. It was the only thing to say.

"So am I. I'm sorry that I ever met you."

His dark eyes flashed, but Sam saw the very real hurt underneath. He turned and strode away the same way she had just come in. It was only when he was safely out the door and into the hotel lobby that Sam let the tears come.

Hurts So Good

Friday morning, 11:05 a.m.

"I'd like an iced coffee," Anna told the waitress, closing her menu.

"And I'd like a Bloody Mary, followed by a Manhattan, followed by a glass of Taittinger. Then come and talk to me about brunch," Sam said crisply.

They were at Geoffrey's Restaurant in Malibu, one of Anna's favorite places, overlooking both the beach and the curve of the coastline heading south toward Santa Monica and beyond. Anna had been awakened by a phone call at nine o'clock, in which Sam had ordered her to join her for brunch. She'd have one of her father's drivers take her up the coast. But in case she keeled over into her tiramisu from exhaustion, could Anna drive her back? Anna assured her that she would. What were friends for?

"Anna, are you going to drink with me?"

Anna shook her head. "All I want is an iced coffee."

"Add some Baileys to it," Sam ordered the tall, thin blond waitress. "I can't stand the thought of drinking alone."

"Will do," the waitress said. "Aren't you Sam Sharpe?"

"No. Iced coffee for my friend. Start with the Bloody Mary for me. Thank you. Consider it an emergency."

"You got it," the waitress told them, and moved off toward the kitchen.

"I don't much feel like being Sam Sharpe today," Sam commented as she watched the wanna-be-actress waitress walk away.

"That's quite all right by me." Anna smiled at her friend. "You picked a great place," she commented.

"If only I'd had my rehearsal dinner here," Sam snorted. "I could have flung myself off the cliff at the end."

Anna tried a joke. "How operatic."

"How difficult to clean up," Sam shot back. She let her head collapse onto her folded arms. "Am I insane?" she moaned.

"You did the right thing," Anna said firmly. Since Sam was showing no sign of lifting her head, Anna looked around. The place was beautiful. The outdoor patio followed the natural curve of the cliffside; the occasional white umbrella shaded some of the tables, but not all, in case diners wanted to enjoy the sun. Morning glories climbed the side of the white main building, and other fragrant flowers bloomed in planters. The clientele was elegant—mostly couples and groups of well-dressed friends, with not a few obvious romances in progress. Diners had the choice of sitting at the large, plush booths or lounging on the elegant low-rise blue-and-white-striped couches that lined the deck. In addition to acclaimed favorites like the Geoffrey's Kobe burger and grilled portobello mushrooms, the menu always featured the freshest seafood available and changed daily depending on the market.

The waitress brought their drinks and said she'd give them some more time to look at their menus. Only then did Sam lift her head.

"Know why I wanted to come here?" Sam asked darkly.

"Because it's not in town?"

"There is that," Sam agreed. "But also because I couldn't stand the idea of going downstairs to have breakfast with my father and Dina. She slept over last night, you know."

Anna peered at her friend. "How do you know?"

"Because we ran into each other at the refrigerator at four in the morning. I couldn't sleep and had to eat my sorrows away. I was thinking pastrami piled on rye. I came downstairs, and she was chowing on exactly that! Can you believe it? At least I know where I get it from."

"Who knew a love of pastrami was genetic?" Anna pushed up the sleeves of her favorite gray cashmere sweater, which she'd worn with a battered pair of jeans. It was cool up here, with the stiff ocean breeze, and she was glad she'd worn it. As for Sam, she was as low-key as Sam Sharpe got. A cast-and-crew jacket from *Ben-Hur* over a long-sleeved black tee, and black DVF trousers.

"I don't know why she's even still here. There's no wedding. She should go back to North Carolina."

Anna risked stating the obvious. "Maybe she likes your dad again. Maybe she'll sleep with him again tonight. Then she'll go home. She has a life, right?"

"I suppose," Sam replied. "But it doesn't involve me."

She raised her glass. "What should we drink to? Not the past. The past reminds me of Eduardo."

Sam's stomach turned. "I broke his heart." Out of the corner of her eye she watched a couple dressed in practically identical white linen ensembles interlocking arms as they clinked champagne flutes and looked deep into each other's eyes.

"But . . . maybe you had to choose between his and yours," Anna offered.

"I'll never get another guy as great as him." Sam stabbed a finger in Anna's direction. "Don't tell me different."

"Okay." Anna smoothed back some hair that had escaped from her ponytail. "But let me just say this one thing. If you find the right guy at the wrong time . . . then he's the wrong guy. You don't even know who you are yet, Sam. I mean, how could you? How could I? We have to live a little first."

Sam rolled her eyes. "You sound like that asshole therapist Dr. Fred."

Anna laughed. "Well, come on. The runaway bride. You're a talk-show segment."

"Lucky me," Sam muttered. She raised her glass again. "How about to the future?"

"To the future it is," Anna agreed, and clinked her iced coffee against Sam's red Bloody Mary.

"Yours starts tomorrow, huh?" Sam asked. "Are you packed?"

"Mostly. I don't have all that much. I'll take a couple of suitcases back to New York and ask my dad to ship the rest."

Sam took a long sip of her Bloody Mary and pronounced it outstanding. "How is your father? When will he be out of the hospital?"

"Tomorrow."

"And you're going back to Yale. And I'm going to film school. Jeez." Sam laughed bitterly. "It's almost like the last eight months didn't happen."

"Oh, they happened all right. So much changed. Me, especially."

"Funny. You look just the same. Only skinnier. Bitch."

The waitress drifted by to take their orders, but Sam waved her away. "I'm not so hungry. Must have been the pastrami. Are you okay with that?"

"I had a bagel before you called," Anna confessed. "I'm fine. Did you talk to your mom last night? Or just grab the pastrami and run?"

"We talked. Dina said she and my dad were proud that I did the right thing."

Anna nodded. "I did the right thing, too. When I told Logan goodbye."

"Cammie's father, Clark? He always says that character is destiny. You're not the kind of girl who'd blow off Yale and go to Bali with some beautiful stranger." Sam nodded definitively, biting into the celery stick that had come with her Bloody Mary.

Anna bristled. "He's not a stranger. I've known him my whole life."

"With a very significant multiyear gap in there. How soon we forget."

Anna looked out at the ocean waves crashing against the shore. Logan was probably packing right now, and by this time tomorrow he'd be gone. When she thought about him, she felt badly at the hurt she must have caused, but she didn't have a moment's regret. She'd made a split-second decision last night, but that didn't mean it was the wrong one. And the fact that she'd made it right after seeing Ben . . . well, she hadn't fully unpacked what that meant yet. She'd spotted him dancing with Cammie soon afterward, and hadn't had the chance to talk to him, what with Sam calling off the wedding and ending the evening so abruptly. She wondered if she'd even have the chance to say goodbye in person before she left for Yale.

"What are you doing tonight?" Sam asked. She downed the rest of her Bloody Mary in one gulp and looked around for the waitress.

"Packing, I guess." Anna stirred her half-finished iced coffee. "What do you have in mind?" What she really wanted to ask Sam about was her screenplay, but once again, this wasn't the right time or place. It would be incredibly selfish of her to bring it up. Sam would get around to reading it. She had more than a little on her mind.

"Let's go out."

"Any special destination?"

"Someplace Hollywood and cool. I'll choose." Sam glanced over at the couple with the champagne. As the girl reached over to pluck an invisible piece of lint from her boyfriend's shoulder, he snatched her hand and kissed it in mock sincerity, and the girl giggled gleefully. "We have to really do it right for your last night in L.A."

"I'd like that." Suddenly, Anna got very sad at the prospect of the day after tomorrow. It was like a heavy weight had settled once again on her shoulders. She was about to ask her friend what she thought that meant when Sam's cell rang.

"Excuse me," she said as she picked up. "Uh-huh . . . uh-huh . . . no . . . you're kidding. You're fucking kidding. You're totally fucking kidding. You're not kidding. . . . Fair enough. Bye." She clicked off, her face pale.

Anna tensed. What could it possibly be? Something about her family? About Eduardo?

"Good news? Bad news?" Anna asked cautiously.

Sam shrugged. "Depends on how you look at it. Those plans we had for tonight? They just changed. Big-time."

Kiss Off

Cammie strode across the thick green grass of Hollywood Forever Cemetery, smiling at Ben as she approached. The cemetery was off Santa Monica Boulevard in Hollywood, near the final resting place of the silent film star Rudolph Valentino, one of the greatest screen lovers in the history of the industry.

She'd dressed down for the occasion, in Frankie B. jeans and a white Petit Bateau T-shirt. For once, she hadn't even bothered with full makeup, just a dab of Smashbox lip gloss and a few spritzes of Narciso Rodríguez eau de toilette. Still, she looked fresh-faced and beautiful.

Hollywood Forever was perfect for this moment. Not just Valentino, but such screen luminaries as Jayne Mansfield and Douglas Fairbanks also had their final resting places there. The facility had a great attitude about life and death. Spread out over sixty well-manicured acres were walking paths, five different mausoleums, and a special building where loved ones could record "Forever LifeStories" about the deceased, featuring interactive audio, visual, and computer displays so the deceased could be seen in death as they had been in life. Best of all, the cemetery showed movies on Saturday night, projecting them against the side of one of the buildings and inviting anyone with a chair or blanket to attend. There was something both creepy and exhilarating about watching *The Sixth Sense* in a place like this.

"Hi." Ben waved his left hand; in his right was a to-go coffee cup from the Coffee Bean. Cammie saw he'd brought one for her, too. It was on the ground near his left foot. He'd come in cargo shorts and a T-shirt from the club.

"Hey, yourself." She eased up next to him. "Want to walk a bit?"

"Love to. Great place for us to meet up. I haven't been here in years."

She slipped her hand into the crook of his arm, and they headed deeper into the cemetery.

"Who do you want to visit? Jayne Mansfield or Douglas Fairbanks?"

"Just us."

"I sense something serious coming," he joked.

"It won't be if you don't make it that way," she replied.

"Then let's sit and talk," he proposed.

They were near a small mausoleum, a paean to one of the robber barons who worked for one of the major automobile manufacturers in the 1920s and 1930s, and who was responsible for tearing up the streetcar tracks that used to crisscross the city. There was a stone bench near the mausoleum, under a spacious chestnut tree that offered shade against the sun. They sat, almost contentedly.

"We've had an amazing summer," Cammie began.

Ben nodded and sipped his coffee. "Yes, we have."

"But the summer has come to an end," Cammie added. "And so have we."

As she said the words, Cammie thought about how far she had come as a human being in the year since Ben had graduated from Beverly Hills High School and gone off to college. She'd had him. Lost him. Semi-gotten him back again. And now she was letting him go. A year ago, she might have done this by e-mail. Or fax. Or even—she shuddered to think about it—text message. How fucked-up was that?

Ben got the implication. He stiffened slightly and pressed his lips together. "You want to keep it strictly business from here on in."

"Actually, Ben, I would say that you're the one who wants to keep it strictly business. Which is fine with me. And speaking of, the club is your business. I was happy to be a part of it. But it was your dream, not mine." She crossed and uncrossed her legs. The stone was cool underneath her.

"It was both of our dreams," he protested, edging closer to her on the bench.

"That's nice of you to say. But it's not true. You came up with the idea, you found the place, you ran the renovation; I just wrote checks and cheered. Mostly."

"You're not giving yourself enough credit."

"Nonsense," Cammie said, shaking her head. She saw a flock of mourning doves land on the lawn near them. They pecked contentedly at the soil, and she wondered idly how close she could step toward them before they'd fly away. "I'm still in on the club financially. But it's kind of boring me, so you won't see me there all that much. I'm going to concentrate on the model-management thing. I love helping Champagne, and I think I can help a lot of other girls, too. Think you can run the place on your own?"

Ben appraised her carefully. "If you're sure you want to do this, then . . . definitely." He was emphatic.

Cammie grinned. "This is why you suck. You should fight for me."

His blue eyes twinkled in the bright sunshine. "I took a punch in the jaw from a guy who wanted to fight for you."

Cammie stood up and stretched languorously, ignoring Ben's comment. If Adam wanted to be with her, he wouldn't have decided to go to Michigan for college. That was two time zones, and two thousand miles, away. How could anyone call that fighting for her?

"It was a fun ride." Ben stood too. "Hey, before we go, I wanted to tell you—what you did for Sam at the rehearsal dinner? That was really amazing." He shoved his hands into the pockets of his cargos. "You didn't stick around long enough to hear, but most of us were cheering. At least on the inside."

Cammie Sheppard prided herself on never choking up. But tears started to well in her honey-colored eyes.

"I'll remember that," she told him. "I—"

Her Razr sounded, and she fished it out of her jeans pocket. "Hello?"

"Hey, it's me, the disappearing bride. What are you up to?" Sam's voice sounded surprisingly upbeat.

"I'm with Ben, at Hollywood Forever."

"Cool. Say hi to him for me. And also Jayne Mansfield. I wonder if her head is buried in one grave and her body in another."

"She died of a broken neck, Sam," Cammie pointed out. "That doesn't mean her head fell off." She turned to Ben. "It's Sam."

"Tell her I hope she's drinking," he joked.

She put the phone to her ear again. "Ben says he wants to know how much alcohol you've had today. Whatever it is, it isn't enough."

"Yeah, whatever. Listen, do you still have your bridesmaid's dress?"

Cammie dug her Sigerson Morrison stacked heel into the ground. No fucking way. Sam was going through with the wedding after all?

"Yeah, I still have it," Cammie began cautiously, "but Sam, I think you really need to think this through—"

"Not 'buts' allowed," Sam decreed. "Cancel whatever plans you had for tonight. I'll see you on the *Look Sharpe* at seven."

Here Comes the Freaking Bride

Friday night, 7:07 p.m.

Ah, the irony.

Anna had spent her first night in Los Angeles, all those months ago, at a Sharpe family wedding: Jackson Sharpe and Poppy Sinclair's, at the Griffith Observatory. That wedding, with three hundred and fifty of Jackson's closest friends, had been Anna's introduction to life in Hollywood. She'd attended as Ben's guest, and it was there that she'd met Sam, Cammie, and Dee.

And now, her last night in Los Angeles would be spent at another wedding, this one out on Jackson's newest yacht, the *Look Sharpe IV*.

The boat had been decorated magnificently for the ceremony. James Cameron himself couldn't have designed it better, and in fact, Dee had brought in the production designer from *Titanic* to set the right mood. The teak banisters were covered with white silk and delicate strands of ivy. The greased mahogany bar shone in the waning light and held bottles of every alcohol imaginable, plus several cases of wine sent by Francis Ford

Coppola from his vineyard in Napa County. In addition to the usual sleek rattan deck chairs, a number of small tables with white silk tablecloths had been set up on the second deck so that guests could eat and mingle as an army of tuxedo-clad waiters circulated with steaming trays of hors d'oeuvres and bottles of Taittinger champagne. The centerpieces were one of a kind—crystal bowls containing brightly colored tropical fish that swam graceful laps around a single purple orchid rising three feet into the air.

The guests—enough celebrities to populate a studio movie premiere, because no one in Hollywood with any sense would decline an invitation involving America's Favorite Action Star—were stylishly and formally attired in the season's latest collections, and seemed to be having the time of their lives. Everywhere Anna looked, she saw elegant men and women, laughing, chatting, and—of course—networking. She realized that eight months ago, she'd have had no idea who these people were, but she sure knew them now. Tom Hanks and his wife were chatting amiably with Paul Haggis. Les Moonves was huddled with Cammie's father, Clark Sheppard.

Anna stood on the starboard side of the hundred-and-seventy-foot, gleaming white, three-decked vessel. She looked out to the glassy calm seas. The Santa Monica coastline was just three miles away, and the lights of the Ferris wheel on the Santa Monica Pier sparkled serenely in the distance. She took a sip of the Taittinger that had been poured for her the minute she'd stepped on board the vessel at the Malibu Yacht Club, clad in her pink bridesmaid's dress, per Sam's instructions. The smell of the salt air, the gentle rocking of the boat, even the soft fabric of the pink bridesmaid's dress that Gisella had designed and sewn for her—it was like a dream.

There was only one discordant distraction. Guests were still being ferried from the Malibu Yacht Club by helicopter and speedboat, and there was a constant *whup-whup* from the choppers and a roar of approaching and departing speedboats. But that would stop soon. The ceremony would start at eight o'clock sharp (no pun intended), when the city had dropped into the night and the moon was rising above the horizon.

Then, everyone would assemble on the rear deck of the vessel, where rows of pink leather and chrome chairs had been set out with a center aisle, pink-and-white rose petals scattered around them. Dee had brought in huge arrangements of pink roses that towered above the seats, and Anna had a matching pink rose in her hair. At the very back of the boat, a variation on a Jewish wedding canopy had been erected, again in a theme of roses. Underneath it was a small table covered in red velvet where the chief justice of the California Supreme Court—a personal friend of Jackson's—would perform the ceremony.

That was it. Simple. Tasteful. And very romantic.

Right now, as a sort of warm-up to the main event, just about everyone was up on the second deck, where a prewedding seafood raw bar buffet had been set out, with oysters, mussels, three different kinds of clam, Alaska king crab legs, and broiled, chilled lobster, plus the tiny sea snails that the French called *boulots*, which Anna had once dined upon during a memorable visit to Normandy. All of Sam's friends were in attendance. Cammie and Dee, of course. Adam and Ben. Parker Pinelli and his brother, Monte, whom Anna hadn't seen in ages. Plus some of the kids she'd gone to BHHS with—Krishna and Blue, who were planning to take a year off to explore Europe before starting college. Some others. They were all up on the second deck. Anna knew she should probably go up there, too, and socialize. That's what bridesmaids were supposed to do. But there was something bittersweet about standing where she was, all alone, letting the memories of the last eight months wash over her. There were so many. And so many of them involved—

"Excuse me? Someone told me you were Anna Percy."

A voice behind her startled Anna. It belonged to an older guy—fifties, unshaven, but discordantly well dressed in an Armani tuxedo with a black silk shirt underneath. He looked vaguely familiar, but she couldn't place him.

"Yes," she replied. "I'm Anna. I'm one of Sam's bridesmaids."

"Marty Martinsen." He held out a beefy hand for Anna to shake. "You know who I am?"

Now Anna remembered. Marty ran Transnational Pictures. He'd hosted the wrap party for *Ben-Hur* a few weeks ago. She and Sam had stayed for a week at his Malibu beach house earlier in the summer, when Marty and his family had been vacationing in Malta.

"You're a friend of Sam's dad, right? You let us housesit at your place in Malibu earlier in the summer—that was so nice of you."

"And I hope you enjoyed it," Marty said smoothly, "as much as I enjoyed reading *The Big Palm*."

It took a moment for what he was saying to register. He had read her screenplay? That had to mean . . . "Sam gave you my screenplay to read?"

"No, she gave me some other screenplay called *The Big Palm* by some other girl named Anna Percy," he replied, deadpan. "Imagine the coincidence."

Anna laughed. "You're right, that was a silly question. It's just that Sam didn't tell me anything about it." She couldn't decide whether to hug Sam or to yell at her when they next crossed paths.

"For a young writer, you've got a lot of talent."

One of the tuxedoed waitstaff passed by with a tray of champagne flutes, and Marty nabbed two of them neatly, offering one to Anna. She took it and set it on the edge of the deck, trying to digest what Marty was saying to her, and why. She nodded slowly, trying to decide if he really meant that or was simply being nice. She knew so many people in Hollywood who would hand out compliments, oozing faux sincerity to a person's face, only to berate and insult them behind their backs as soon as they were out of sight. Finally she smiled. "That's very kind of you."

Marty snorted, then swiped a knuckle against his stubbly chin. "You don't know me yet. You'll come to find out that I'm rarely kind. It's a highly overrated character trait." He swirled his Taittinger around in his flute, the bubbles glistening in the late-evening light. "So here's the thing, Anna. I was going to call. But hey, here you are—we might as well discuss it face to face. I want to make you an offer. If we can reach a satisfactory deal, Transnational will make your picture."

Anna scratched at her ear, as if to make sure she had heard correctly. The noisy choppers made it difficult to understand what he was saying. "Excuse me?"

Marty swallowed half of his champagne in one gulp. "I've got a new low-budget division in the works for the fall, and I've been looking for a good first niche project. I think we can do it for under ten mil, which is less than I spend on craft service for one of Jackson's babies." He laughed dryly and grabbed a piece of shrimp from a passing waiter, tossing it into his mouth.

Anna put her champagne down on a nearby banquette and blinked twice. "You're making my movie," she said slowly, as if English weren't her first language.

"If we can reach a deal, I don't see why not. I need a project like it, this film needs studio support, and if we can get the right cast—Hayden Panettiere or that cute redhead Amelie Adams for the girl, maybe Michael Graziadei for Brogan—I'd say we shoot on location in New York, then come back here. I'm thinking mid-October. It's a little rushed, but I say, what the fuck. These small movies we can go wham, bam, thank you, ma'am, put it out next summer, do some kind of commercial tie-in with BMG Music or MTV, open it fast, close it fast, be on video by Columbus Day. So who are your people?"

Her *people*? Was he asking about her family? "Well, I grew up in New York. My mother is in Italy now—"

Marty held up a meaty hand to interrupt. "Who handles your material, Anna? Who's your agent?"

Anna colored. *Of course* that was what he meant. But she didn't have an agent. Or a manager. Or a lawyer. Or anyone else whose job it would be to negotiate a movie deal, because the idea that she would be making a movie deal on the day before her departure to Yale was so remote as to be laughable.

A name flew into her head.

"Clark Sheppard," she said smoothly.

Well, why not? Cammie's father was one of the biggest agents in town; in fact, she'd briefly worked for him as an intern. No way on this planet would he represent a writer as young as she was, someone who had never sold anything. But she needed something to tell Marty— maybe she could ask Clark to recommend her to someone else at his agency, a junior agent or someone—and she could see that the CEO of Transnational was suitably impressed.

"Clark Sheppard, huh? Well, I shoulda figured it— that I'm not the only one who knows a good script when he reads it." He finished his champagne and poured the remaining drops in his glass over the side of the *Look Sharpe* for good measure. "Now I have to negotiate with the son of a bitch." He waved a hand in the air. "Fine, fine, I'll have one of my business-affairs people give him a call. Just don't expect the moon."

Anna nodded. She didn't expect the moon. She'd come to learn during her time in Hollywood that as a new screenwriter on her first film, she could barely expect to be a guest on her own movie set. There was every chance, too, that the studio would bring in another writer to rewrite her, and that she'd be forced to share credit.

On the other hand, she didn't have to have this movie made. She had plenty of money. She had plans for the fall, and for her future. Which was why she was willing to make an audacious request.

"This all sounds good. But I'd like to select the director."

Marty's graying eyebrows went up into his forehead. "You're shitting me."

Anna's heart pounded, but she stood her ground opposite the powerful executive. "I'm not. I'd like Sam Sharpe to direct. I know you probably think of her as a kid, the daughter of your friend, but she really is brilliant—"

Marty threw his head back and laughed. "You're good, you." He wagged a finger at her. "You had me going there. Some little birdie told you I was gonna have her direct, am I right? She brought me the screenplay, it's part of the deal."

It was? "Well, great, then." Anna held out her hand. "My people look forward to hearing from your people," she finished, feeling like she might laugh out loud hearing those words come out of her mouth.

Marty shook her outstretched hand, a bemused look on his face. "Congratulations, Anna. You wrote a fine script. We'll talk soon." He moved off, nabbing one more flute of champagne from a passing waiter as he did.

Anna felt faint, her knees actually weak. She wanted to sit, to breathe, to play over again in her mind what had just transpired with Marty.

She spotted a single empty rattan deck chair and made for it. Just as she did, Sam appeared from the steps to the upper deck and blocked her path. She wore a beautiful pink Chloé sundress; Anna knew she would be changing clothes very soon.

"Hi," her friend said with studied nonchalance. "What's new?"

"I just got the shock of my life. You gave my screenplay to Marty Martinsen! Why didn't you tell me?" Anna demanded.

Sam grinned, her brown eyes gleaming with excitement. "Come on. And ruin the surprise? Besides, I only found out he wanted to buy the script this afternoon. I thought he'd passed. If he had, I wasn't going to say a word. Call it kindness by omission."

Anna made a face. "Marty says that kindness is a highly overrated quality."

"If you're a studio chief, it probably is," Sam acknowledged. "But I have a confession. Marty had me standing on the upper deck right above you so I could listen in."

Sam pointed. Right above where Anna and Marty had been discussing the movie, the second level of the *Look Sharpe* dipped a bit. It would have been easy for Sam to stand there and hear everything.

"Isn't that against the law?" Anna mock-chided.

Sam laughed. "This is the movie business It's the law of the jungle. What I want to know is, you got an offer from a huge producer to make the very first movie you ever wrote. And you were going to turn the deal down unless *I* got to direct?"

"Yes," Anna confirmed.

"You are either a total idiot or the best friend I ever had, or both," Sam said, the emotion clear in her voice.

"You gave him my screenplay without telling me," Anna pointed out. "I'd say it was a fair trade."

"True," Sam acknowledged. She glanced at the antique

gold watch that she'd acquired at a Sotheby's auction a couple of years before. "I don't have much time. I needed to change like five minutes ago. But listen. I've been thinking about the title. *The Big Palm* sucks ass."

"You have a better idea?" Anna asked.

"Definitely. *The A-List.*"

"*The A-List.*" Anna considered the title. "I like it." Then another thought occurred to her. "I wonder if Yale will let me start late. What if they won't? That is, if you even want me on the set."

Sam howled with laughter. "See, your problem, Anna, is that you write about the A-list but then you don't act like you're part of it. I talked to the dean of the film school at USC. They'll give me credit to direct. Call Yale. Don't ask them. *Tell them* you've written a studio picture, that it's shooting in the fall, and that they have to make some accommodation for you. If you don't want to do it yourself, let Cammie's father do it. He went to Yale too."

"He did?" Anna was astonished. "I didn't know that."

"You probably never asked."

Anna gazed out at the coastline. It was all just so overwhelming. Just when she thought her life would never really change, it did. Simple as that.

Sam took her arm for a moment, and they stared out to sea together. The darkness had fully descended and the sky was now a gorgeous midnight blue, the ocean a few shades darker. They stood in silence, joined only at the elbow, Sam's skin warming Anna's own against the stiff ocean breeze.

Finally Sam pulled away, glancing at her watch. "Well,

I gotta get changed for the main event. Ready to watch me make a fool of myself?"

Anna smiled back at her. "Always."

"Cool. Wish me luck. And pray I don't trip walking up the aisle."

"Why the fuck not?" Cammie asked herself rhetorically. There was a first time for everything.

Adam was standing on the bridge of the *Look Sharpe*, talking quietly with the black-uniformed captain, a gentleman straight out of central casting for a remake of *The Poseidon Adventure*, with his chiseled chin, silver moustache, gold brocade on his shoulders, and white captain's hat.

Cammie Sheppard never approached guys, and she never, ever approached guys who had dissed her. She always waited for them to approach her, because they always did. Even the ones who were foolish enough to get on her shit list.

But dammit, here they were. She, here on the top deck outside the bridge, and Adam inside with the captain. She had nothing to lose—Adam would be leaving for the University of Michigan in a few days. The thought of that made her heart clutch.

"Adam?"

The captain grinned as Adam turned to face her. A slow smile slid across his face. He'd worn a black Ralph Lauren tux, with a typical Adam-like touch: a violet polka-dotted bow tie and matching cummerbund.

Adam touched the captain lightly on the shoulder. "You'll excuse me. I've got something important to attend to."

"I don't blame you one bit. You want to help me bring her—this ship, not the girl—back to harbor, come up here later."

"I'd like that."

Cammie watched as Adam and the captain shook hands, and Adam stepped out of the bridge to join her on the uppermost deck. From down below, on the first level, they could hear Django playing the Steinway grand piano that Dee had arranged for the boat, along with the low buzz of conversation as the guests assembled for the actual nuptials. Cammie knew she didn't have much time. Ten minutes, maybe. But it would be enough to say what had to be said.

"So," Adam said when he reached Cammie's side.

"So. There's a few minutes until the ceremony starts. We need to talk."

"There are some deck chairs in front of the bridge," Adam pointed out. "No one's there."

"Works for me."

They skirted the bridge via a narrow walkway to its left, on the ocean side of the vessel. Just as Adam had promised, there was a pair of white deck chairs with a low gleaming white table in between. Adam sat in one of them; Cammie dropped into the other. She looked out at the open expanse of sea, pitch black except for the glittering light that reflected off the water. The night was unusually clear for Los Angeles, and the stars were out in force, filling the sky.

Adam scratched at the star tattoo behind his ear while he waited for her to speak. That was a good sign; a typical nervous gesture. Nervous was good. She didn't want to be the only one who was nervous in this conversation.

"I'm glad we got a chance to talk at the rehearsal," she began.

"He raised his eyebrows. "Instead of throwing things at each other? That would have been fun. But messy."

"You pissed me off last month. When you were in Michigan. And didn't want to come back here."

He shrugged. "I was conflicted. You've never been conflicted?"

"Never," Cammie insisted, proudly tossing her strawberry-blond curls over her shoulder. She looked at Adam's open, honest face. "Okay. That was bullshit. I felt conflicted when Sam asked me to wear this goddamn pink bridesmaid's dress. Okay, that's bullshit too. I feel conflicted almost all the time."

"Nice to hear you admit it." He crossed one leg over another, and Cammie saw he'd added another typical Adam touch: instead of black patent leather tux shoes, he'd worn black-and-white sneakers.

"Fine. I admit it." She couldn't quite look at him as she continued. "I have a few other things to admit, too. I wasn't just pissed off. I was hurt. I admit that the only bad thing about working on the new club with Ben was that I wasn't working on it with you. I admit that no matter how much I tried to kick you out of my brain, you kept sneaking back in. I admit that I like myself a lot better when I'm with you, and I admit that the idea of you going back to Michigan and me staying here in Los Angeles makes me feel like I can't breathe. I admit that—"

He held up one finger to his lips. "Stop. That's enough for one session on the witness stand."

"But I'm not done."

"Actually, you are." He leaned toward her and pressed his lips against hers. Slowly, gently, then more insistently. She couldn't speak. She could hardly breathe.

When she came up from the sizzling kiss, she cautioned, "There is more to discuss."

"There is, is there?" A smiled played across Adam's lips as he pulled back. He leaned against the table, and she stood in front of him. "Then spill."

"Fine." She paced a few steps away before turning back to him. "I need to know: what's the weather like in Michigan this time of year?"

Adam's face was clouded with confusion.

"I need to know what to pack." She hoped that clarified it for him, because it was too embarrassing to repeat.

"Who said anything about Michigan?"

"Don't joke, this isn't funny. I, Cammie Sheppard, have just offered to accompany you to what I can only imagine is the armpit of America—"

"Michigan happens to be wonderful, and you are an unadulterated snob," Adam corrected. There was no malice in his voice.

"Fine. It's wonderful. I'm sure I'll love it," Cammie said sweetly.

"Great," Adam agreed. "But I don't know why you're going there."

Did she have to spell *everything* out?

"For you, asshole."

He ran a hand through his short dark hair. "Well,

that's going to be a helluva commute, since I'm going to Pomona."

"What?" Cammie put her hands on her pink-clad hips and stared at him. "Pomona College? As in, like, fifty miles away in Claremont?"

"Yep. I was thinking about changing schools. I told you that. But I finally decided to stick around here. I figured you'd come to your senses eventually." He stood with a devilish smile and stepped over to her. "I was right."

"Adam Flood, you did not say one word about Pomona!" she cried, batting him lightly with a manicured hand.

"Cammie Sheppard, we're not always going to play everything your way."

For the briefest moment, she felt her temper flare. But then she realized: if he had been willing to play everything her way, he wouldn't be the guy he was, the guy she wanted.

"Okay."

His eyebrows rose. "You agree with me?"

"I do. So, want to come with me to look at some commercial space tomorrow? For my modeling agency? I'm meeting a broker."

He entwined his fingers with hers. "Want to look at apartments in Pomona with me?"

Cammie flipped her golden curls. "I don't do apartments. But I *do* do helicopters, which happen to fly from my dad's helipad at Apex out to Pomona. And I *do* do you. Given proper motivation, of course."

"I'm going to kiss you again," he murmured, bringing her face close to his with one hand on her chin.

"Don't say it, Adam. Just do it."

And he did.

City of Angels

Friday night, 8:20 p.m.

Anna stood to the left side of the ten-foot arch of exotic flowers—candy pink anthuriums, crimson heliconias, and birds-of-paradise in every hue—and looked back toward the one hundred and fifty guests who were seated on both sides of the aisle. Dee had pulled it off. The wedding was going to happen. The sun had gone down completely, and tiny lights outlined the yacht. Others, recessed and subtle, washed the throng of people in a rich, golden ochre. The ocean lay inky beyond the confines of the boat. When Anna tilted her head back to look, she saw a sky full of stars.

To her left and right stood Dee and Cammie, each in a pink bridesmaid's gown identical to Anna's. Back in January, she would never in a million years have imagined herself at another wedding with these girls, much less being members of the same wedding party together. Now, here they were in August—if not exactly friends, something much less than enemies. The thought pleased her. In fact, it pleased her a lot.

The chief justice of the state Supreme Court stood directly in front of Anna. Like the ship's captain, he looked the way a judge was supposed to look. Tall and regal in his black robes, with thick silvery hair and intense dark eyes. He held up one hand for quiet. The audience hushed. Then he gave Django—who was sitting at the grand piano—a little nod. Django started to play an old love song Anna vaguely recognized. And then it came to her. It was "As Time Goes By," from the movie *Casablanca*. Anna smiled. How apt. How fitting. How perfect.

"Here comes Sam," Dee whispered.

Right on cue, Sam stepped out of the *Look Sharpe*'s cabin as everyone beamed at her. Her face shone above her beautiful white dress. Anna didn't think she'd ever seen her friend look quite so luminous. There were actual shouts of, "Bravo, Sam!" as she took confident steps down the aisle toward the wedding party. Then, along with everyone else in attendance, she turned to face the main cabin as Django segued into, "Here Comes the Bride."

Here she came. As the assembled guests rose as one, Dina—dressed in a simple pale blue evening dress designed by Gisella—walked alone down the aisle, tossing red and pink roses to cheers from the crowd. And making a movie star's entrance was her former husband, Jackson. He sneaked out from behind the wedding canopy to more cheers from the crowd, wearing a black Ted Lapidus tux with a pale blue cummerbund. Dina's former husband . . . who was about to become her husband again.

Sam had given Anna the shorthand version of what had happened. Evidently Jackson and Dina had been seeing each other. Sam knew they'd gotten friendly. But she had no idea that they'd gotten this friendly, until the night of the rehearsal dinner. Even then, neither of them had made a big deal of their reconnection, since they didn't know if anything would come of it.

Well, something had come of it. The love they'd shared when they were young and struggling had bloomed again. They were older. Definitely wiser. Evidently, Jackson's type did go beyond vacuous young lollipop blondes with fake pneumatic breasts.

Anna had to smile at the irony of it all. Did people ever really change, or did they all just run in circles only to end up where they'd been at the start? Or maybe the truth was more like in *The Wizard of Oz*. You could go on the longest journey only to discover that what you wanted was something you had all along.

It took a long time for the cheers to die and the judge to begin.

"We are gathered here this evening for a very special occasion," he declared.

The ceremony was short, the vows traditional. Sam stood between Anna and Cammie, with her parents just in front of her. When the judge pronounced them husband and wife and said Jackson could kiss his bride, Anna saw tears in her friend's eyes, and realized that she was looking through some tears of her own.

"Don't ever tell anyone I'm this sentimental," Sam whispered.

Anna playfully nudged her hip into Sam's. "Your secret is safe with me."

The ceremony ended with Django playing Bob Seger's "Old Time Rock and Roll." As the tuxedoed waitstaff whisked the chairs away and began setting up for dinner, guests crowded around Dina and Jackson, offering congratulations.

Anna and Sam got champagne from a passing waiter and toasted each other.

"Here's to the power of my father," Sam proposed. "Getting a divorce from Poppy through the courts of California in record time. It helps to have a friend who's on the Supreme Court."

"But what about your mother?" Anna asked. "Wasn't she married too?"

Sam shook her head. "Nope. Just had a boyfriend back in North Carolina. Emphasis on the past tense. Had."

Sam clinked her champagne flute against Anna's. "Here's to us, Anna Percy. You have changed my life. Thanks."

The clink of their glasses was lost to the growing *whup-whup* of a helicopter approaching the yacht.

Sam cursed. "I bet the captain radioed in our coordinates. How much do you think the tabloids are paying him?"

This, however, was no mere photographer's helicopter. From the way it hovered over the floodlit helipad on the yacht, it was clear that its intent was to touch down.

"Come on," Sam urged, as she led Anna to the helipad. "I just want to see what asshole from what rag had the nerve to do this."

Whoever it was, Anna thought, they wouldn't get far. A dozen burly security guards in blue uniforms circled the helicopter as it touched down. From their intense expressions, it was clear that whoever was in that chopper was going to go right back into the air, with or without the benefit of the helicopter.

Only it wasn't a reporter or a photographer who sprang lithely from the helicopter's interior.

It was Eduardo. He wore an Armani tux, white shirt, and black bow tie, as if he himself was to have been the groom.

Anna had to steady Sam so that she wouldn't fall overboard.

"It's all right," Sam managed to call to the head of security, since the force looked like they were about ready to take Eduardo down. "I know him."

An interesting understatement, Anna thought.

The people who recognized Eduardo applauded his grand entrance, and the crowd dispersed. Eduardo walked over to Sam and said, "We need to talk."

Sam figured the stateroom of her father's newest yacht was roughly the size of a decent-size three-bedroom apartment in Sherman Oaks. Not that she'd ever set foot in such an abode, but she was an artist. She had an imagination. The room was done in royal purple and black marble, with gold-leaf fixtures on the chandelier, the doorknobs, and headboard of the king-size four-poster bed.

Eduardo seemed to be paying no attention to the décor at all. His eyes were fixed on Sam. "I didn't mean what I said to you last night," he began. "And I couldn't go to Paris and leave things like that between us."

"You're not the one who should be apologizing," Sam protested softly. "What I did to you was terrible, unforgivable—"

"I am chalking it up to your youth," Eduardo surmised, raising a hand in protest.

"Maybe," Sam agreed. "Maybe even probably. I just don't know. I've never been any older than I am right now."

That got a small smile from him.

"I wish I had been brave enough to tell you the truth sooner." Sam walked over to the stateroom window and looked out. People were partying and dancing. She saw Dee swaying in Jack's arms. Parker was dancing with Citron. It made her happy and sad at the same time. Couples in love. With a future. "I was blinded by how wonderful you are, by how much you love me, by what a miracle it was that you thought I was beautiful—"

Eduardo came up behind her and turned her toward him. "Because you are," he insisted, his dark eyes earnest. "And I still think it."

"But even with all of that, Eduardo, it's not enough to get married. My parents? They married each other again tonight. But me? I'm not ready. For any of it. But I was so afraid I would lose you. . . ."

He put his strong arms around her, and she leaned into him.

"I'm sorry," she whispered. "I'm so sorry."

"I forgive you," he said simply.

She burrowed into his chest, where it felt safe and warm, and for the briefest moment she wanted to beg him to take her back.

But no. She had something to prove. A lot of things to prove. She wanted to prove that she could be part of a family, with an actual mother and an actual father.

She wanted to prove her talent to a town that too often thought of her as nothing more than Jackson Sharpe's daughter. Most of all, she had something to prove to herself.

She stepped out of Eduardo's embrace.

"Until we meet again, beautiful Samantha," he said.

"I hope we do, Eduardo. I hope we do."

He kissed her hand. Then she watched again through the window as he stepped out of the stateroom, made his way along the deck and to the chopper, and zoomed off into the night.

"Prodigious. Cacophony. Hypotenuse."

Anna knew who it was before she saw him. She had always, always been able to recognize his voice. It had given her chills that very first day on the airplane, and it gave her chills now, as she turned away from the stern of the *Look Sharpe*, where she'd been watching a pod of porpoises leaping in the vessel's slow wake.

"Hi, Ben."

He moved next to her. "Remember the day we met, on the plane? When you whispered big words into my ear? That was so hot."

She laughed. "Good to know. And your pronunciation is perfect."

He wore a black Calvin Klein suit instead of a tux, over an open white shirt, and he looked as good as that day on the plane, right down to the cleft in his chin. Better. There was a fresh confidence that hadn't been there before.

"The wedding was great, huh?" Ben asked. He turned to face her, leaning his elbows against the railing.

"Amazing," Anna agreed.

"I heard your good news. About the movie."

Anna was surprised. She hadn't mentioned it to anyone. "From—?"

"Sam, of course," Ben replied. "I'm really happy for you, Anna. Can you work on the movie and go to school at the same time?"

"I'm not sure. There's no way I'm not going to work on the film. It's too big an opportunity to miss. Maybe they'll let me start late. If I have to defer for a year, I'll defer."

Well, well. That was it, then. The decision she'd agonized over for so long had been made. The words came out of her mouth so easily, it was almost like she'd had them planned. Maybe all that overthinking wasn't such a waste of time. Or maybe it didn't go on forever.

He grinned. "That means you'll be here for the fall."

"I guess I will."

"That's . . . great. Your dad will be psyched. How's he doing?"

Anna raised her eyebrows and blew out some air. "Better each day. Back to work in three weeks. Can't wait to get out of the hospital."

"I'm happy for you." His blue eyes shone. "For so many reasons."

"And I'm happy for you," she echoed. "The club is a huge success. And you and Cammie . . ."

Her voice trailed off as she waited for him to fill in just what he and Cammie were to each other.

"Let's leave Cammie out of it. I've been trying to figure," he mused, scratching his neck, "how things got so complicated between us."

Anna shrugged. "Maybe we just weren't meant to be."

"You don't really believe that."

"No," she admitted. "I don't believe that. 'Meant to be?' It's just something people say so that they don't have to look at all the things they did wrong and wish they could take back. Only by the time they figure that out, it's too late."

"Bullshit," Ben said roughly. He turned back to the ocean as a cheer went up from the upper deck, and the crowd up there started to chant for Jackson to kiss Dina, or vice versa. Anna had to strain to hear him over the noise. "Don't tell me it's too late."

And so it came down to this. This moment. This boy. It had always been him, from the moment their eyes had met in the airplane's aisle. From the first moment his hand had touched her arm. From that insane moment in the plane's bathroom, when she'd found herself in his arms, his lips on hers, and she had never, ever wanted it to end.

He turned again to face her. "The night of the crash landing—remember that huge crowd of people in the terminal, after you all were safe? I was there."

"What?"

"I saw the news. I was at the club with Cammie and Adam, but I left. They thought I went home. I went to the airport."

"But why? And why didn't you say anything?"

"Anna—you kissed Logan in front of Sam, and Eduardo, and your dad. I was there. I was there—about thirty feet away. Close enough to see the slippers on your feet. Close enough to see how happy you looked."

She swallowed hard. Yes. That was how it had happened. She had been so overjoyed, so relieved to be alive, she'd kissed Logan on impulse.

"You looked happy *together*. And if that's what you want—"

"It's not," she insisted, cutting him off with a whisper. "What I want is . . ."

In the background, Citron's voice sang "Unforgettable" amid the tinkle of cocktail glasses.

"I love you, Ben," she said. "That you came to the airport just makes me love you more. I don't care who knows or who likes it or who approves. I don't care if you go back to Princeton or open ten nightclubs or give it all up to sail around the world. If you want to sail around the world, I'll sail with you and write a screenplay about it. I want to stop thinking and planning and worrying and just be with you, only you, forever and ever and—"

There were probably ten or twenty more "forevers" where those had come from, but Anna never got to utter them. Instead, her arms went around him, and she kissed him.

Their first kiss, eight months ago, in the first-class lavatory of a Delta jet, had been amazing. Breathtaking, even. This one, in the middle of the inky Pacific Ocean, under the twinkle of a million stars overhead, with the glittery lights of the City of Angels shimmering in the distance, was forever.

THE A-LIST

Sam Sharpe, Cammie Sheppard, and
Anna Percy were the most glamorous
faces of Young Hollywood.

But it's a new year at Beverly Hills High—
and there's a fresh cast of scandalous
A-Listers ready to become the toast
of Tinseltown.

L.A. will never be the same. . . .

Coming January 2009

Something wild and wicked is in the air.
The Carlyle triplets are about to take Manhattan by storm.

Lucky for you, Gossip Girl will be there
to whisper all their juicy secrets.

Turn the page for a sneak peek of

gossip girl
the carlyles

Created by the #1 *New York Times*
bestselling author Cecily von Ziegesar

hey people!

Surprised to hear from me? Don't be.

Something's happened and as you already know, I'm never quiet when things get interesting. And the Upper East Side just got a lot more exciting: We have a new threesome in town. And they're far too exquisite not to talk about . . .

But first, I'll need to back up a little.

As we all know, the beloved Avery Carlyle passed away this summer. She was the elegant, silver-haired woman who gave away her money to museums, libraries and parks the way other people donate last season's dresses to St. Géorge's thrift shop. At seventeen, she made headlines dancing on tables. At twenty-one, she married (for the first time) and moved into the famous peach-colored townhouse on the corner of 61st and Park. And at seventy-two, she still drank Coke and Gin and was always surrounded by fresh-cut peonies. Most importantly, she was the queen of getting exactly what she wanted from anyone. A woman after my own heart.

So how does this affect me, you ask? Keep your panties on, I'm getting there. Avery Carlyle's wayward daughter, Edie—who ran away to Nantucket to find herself through art after college—was called back to New York to sort through her mother's affairs. Judging by the bookcase of leather-bound journals (and the six annulled marriages) Mrs. Carlyle left in her wake, that process may take a while. Which is why Edie shut down the Nantucket house and moved her family into **B**'s old penthouse. Since the *père* Carlyle isn't in the picture, the cozy family of four consists of mother Edie and her triplets, **A, O,** and **B.**

Meet the Carlyles: There's **O,** buff bod, golden blond hair . . . looks good so far. Then there's **A,** blond hair, blue eyes, a fairy-tale goddess robed in J.Crew. And lastly **B,** which stands for Baby. *Aw.* But just how innocent is she?

Then of course, our old friends are up to some new tricks. There's **J,** last seen drinking Tanqueray gimlets on a yacht in Sagaponack. But why was she there, when she was supposed to be doing arabesques at the Paris Opera House? Did the pressure get to her, or was she just homesick for her tycoon-in-training boyfriend, **JP**? . . . And what about the impeccably mannered **R,** swimming laps on the rooftop pool of SoHo House while his mother did a piece on summer entertaining for her television show *Tea with Lady Sterling.* We all know Lady **S** can't wait to plan his fairy-tale wedding to long-time girlfriend, **K.** But can young love endure? Especially when **K** was seen in the confessional at St. Patrick's . . . What's to confess, Kitty Cat?

What will the old crowd think of the new additions to our fair island? I, for one, can't wait to see if they sink or swim. . . .

your e-mail

Q: Dear GG,
So, my mom went to Constance Billard like a million years ago with the triplets' mom and she told me the reason they moved here is because **A** slept with the entire island—boys and girls. And then **B** is like, this crazy brilliant genius that's mentally unstable and never washes her clothes. And **O** apparently swims up to Nantucket on the weekends in a Speedo. Is that true?
—3some

Dear 3,

Interesting. From what I've seen, **A** looks pretty innocent. But we all know looks can be deceiving. We'll see how brilliantly **B** does in the city. As for **O,** Nantucket's a long way away, so I doubt he can swim that far. But if he can . . . I've got one word for you: Endurance. Exactly what I look for in a man.

—GG

Dear GG,

So, I just moved here and I love New York!!!!! Do you have any advice to make this year the best year ever?

—SMLLTWNGRL

Dear STG,

All I can say is be careful. Manhattan is a pretty small place itself, albeit much more fabulous than wherever you came from. No matter what you do, and no matter where you are, somebody is watching. And it's not going to be gossiped about in your high school cafeteria—in this town, it's bound to hit Page Six. If you're interesting or important enough to be gossiped about, that is. One can only hope.

—GG

Dear GG:

I bet you're just saying you deferred from college because you didn't get in anywhere. Also, I heard that a certain monkey-owning dude never made it to West Point and I think it's pretty mysterious that he's still here and so are you. Are you really a girl?? Or are you even a senior? I bet you're just some nerdy thirteen-year-old.

—RUCHUCKB

A: Dear RUCHUCKB,

I'm flattered that my continued presence is spawning conspiracy theories. Sorry to disappoint, but I am as feminine as they come, without a pet monkey in sight. My age? As the venerable elder Avery Carlyle would say: A real lady never tells.

—GG

Sightings

This just in, from the newbies: **O** running in **Central Park,** without a shirt. Does he own any shirts? Let's hope not! . . . **A** trying on a silver sequined Marni minidress in the dressing room of **Bergdorf's**. Didn't anyone tell her Constance has a dress code? . . . And her sister **B** in **FAO Schwartz,** clinging to a guy in a barn-red NANTUCKET HIGH hoodie putting stuffed animals in inappropriate poses and taking pictures. Is *that* what they do for fun where they're from?

Okay, ladies and gents, you all probably have to go back-to-school shopping—or for those of you who've headed off to college, read Ovid and chug a beer in your new 8 x 10 dorm room. But don't worry; I'll be here, drinking a glass of Sancerre at Balthazar, reporting on what you're missing. It's the dawn of a new era on the Upper East Side, and with these three in town, I just know it's going to be another wild and wicked year. . . .

You know you love me,

gossip girl

welcome to the jungle

Baby Carlyle woke up to the sound of garbage trucks beeping loudly as they backed up Fifth Avenue. She rubbed her puffy eyelids and set her bare feet on the red bricks of her family's new terrace, pulling her boyfriend's red Nantucket High sweatshirt close to her skinny frame.

Even though they were all the way on the top floor, sixteen stories above Seventy-second and Fifth, she could hear the loud noises of the city coming to life below. It was so different from her home in Nantucket, where she used to fall asleep on the beach with her boyfriend, Tom Devlin. His parents ran a small bed-and-breakfast, and he and his brother had lived in a guest cottage on the beach since they were thirteen. He'd come to visit for the weekend, and after he left last night, Baby dragged a quilt onto the terrace's hammock and fell asleep in a Frette duvet cocoon.

Note: Sleeping al fresco is a worst-case-scenario situation. Never done willingly (i.e., only if your cruise ship hits an iceberg or your elephant loses a leg on safari).

Baby shuffled through the sliding French doors and into the cavernous apartment she was now expected to call home.

The series of large rooms, gleaming hardwood floors and ornate marble detail was the opposite of comfortable. She dragged the duvet behind her, mopping the spotless floors as she wound her way to her sister Avery's bedroom.

Inside, Avery's golden-blond hair was strewn across her pale pink pillow, and she sounded like a broken teakettle. Baby pounced on the bed.

"Hey!" Avery Carlyle sat up and pulled the strap of her white Cosabella tank top. Her long blond hair was matted and her blue eyes were bleary, but she still looked regally beautiful, just like their grandmother had been. Just like Baby wasn't.

"It's morning," Baby announced, bouncing up and down on her knees like a four-year-old high on Sugar Smacks. She was trying to sound perky, but her whole body felt heavy. It wasn't just that her whole family had uprooted themselves from Nantucket last week, it was that New York City had never—*would never*—feel like home.

When Baby was born, her emergence had surprised her mother, and the midwife, who thought Edie was only having twins. While her brother and sister were named for their maternal grandparents, the unexpected third child had simply been called Baby on her birth certificate. The name stuck. Whenever Baby had come to New York to visit her grandmother, it was clear from Grandmother Avery's sighs that while twins were acceptable, three was an unruly number of children, especially for a single mother like Edie to handle. Baby was always too messy, too loud, too much for Grandmother Avery's presence, too *much* for New York.

Now, Baby wondered if she might have been right. Everything, from the boxy rooms in the apartment to the grid of New York City streets, was about confinement and order. She sighed and bounced on her sister's bed some more and Avery groaned sleepily.

"Come on, wake up!" Baby urged, even though it was barely ten, and Avery always liked to sleep in.

"What time is it?" Avery sat up in bed and rubbed her eyes. She couldn't believe she and Baby were related. Baby was always doing ridiculous things, like teaching their dog, Chance, to communicate by blinking. It was as if she were perpetually stoned. But even though her boyfriend was a raging stoner, Baby had never been into drugs.

It doesn't really sound like she needs them.

"It's after ten," Baby lied. "Want to go outside? It's really pretty," she cajoled. Avery looked at Baby's puffy brown eyes, and knew immediately that she'd been crying over her loser boyfriend all night. Back in Nantucket, Avery had done everything possible to avoid Tom. This past weekend, it had been impossible. Even though their apartment took up half the top floor of the building, it wasn't large enough to escape his grossness. Every day, she'd found something more disgusting about him, from the stained white Gap athletic socks he'd ball up and give to their cat, Rothko, to play with, to the one time she had walked in on him wearing Santa Claus–print boxers and doing bong hits on the terrace. She knew Baby liked that he was *authentic*, but did authentic have to mean appalling?

Short answer? No.

"Fine, I'll come outside." Avery pulled herself out from under her 600-thread count Italian cotton sheets and walked barefoot onto the terrace, and Baby followed. Avery squinted her eyes in the bright sunlight. Below her, the wide street was empty except for an occasional sleek black towncar whooshing down the avenue. Beyond the street was the lush expanse of Central Park, where Avery could just barely make out the tangled maze of paths winding through its greenery.

The two sisters sat together, swinging in the hammock and overlooking the other landscaped Fifth Avenue terraces and balconies, empty except for the occasional rooftop gardener. Avery sighed in contentment. Up here, she felt like the Queen of the Upper East Side, which was exactly what she was born to be.

Was she really?

"Hey." Owen Carlyle, six foot two and shirtless, stepped onto the terrace carrying a carton of orange juice, a bottle of champagne, and wearing just a Speedo, a maroon towel knotted around his slim hips. Avery rolled her eyes at her swimming-obsessed brother, who could easily drink anyone under the table and then beat them in a 10K.

"Mimosa anyone?" He took a swig of orange juice from the carton and grinned at Avery's repulsed grimace. Baby shook her head sadly as her tangled hair brushed against her shoulder blades. Always tiny, Baby now looked absolutely fragile. Her tangled brown hair had already lost the honey highlights that always showed up during the first weeks of a Nantucket summer.

"What's up?" he asked his sisters companionably.

"Nothing," Avery and Baby answered at the same time.

Owen sighed. His sisters had been so much easier to under-
and when they were ten, before they'd started acting all coy and mysterious. If girls weren't so irresistible in general, he might have given them up and become a monk. Case in point: The only reason he was up so early was the semi-pornographic dream that had forced him out of bed and on an unsuccessful hunt for a pool.

Dream about whom? Details please.

He placed the unopened bottle of champagne in a large daisy-filled planter and took another swig of OJ before squishing into the hammock next to his sisters. He glanced down at the mass of trees, not believing how small Central Park seemed. From up here, everything looked miniaturized. He just wished he had an expanse of dark ocean in front of him, like he'd had back in Nantucket.

"Helloooooo!" The sound of their mother's voice and the jangling of her handcrafted turquoise and silver bracelets carried out onto the terrace from inside. Edie Carlyle appeared in the French doorway. She wore a blue Donna Karan sundress, and her normally blond-streaked-with-gray bob had been knotted into a hundred tiny braids. She looked like a scared porcupine rather than a resident of Manhattan's most exclusive zip code.

"I'm so glad you're all here," she began breathily. "I need your opinion on something. Come, it's inside." She gestured toward the foyer, her chunky bracelets clanking against each other.

Avery giggled as Owen dutifully slid off the hammock and wavered into the apartment, following Edie's long stride. For the past week, Owen had been acting as Edie's de facto art adviser. He had been to an opening almost every night, usually in an overcrowded, patchouli-ridden gallery in Brooklyn or Queens where he drank warm Chardonnay and pretended to know what he was talking about.

The expansive, wood-paneled rooms that had once housed toile Louis XIV Revival chaises and Chippendale tables were now empty except for a few cast-offs Edie had found through her extensive network of artist friends. Avery had immediately ordered a whole ultramodern look from Jonathan Adler and Celerie Kempbell, but the furniture hadn't yet arrived. In the interim Edie had managed to find an orange moth-eaten couch to place in the center of the living room. Rothko was furiously scratching at it, his favorite new activity since moving to New York. Most of their pets—three dogs, six cats, one goat, and two turtles—had been left in Nantucket. Rothko was probably lonely.

Not for long.

Sitting next to Rothko was a two-foot-high plaster chinchilla, painted aquamarine and covered in bubble wrap.

"What do you think?" Edie asked, her blue eyes twinkling. "A man was selling it for 50 cents on the street down in Red Hook when I was coming home last night from a performance. This is authentic, New York City found art," she added, rapturous.

"I'm out of here," Avery announced, backing away from the plaster sculpture as if it were contaminated. "Baby and I are going to Barneys," she decided, locking eyes with her sister and willing her to say yes. Baby had been moping around in Tom's stupid sweatshirt all weekend. It had to stop.

Baby shook her head, pulling the barn-red sweatshirt tighter against her body. She actually kind of liked the chinchilla. It looked just as out of place in the ornate apartment as she felt. "I have plans," she lied. She'd decide what those plans were just as soon as she was out of her family's sight.

Owen gazed at the statue. One of the chinchilla's heavily lidded eyes looked like it was winking at him. He really needed to get out of the house.

"I, uh, need to pick up some swim stuff." He vaguely remembered getting an e-mail saying he needed to pick up his uniform from the team captain at St. Jude's, his new school. "I should probably get to it."

"Okay," Edie trilled, as Avery, Owen, and Baby scattered to opposite ends of the apartment. School started tomorrow and all three knew it was the dawn of a new era.

Edie tenderly carried the chinchilla sculpture into her art studio. "Have fun on your last day of freedom!" she called, her voice echoing off the walls of the apartment.

Like they don't *always* have fun?

gossip girl
the carlyles

Coming May 6th

Five Spectacular Stories.
One Ah-Mazing Summer.

THE CLIQUE
SUMMER COLLECTION

MASSIE
APRIL 1, 2008

DYLAN
MAY 6, 2008

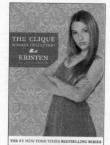

ALICIA
JUNE 3, 2008

KRISTEN
JULY 1, 2008

CLAIRE
AUGUST 5, 2008

Spend Your Summer with THE CLIQUE!

poppy
www.pickapoppy.com

Welcome to Poppy.

A poppy is a beautiful blooming red flower
(like the one on the spine of this book). It is also
the name of the new home of your favorite series.

Poppy takes the real world and makes it
a little funnier, a little more fabulous.

Poppy novels are wild, witty, and inspiring.
They were written just for you.

So sit back, get comfy, and pick a Poppy.

poppy

www.pickapoppy.com

gossip girl

THE A-LIST   THE CLIQUE

the it girl   POSEUR